THE BIG UNEASY

BOOK TWO IN THE AROUND THE WORLD SERIES

A.E. RADLEY

SIGN UP TO WIN

Firstly, thank you for purchasing *The Big Uneasy* I really appreciate your support and hope you enjoy the book!

Every month I run a competition and randomly select three subscribers from my mailing list to win free eBooks. These books can be from my back catalogue, or one of my upcoming titles.

To be in with a chance of winning, and to hear more about my upcoming releases, click the link below to subscribe to my mailing list.

http://tiny.cc/aeradley

REVIEWS

I sincerely hope you will enjoy reading The Big Uneasy.

If you do, I would greatly appreciate a short review on your favourite book website.

Reviews are crucial for any author, and even just a line or two can make a huge difference.

DEDICATION

I am blessed to have so many lovely readers who have supported me in my author career, this book is dedicated to one reader who has been there from the beginning; Jenn Brown. Thank you for all your support.

1

THE ARRIVAL

It was another blisteringly hot day on Bourbon Street. The broken red tiles of the sidewalk were soaked with rainwater from one of the frequent and much-needed storms that were common in New Orleans during the height of summer.

The thirty-minute downpour had done nothing to cool the air. Early morning tourists walking up the iconic street complained about the unforgiving heat, but locals like Jenn Cook were simply happy for the brief respite the storm had offered. Even if it was hardly noticeable now the rains had stopped.

The doors and shutters to CeeCee's Bar were all wide open, but there was still zero airflow. Jenn plunged her hands into the ice bin behind the bar. Bottles of water and beer and half-melted ice cubes bounced around on the top of the cool water.

She blew out a deep breath and turned to face the antiquated fan that whirred behind the cash register. It blew warm air in her face, but she'd take that over no air at all.

It was ten o'clock in the morning on a Tuesday in July. Already some tourists were starting to make their way up Bourbon Street. It may have been before lunch, but CeeCee's Bar, like so many others in the area, was open and ready to sell alcohol. Jenn had already served a few people that morning, pouring frozen cocktails into plastic to-go cups. Tourists loved the fact that alcohol was cheaply available, and that it was perfectly legal to walk around with a cup of whatever, unlike many other places.

Personally, Jenn couldn't think of anything worse than imbibing alcohol at ten in the morning, but heat made people do strange things. In fact, *New Orleans* made people do strange things.

In the five years Jenn had lived in the city, she'd seen things she would never have believed if she hadn't seen them with her own eyes. A city didn't earn the nickname 'The Big Easy' for nothing, and millions of tourists packed the narrow streets each year to see what all the fuss was about.

New Orleans had a unique culture, something that couldn't be found anywhere else in the world. A blend of jazz, architecture, history, and food made it a one-off. But it was the people who really brought New Orleans to life, from impromptu jazz sessions that would pop up on a street corner to the party animals who filled the French Quarter each and every night.

Jenn was blinded by New Orleans when she had first arrived as an unemployed twenty-three-year-old post-grad-uate. She had expected to use her degree to obtain a respectable office job, which would allow her to spend her evenings strolling around admiring the nineteenth-century architecture. Or to take a trip down to the Mississippi and soak up the atmosphere as she watched an old paddle-wheel steamboat sail by.

That hadn't quite worked out.

She had quickly blown through her savings, and, before long, she had to abandon her hunt for work in the Business District and turn her attention to the party zone: the French Quarter. Necessity caused her to take any part-time job she was offered. Five years later, nothing had changed. She loved her life and the freedom the multiple jobs offered her.

CeeCee's was the first place to give her a chance. Even though Jenn loved it, she knew there was no getting away from the fact that it was an absolute dive. The entire bar was only five metres by fifteen metres in size. Just enough room for patrons to walk in one of the many open doors and order a drink at the long bar.

The main selling point of CeeCee's was the brightly coloured slushie machines that churned out neon alcoholic ice cocktails all day and all night. Each machine had a scrappy piece of paper taped to it with a scribbled description of the contents: Piña Colada, Margarita, Daiquiri, Rum Punch, and the famous Hurricane.

Now and then a special would crop up, usually in the guise of a fruit or some inexplicable name like the Terminator or the Mind Number. People bought the drinks regardless of the name or presentation. That was New Orleans for you; it never claimed to be classy.

The bar was open twenty-four hours a day, mainly

because the rickety old doors on the building didn't close. Five double-shuttered doors allowed entry into the bar. Half of the shutters were missing, and the others were so old they were being held together by flaking paint.

The effect was as if there was nothing separating people walking along Bourbon Street from the hypnotic churn of the slushie machines. It was easy to step in, part with a staggering eleven dollars for a souvenir cup and grab a frozen drink to go.

And many people did, no matter the time of day or night.

Each night Bourbon Street came to life and partied like it was the last night on earth. The street, road, and sidewalk would be packed with people talking and walking from bar to bar, picking up cheap drinks as they went.

The balconies above the street would be filled with well-dressed people slow-dancing to traditional Dixieland jazz, occasionally toasting the rabble below them.

During the day, Bourbon Street was sparsely populated with curious tourists, fellow business owners, and the people who lived in the apartments that overlooked the street. But all the nightlife businesses that thrived during the darkened hours still opened their doors during the day. Which was why it wasn't unusual to find a drunk literally sleeping in the gutter outside the bar, or unsuspecting tourists being pulled into daytime shows in strip clubs.

Despite some of the seedier elements of New Orleans, Jenn adored the vibrant city and the freedom and equality it offered all who visited.

A young tourist couple entered the bar, interrupting

the thoughts the rainstorm had sent her. Jenn took her hands out of the ice bin and shook the cold water off them, enjoying the feel of the cold drops on her bare legs.

"Hey guys." She blew a stray lock of long, blonde hair out of her face. "What can I get you?"

The young man ordered two of the strawberry daiquiris. Jenn picked up two plastic cups and placed them under the taps on the slushie machine. She pressed a button and watched the neon icy drink automatically drop into the cup.

She turned around to face her customers. "Got any plans for this beautiful day?"

"Melting," the woman answered with a laugh.

Jenn smiled. "It is a hot one, be careful out there."

"Where's the voodoo museum?" the guy asked.

Jenn leaned over the high bar and pointed down the street. "Keep on down Bourbon for about three more minutes. After that, you'll come to the lobster place on the corner. Turn right there and you can't miss it."

She grabbed the drinks from the slushie machine and placed them on the bar. She stabbed a straw into each before pushing them towards the couple.

"Great." He handed her some bills. "Keep the change."

"Thanks." Jenn beamed. "Y'all come back tonight for happy hour. Half price on all Hurricanes!"

The couple picked up their drinks and sauntered out. Once they left, Jenn wiped down the wet residue left on the bar and checked the temperature gauges on the slushie machines. She walked around the bar, straightening stools, and checking that everything was clean. It had only been an hour since her previous check, and with less than five customers, everything was as she had left it.

She sighed as she sat on the rickety wooden stool behind the bar and watched the street through the open doors.

A few moments later, a black sedan pulled up on the opposite side of the street. The driver's door flew open and a tall, well-dressed redhead got out. She strutted to the rear of the car where the trunk popped open.

A few seconds later, the front passenger door opened, and an attractive brunette got out of the car. Jenn thought she'd be more attractive if her expression wasn't bordering on rage. She stormed to the back of the car and started arguing with the redhead.

A nearby saxophone played a soulful jazz tune, which Jenn would have usually enjoyed. But at that moment, she was curious, and it was preventing her from hearing what was being said.

The redhead pulled a small suitcase out of the trunk and placed it on the sidewalk. She turned back to the trunk and started to pull a second, larger case from the car. As she did, the brunette picked up the small case from the sidewalk and attempted to put it back into the trunk.

Jenn laughed at the ridiculous sight of the two suit-clad women wrestling with their luxury luggage. She grabbed a moth-eaten old broom and headed to the side-walk in front of the bar where she pretended to sweep. Luckily, the women were shouting so loudly she didn't need to strain to hear what was being said.

"I've literally had it up to here, Kathryn!"

Jenn tilted her head. The redhead was addressing the

brunette. Jenn thought she looked like a Kathryn. Short-sleeved white blouse, tight black work skirt, pantyhose, and high heels. Clearly no idea how to dress for the exhausting New Orleans heat.

"Stop moving my suitcase, Erica," Kathryn shouted back.

Jenn leaned on the handle of the broom and watched as the two women struggled with the suitcase. One blocked the path to the trunk, while the other tried to get around her.

"No. I'm serious! You're staying here," Erica replied.

"I am not staying in this sordid hellhole one more minute," Kathryn replied.

Jenn raised an eyebrow. She had to admit it; Kathryn was brave to call New Orleans a sordid hellhole in a screaming match in the middle of Bourbon Street.

Stupid, but brave.

"Well, that's tough. Because I booked you into the hotel for two weeks," Erica said. "You need to get yourself together. You can't go on like this anymore."

"I'm fine!" Kathryn shouted back. "And why the hell would I want to stay in this grubby, sleazy cesspool for two whole weeks? And even if I did, what was wrong with the perfectly good hotel we just came from? Why do I have to stay with the drunks and drug-pushers?"

Jenn winced. She looked around the street to see if anyone could hear the select adjectives this woman was using to describe their hometown.

"Because that was a business hotel, for conventions," Erica explained, like Kathryn was five. "This is a hotel and spa, for relaxing."

"I don't need to relax. I need to work," Kathryn said.

"No, you need to take some time for yourself. Time you should have taken before."

"I'm fine," Kathryn argued.

"You're not fine. And you know that. You're… you're like a husk of the person you were before the—"

"Erica!" Kathryn's shriek cut her off.

Before the what? Jenn wondered to herself. The day had been shaping up to be another quiet and dull Tuesday morning until these two turned up and put on an impromptu show.

Erica used Kathryn's distraction to toss one of the suitcases away from the car. It flopped into the road.

"New Orleans is far enough away from home for you to not cause any more problems for Mother. And if there's one place on earth that even *you* will have to eventually crack and enjoy yourself, this is it. Think of it as a vacation. A nice break."

Kathryn stalked towards her case. She picked it up and spun around, fixing Erica with a glare that could melt steel.

"A *nice* break? Are you out of your mind? *Her*e?"

"Soak up the atmosphere," Erica instructed. "Take some time to reflect on… things."

"You can't *force* me to take a vacation."

Erica raised an imposing eyebrow. "If you come home before the fifth of next month, then I'll tell Mother about Addison."

Jenn deemed the threat a good one if Kathryn's shell-shocked face was anything to go by.

"You wouldn't dare," she seethed.

11

"Oh. I would." Erica picked up the other case and placed it on the ground. She slammed the trunk shut. "Two weeks, Kathryn. Take some time for yourself."

Kathryn dropped her suitcase and marched over to Erica. She stood in front of her, toe to toe with arms folded. "So, dragging me down here for that conference was a ruse? All so you could dump me here?"

"Yep. Gotcha." Erica smirked.

"This is ridiculous!" Kathryn flailed. "I don't need a vacation. I need to go back to work."

"You really don't," Erica replied. "There's an envelope in the front pocket of your suitcase with all the information about your hotel. Remember, if you don't stay here… I will tell Mother."

"I can't believe you're blackmailing me," Kathryn growled.

"Well, I am. And I know you don't believe me, but I am doing this for your own good." Erica got into the car and wound down the window. "By the way, I've had your cell disconnected. Just so you don't try to do any work. There's the oldest possible, non-Internet enabled burner I could find in your bag. Just in case there's an emergency. I'm not a monster, after all." She looked Kathryn up and down before rolling the window back up. "All right, see you next month!"

Kathryn pitched towards the car in what looked like an attempt to strangle Erica, but the redhead sped away.

Jenn watched as the black sedan rounded a corner and disappeared from sight. She decided the show was over and that being anywhere near the irate brunette wasn't a good idea. She gave up her pointless sweeping and went back into the bar.

Inside, she picked up a cloth and started to wipe the bar down, wishing that someone would give her a two-week all-expenses-paid spa vacation in New Orleans.

She heard someone mumbling curse words under their breath and looked up to see Kathryn struggling into the bar with her suitcases.

Jenn let out a small sigh. It was just her luck that the troublesome woman would come in. She watched as Kathryn stacked the suitcases beside a bar stool and then sat down.

"Hey, what can I get you?" Jenn flashed Kathryn her friendliest smile.

Kathryn regarded the slushie machines and rolled her eyes. "Water."

Jenn picked up a bottle of water from the bucket of half-melted ice and placed it on the bar in front of Kathryn.

Kathryn raised an eyebrow and looked with displeasure at the wet bottle. "Do you not have cups?"

Jenn plucked a plastic to-go cup from the large stack by the slushie machine and placed it beside the dripping water bottle.

Kathryn looked at the two objects as if they were completely foreign to her. She sighed and pulled a couple of paper napkins out of the metal box on the bar. She placed one on the bar and wiped the bottle dry with the other before placing the bottle on the dry napkin.

Jenn watched with amused interest as Kathryn plucked another napkin and dried her hands before finally opening the bottle and pouring some of the water into the cup. It was the least New Orleans thing she'd ever seen.

Jenn picked another water bottle out of a box and put it in the bucket of icy water.

"So, are you in New Orleans long?" she asked.

Kathryn laughed sarcastically. "Please, like you didn't hear it all."

Jenn considered pretending she hadn't been listening but thought she might get more gossip if she admitted it. She took the middle road and shrugged her shoulders.

Silence loomed over them.

Jenn realised she wasn't going to get anything else out of the woman. She wrapped her foot around the leg of her own rickety bar stool and dragged it over to the slow-moving fan. She picked up a magazine and started to flick through it.

After a couple of minutes of head-shaking and slowly sipping water, Kathryn bent down and opened the front pocket of one of her suitcases. She pulled out an envelope and slammed it down on the bar angrily.

Jenn attempted to ignore the brunette, but it was impossible. She watched as she noisily sighed, ripped open the envelope, and pulled out some pieces of paper.

"Hey!" Kathryn called without looking up. She flicked a disinterested hand in Jenn's direction. "Where is this hotel?"

Jenn stared at Kathryn in disbelief. Not that it mattered, Kathryn wasn't looking at her. She slowly pushed herself off of the stool and ambled back towards the bar. She snatched the piece of paper out of Kathryn's hand.

"The Royale. Nice," Jenn said with a dreamy sigh. "You want to walk down Bourbon, turn left by Dixie's Bar, and then take the next right."

Kathryn turned around and regarded Bourbon Street with a sneer. "Unbelievable," she muttered as she snatched the paper out of Jenn's hand.

"I'm beginning to understand why she dumped you here instead of driving you to the hotel," Jenn mumbled under her breath as she returned to her stool and her magazine.

She didn't bother to look up to see if Kathryn had heard her words.

"How much for the water?" the woman asked.

"On the house. Consider it some Louisiana hospitality," Jenn said without looking up from her magazine. "Courtesy of the sordid hellhole."

"Oh, great. You heard that?" Kathryn muttered.

"*Everyone* heard that."

A few more silent moments passed before Jenn heard Kathryn pick up her papers and shove them back into the front pocket of her suitcase. She refused to look up at the rude woman. She simply wasn't worth her time or energy.

At the sound of suitcase wheels trundling into the distance, Jenn let out a sigh and looked up to see the empty bottle and cup and a handful of screwed-up napkins lying on the bar.

2

GRUMPY TRAVELLER

Arabella Henley nodded a silent greeting to the doorman at the Royale Hotel as she passed by. She crossed the lobby, not paying much attention to her surroundings. She was exhausted and what she most wanted was to check in, get to her room, and finally rest. She approached the front desk and lowered her handbag onto it.

"Arabella Henley, checking in," she said.

She turned around and saw Rebecca was following her. She'd been speaking to the bellboy who was now dealing with their luggage.

"And Rebecca Edwards, separate booking," she added.

She watched as Rebecca looked around the ornate lobby with fascination. Arabella followed her gaze. There was a sumptuous chandelier hanging from the ceiling. Rebecca took her phone out of her pocket and snapped a couple of pictures.

Arabella smiled to herself as she watched Rebecca taking in the splendour of the room. She'd walked straight past without a second thought, hadn't even noticed the beauty of the surroundings that entranced her travelling companion. She knew she could do with taking a leaf or two out of Rebecca's book, learning to stop and smell the roses now and then.

"Would you like a connecting room?" the receptionist asked.

Arabella turned back to face the man. She didn't know. It wasn't something they had discussed. Was it presumptuous to request one? Did asking for a connecting room imply that she intended to use it? Worse, what did *not* requesting one say?

She sighed at her internal fretting. She was putting too much emphasis on an innocent enough question.

She nodded. "As long as the rooms are well away from the elevators."

"Hemingway stayed here," Rebecca said as she joined Arabella by the front desk.

Arabella raised her eyebrow and looked around the lobby. It was all marble columns, gold leaf, and chandeliers. "Really? I thought he liked... understated things."

"May I have your passport and a credit card?"

Arabella reached into her handbag and handed over the items. Rebecca took her rucksack from her back and did the same.

"Are you from England?" the receptionist asked once he looked over their passports.

Arabella looked at his name badge. *Tommy.* She sighed. Why did she always get the chatty ones? Especially after a long journey.

"We are," Rebecca answered. "London."

"I've always wanted to visit London," Tommy confessed.

Arabella rolled her eyes and turned away. She just wanted to check in, unpack, and maybe have a shower. If she could manage to stand up long enough to do so.

The ten-hour flight, the three-hour check-in before that, and the hour's drive from the airport to the hotel had completely sapped her energy. She'd been looking forward to a holiday away from the stresses of work, but simply the journey to the hotel had her longing for a twelve-hour shift at her desk.

Her desk. She blew out a breath as she recalled the mountain of work she had been forced to leave for her colleagues. It had been a busy first half for Henley Estates, and staff upheaval meant that it had been busy for everyone for a number of months.

Eventually, she decided that waiting for the office to quiet down would be like waiting for a watched kettle to boil. There was no good time to take a holiday, so she might as well do it anyway.

But that didn't stop her worrying about the work she had left behind. Rebecca had reminded her that she was the boss, and she should learn to delegate and trust her staff. Which just showed how little Rebecca knew the staff members in question.

She shook the thought from her mind. She was here to relax, not fret about work.

"I need to make a copy of these, I'll be back in a moment." Tommy disappeared into a room behind the front desk.

"You get grumpy when you travel," Rebecca noted

with a grin.

"I'm tired," Arabella corrected.

"Grumpy." Rebecca picked up a couple of leaflets from the desk. "You were like this in Portugal, too. I thought you were a grade A bitch, but you just don't like travel, do you? You could have mentioned that before we agreed to travel together."

"I'm *tired*," Arabella repeated. "It was a long flight."

"Long?" Rebecca laughed. "That was nothing. Just wait until we go to the Far East. Oh god, actually, no. If you're this bad after a mid-haul flight to America, I can't imagine you after a long trip with a changeover."

Arabella felt her cheeks flush. She coughed and turned away, pretending to read some historical facts that were framed on the wall beside her.

She hated Rebecca seeing the worst of her.

"If you want to travel with me in the future, that is," Rebecca added.

"Of course, I do," Arabella said quickly.

She did. The idea of travelling with Rebecca was scary but exhilarating. Not because of where they could go or what they could see, but because of how Arabella felt. She was pretty sure she was falling for Rebecca, despite six months ago being engaged to a man and planning her wedding.

The relief at the ending of that particular relationship was still palpable.

She had Rebecca to thank for it. Without that fated trip from Portugal to London the previous Christmas, she would have blindly walked into a marriage with a man she didn't really love. Unaware of what love really was.

But with the certainty that she was doing the right thing by ending the engagement, came confusion regarding her feelings for Rebecca. They'd kissed. A few times. Tentative, unsure kisses but nothing else. No conversation, no understanding of where they were heading.

Arabella had asked for time to sort out her feelings and figure out what it meant to be, quite suddenly, attracted to a woman. And Rebecca, damn perfect Rebecca, had given her time.

And continued to do so. The long overdue conversation hung between them. Arabella was too frightened to even think about her feelings, never mind discuss them. And Rebecca was generously giving Arabella all the time she needed.

The proposed trip to Scotland had been a disaster. It took a few weeks for the pair to even start talking again after the aborted adventure. Eventually, they picked up and continued to socialise, this time just as friends.

The free-spirited Rebecca had continued with her travel plans, taking short, solo trips here and there. Each time Rebecca went somewhere, she invited Arabella, and, each time, Arabella said no. She said no because she was scared of a repeat of Scotland, but she always told Rebecca it was bad timing or some other excuse. The enormous workload at the office had become a convenient justification.

Then Rebecca mentioned New Orleans, a trip to see a good friend of hers, and Arabella knew that she had to say yes to this particular trip. The strain on their friendship was beginning to pull a little too tightly. If she didn't say yes, she might lose Rebecca. Lose a chance at finally figuring out what she wanted.

But now they had arrived, she felt much as she had on the way to Scotland. Fearful. She swallowed down the emotion and forced herself to remain calm.

"Thank you for coming," Rebecca said softly.

"Thank you for inviting me."

"Of course. At least we made it here. Better than our first attempt to travel together to Scotland—"

"Let's not talk about that," Arabella pleaded. Clearly, she didn't need a reminder.

She heard a commotion at the front entrance and turned to see a brunette with two cases struggling to get up the short flight of stairs. The doorman was offering to help her, but she seemed determined to do it alone.

"Thank you, ladies." Tommy had returned and placed their passports and credit cards on the desk. "I have you booked into 612 and 613. A lovely view of the city. You can even see the Mississippi."

"Oh, cool!" Rebecca enthused. "And there's a roof terrace, right?"

"There is," Tommy confirmed. "On the ninth floor. There's a fitness suite and a roof terrace. Great views, especially at night."

Arabella took a step to the side to accommodate the brunette with her luggage. She regarded the harassed woman with a raised eyebrow. She was pretty sure she had that skirt.

"Kathryn Foster," the woman said. "Apparently you have a room for me?"

Arabella turned her attention back to her travelling companion.

"Told you there would be a gym," Rebecca said, continuing where Tommy had left off. "So you can keep up with your ridiculous exercise schedule that could kill a horse."

"I'm in training," Arabella explained for the fiftieth time.

"Supposedly."

"I'm doing the London marathon!"

"Supposedly," Rebecca repeated with a knowing grin.

Arabella hated how well Rebecca knew her. She'd started a strict gym schedule not long after she started questioning her sexuality. She claimed it was to get her into peak fitness to take on the annual London Marathon. In truth, it was something to fill the long and lonely nights when her mind ran rampant with questions she didn't have answers to.

She hoped that New Orleans would give her some answers. That she'd find the courage to have a proper conversation with Rebecca and figure out what they were, or what they could be.

"Shall we have an hour or so?" Rebecca asked. "We can unpack, shower… take a nap if you like, Grumpy."

Arabella smirked. "You know, I have no idea why I'm travelling with you. You're mean."

Rebecca chuckled. "Aww, can I make it up to you by buying you beignets?"

Arabella picked up her luggage and headed, blessedly, for the elevators. "If you think I'm that cheap, you're very much mistaken."

3

INVEST IN A MAP

Jenn had become a fan of the afternoon nap since moving to New Orleans. When she first arrived in the city she had mistakenly believed she would be able to work through the day and even into the evening with no ill effects.

Then, she worked straight through Louisiana's exhausting midday sun and almost certainly suffered from heat exhaustion as a result. She had stumbled along Basin Street towards her part-time job in the tourist office. When she arrived, she was immediately lectured by her co-worker, Miss Mae, who informed of the importance of the two R's—Rest and Rehydration.

Since that day, she always ensured that her hectic schedule kept her out of the furious heat from midday until two o'clock and that she always carried a full bottle of water with her.

She noticed that many tourists were also caught out by the heat. After the third occasion that an exhausted tourist passed out in front of her, she decided it was time to do something about it. She spoke to Mr Webb, her manager at the tourist office, and said that she was interested in taking a first aid course. He readily agreed, and Jenn enrolled in one, which she passed with flying colours.

It wasn't long before she realised that walking into the tourist office with her shiny new certificate was a big mistake. As one of the very few qualified first aiders on the tourism team, she was quickly signed up to be one of the many marshals along the routes of the parades that were a frequent feature of the French Quarter.

Parades zigzagged their way across the city on a daily basis, and it wasn't unheard of for there to be two parades on any one day. Half the time the locals had no idea what the parade was actually for. Not that it mattered, as most would happily cheer and wave regardless.

Jenn loved the parades. The first time she saw one, she had only been in New Orleans for two days and was eating lunch at a café on Bourbon Street. Engrossed in a local newspaper and looking for jobs, she hadn't heard the parade until it was practically in front of her.

She'd decided to have lunch at an indoor café with air conditioning and had sat at a bar table right in front of the window overlooking the busy street. Towards the end of her sandwich, and while reading, she distractedly noticed that her drink was vibrating. She stared at the rings forming on the top of the clear liquid as her brain attempted to figure out what was happening. It was then that she realised it wasn't just the drink, it was the whole table. She could hear a brass band and heavy feet marching in time to the tune.

Looking through the window, she could see a parade coming down the street. For the next ten minutes, she was absolutely mesmerised by the sight. Ceremonial uniforms with shining buttons and extravagant hats adorned with feathers were the first things she noticed. Then she became aware of the instruments, drums of all shapes and sizes and shining brass instruments that gleamed brightly in the sun. It was only halfway through that she realised the majority of the marchers were teenagers, with young dancers twirling batons and weaving in between the musicians with grace.

Crowds were stopping on the sidewalk. As they watched the spectacle making its way down the narrow street, people cheered and applauded. Everyone became caught up in the carnival atmosphere.

Jenn had asked her waitress what the parade was for. The young woman had no idea, stating there were so many displays that she lost track.

As the end of the parade passed by the window, Jenn noticed that people had randomly joined in, dancing, skipping, and clapping in time to the music. Random strangers who seemed to have nothing to do with the parade were happily getting involved and pulling other spectators along with them. With a laugh and a shrug more and more people joined the end of the party. By the end of the street, the procession had doubled in length.

That was one of the many times that Jenn found herself falling in love with the city.

Unfortunately, being a token first aider did take some of the shine off of a parade. All parades needed permits, and the organisers often provided their own first aiders.

But the tourism office liked to provide a few extra bodies to help out, especially with so many tourists being caught unaware by the summer heat.

Jenn had quickly realised that nothing was less fun than watching other people watching a parade.

On the positive side, being a marshal meant patrolling the route with the police and, even though Jenn hated to admit it, she loved the uniform. If she was going to have to attend a parade and miss out on all the fun the least she could do was take in a little eye candy along the way.

"Hey, Jenn!"

Jenn looked up to see Officer Aude Durand, a beautiful black woman she often saw patrolling the parades and with whom she had struck up a conversation once or twice. Her slight French accent always made Jenn a little weak at the knees.

"Afternoon, Officer Durand." Jenn smiled back.

"You pulled the short straw, huh?"

"Yep." Jenn laughed as she tugged on her lime green high-visibility vest. "The perks of that first aid certificate are literally endless."

"At least the vest matches your eyes." Durand winked as she threaded her thumbs through her belt loops and strutted away from Jenn.

Jenn regarded the woman and sighed. Being interested in women in New Orleans was hard. Though it was one of the most gay-friendly places that Jenn had ever been to, which was undoubtedly a good thing, that meant her misfiring gaydar struggled here more than usual.

With the odds of finding a same-sex partner dramatically higher in New Orleans than in many other places,

Jenn had thought it would be simple to find a girlfriend. But she hadn't factored in the famous Deep South hospitality. Everyone she met was fantastically friendly. While that was a great thing, it did mean that Jenn was now becoming an expert at hitting on straight women.

In a city supposedly bursting at the seams with gay women, Jenn could only find the straight ones. Even in gay bars Jenn seemed to spend her time befriending straight women that their gay male friends had brought along to cheer up due to some straight relationship drama.

"Oh, it's you again," a voice said. "What is that tremendous racket?"

Jenn didn't even have to turn around to know that the acerbic voice behind her belonged to the woman from the bar earlier that day. Kathryn.

"And why are you wearing that hideous thing?" the woman continued.

Jenn kept looking across the road, not wanting to turn around and look at the irritating woman.

"I'm a first aider. There's a parade."

"A parade?" Kathryn laughed derisively. "For what?"

"Celebrating."

"Celebrating what?"

Jenn turned around. "Why, your arrival, of course!"

Kathryn regarded her with a passive expression before replying, "Sarcasm doesn't become you."

"Are *you* honestly questioning *my* personality traits?" Jenn shook her head. She turned back towards the street and wished that the parade would hurry up and arrive. The sound of the band could be heard in the distance. She desperately wished for it to be closer, just so it could drown out anything else Kathryn might say.

No luck. "I thought you worked at that dingy bar," she said, loud and clear.

"I do. I have more than one job," Jenn explained through gritted teeth.

"Well, I suppose this is a step up," Kathryn drawled. "Where is Basin Street?"

Jenn turned around and regarded Kathryn with a suspicious frown. "Why?"

Kathryn gave Jenn a pointed look. "Because I've been led to believe that there is a tourist center there and I'm a tourist."

"A few hours ago, you were furious for being dumped here. Now you're looking for restaurant recommendations?"

Kathryn sniffed. "I spoke with my sister again. We've agreed that I'll stay here for two weeks, so I might as well fill my time with something productive. Educational, perhaps. If such a thing exists here, you know, between the drinking."

The parade was starting to get closer, and a few people were beginning to gather. Jenn looked from Kathryn to the approaching parade.

"So, where is Basin Street?" Kathryn repeated.

"You know I'm not your personal map, right?" Jenn rolled her eyes.

"Well, I'd use my cell phone, but, as I'm sure you overheard, it's from 1992." Kathryn folded her arms across the long-sleeved, blue, silk shirt she had changed into.

Jenn took in Kathryn's outfit with a shake of the head. "You changed into a long-sleeved shirt? Really?"

"I asked for directions, not fashion advice."

"It may have escaped your notice, ma'am, but it's kinda hot," Jenn said. The sound of drums was getting louder. The parade was nearly upon them.

Kathryn shrugged. "It was cold in my hotel room."

"And pantyhose? Who wears pantyhose and heels in this heat?"

"Basin Street," Kathryn articulated slowly.

"Fine." Jenn let out an aggravated sigh. "Walk up this road until you get to the Dixieland Jazz Bar, turn left, and then keep walking until you get to the church. After the church, turn right, and it's on the other side of the road. But, seriously, you might wanna get changed or at least take some water with you."

The end of Jenn's sentence was wasted. Kathryn turned and started to walk into the distance.

"And invest in a map!" Jenn shouted at the retreating figure.

4

POWDERED SUGAR

Rebecca bit into the warm, sugary beignet and let out a loud moan. She closed her eyes and enjoyed the exploding flavours in her mouth. She chewed slowly and then swallowed. Her eyes snapped open, and she dunked the remaining part of the beignet into the pile powdered sugar on the plate.

She realised that eyes were boring into her and looked up. Even through the dark glass of Arabella's large sunglasses, she could see a raised eyebrow.

"Enjoying that, are you?" Arabella asked.

"It's phenomenal," Rebecca replied. She pushed the plate closer to Arabella. "Try one?"

She knew her beignets were safe. Arabella was fastidious about looking after her health, specifically her weight. Not that she needed to. Yes, she was a little curvy, but Rebecca thought she looked incredible. And she'd continue to do so even if she ate all the beignets in New Orleans.

Arabella's lips pursed, and she looked away.

Rebecca sighed and pulled the plate back towards her.

Arabella had been in a strange mood since they arrived. Well, since they arrived at Heathrow, to be exact.

The day before she had been excited and happily discussing what they would be doing in New Orleans. The nerves were slightly visible, but she was soldiering on in her attempt to cover them up.

Then they'd arrived at the airport, and acerbic, scared Arabella was back.

Rebecca wished she knew what Arabella was so nervous about. She had joked earlier that travel made Arabella grumpy, but she knew it wasn't that. She'd hoped the quip would get Arabella to open up. No such luck.

Ever since their abandoned trip to Scotland, Arabella had been out of sorts. Rebecca was desperate to get to the bottom of it, but any time she tried, Arabella pushed her away. So, Rebecca decided to give her space and time to figure things out. She'd rather have Arabella's company than force a permanent wedge between them.

She could tell that Arabella was trying. She was obviously struggling with something, and Rebecca figured she'd tell her about it in her own time.

"So…" Rebecca reached into her rucksack and pulled out her travel notepad. "I've written down a few things that I want to do while we're here. You're more than welcome to join me at any time. But, if you want to do your own thing, then that's fine, too."

She opened the notepad and removed the pen from the spiral spine. She placed the book and the pen in front Arabella.

Arabella turned her attention to Rebecca's list of sights to see.

Rebecca turned *her* attention to the remaining beignets.

"When are we meeting your friend?" Arabella asked.

"She's working tonight, so we decided to meet tomorrow for dinner. I may pop over and see her before then, if she's free. She's going to message me her schedule." Rebecca licked the powdered sugar off her fingers. "She's looking forward to meeting you, if you're free. If you don't want to do dinner tomorrow, then we can meet up some other time."

"Dinner tomorrow sounds lovely," Arabella agreed. "If we have nothing planned, maybe we could explore the area this evening?"

"Sure, we could walk around the French Quarter and grab some dinner. How are you feeling? Jetlagged yet?" Rebecca asked.

"No, not yet." Arabella looked up. She smiled and reached forward and ran her thumb along Rebecca's chin.

Rebecca's breath caught in her chest. It wasn't the first time Arabella had touched her, but it was rare enough that it took her breath away every time. She tried to look unfazed, but inside she was screaming with joy.

"Sugar," Arabella explained. She wiped her thumb on a napkin. Rebecca mourned the missed chance to see Arabella lick the residue off her thumb. Or even better, to guide Arabella's thumb into her mouth and lick it off herself.

Arabella returned her attention to the list. Rebecca resisted the urge to plunge her face into the plate of sugar.

She took a sip of water and tried to calm down. She reminded herself that she'd promised to give Arabella as much time as she needed. To go from being engaged to a man to being unsure about your sexual preference in a few short weeks was bound to be disorientating. And Arabella didn't seem like someone who handled change very well.

"Remember that it's your holiday, so feel free to do whatever you want to do," Rebecca said. "The main thing is that you relax and have a great time. Let me do all the organising."

"I'll hold you to that," Arabella said. "With how my work schedule has been lately, I'll be glad to never see another month planner ever again."

At first, Rebecca had thought that Arabella had used work as an excuse to avoid her. Then she visited her a couple of times in the office and saw for herself that it was absolute pandemonium. Apparently, everyone wanted to move before their summer holiday, and so Henley's Estate Agency was rushed off its feet for a few months. No one more so than one of their top executives: Arabella Henley.

For a while, Rebecca was seriously worried that Arabella was going to burn out. The stress definitely put a wedge between them. She'd assumed that was what had happened on the way to Scotland. But each time they argued, Arabella would come back to her, apologising for her words and behaviour.

Soon they were spending more and more time together. Sadly, it was platonic time. Arabella's sexuality was never brought up. They exchanged innocent cheek kisses but nothing more.

Rebecca enjoyed Arabella's company so much that she

didn't say anything. She had previously promised to give Arabella time, and that's what she would do. It wasn't like she was in a hurry. Her mum had only passed away six months before, and her life had completely turned upside down since then. She was finding her own feet, so she had time to give Arabella, too.

She figured that things would sort themselves out eventually. And the unlikely friendship she had developed with Arabella was more important to her than potentially ruining everything by demanding answers that she was sure Arabella didn't have.

"May I?" Arabella picked up the pen and gestured to the paper.

"Sure."

Arabella drew stars beside a few of the things Rebecca had planned.

"If you don't mind me tagging along, these things sound interesting."

"I'd love you to tag along," Rebecca confessed.

In between the blow-up on the road to Scotland and finally getting Arabella to travel to New Orleans, Rebecca had undertaken a few trips on her own. She'd enjoyed them, and she'd taken some amazing pictures along the way, but something was missing. She always felt lonely.

"I think I'd like to relax tomorrow," Arabella said. She sipped at her freshly squeezed orange juice. "I was looking at the brochure for the hotel spa and it sounds wonderful."

"Cool. I was going to head out and see a couple of things, maybe catch a boat on the Mississippi. As I say, you're welcome to dinner, but if you want to take a break don't feel obligated to come—"

"Of course I'll be there," Arabella said as if it were obvious. "I'll have breakfast and dinner with you. We can just do our own things during the day. Unless you want to join me at the spa?"

Rebecca felt her eyes bug at the thought. She was thankful for her own sunglasses. She'd love to join Arabella at the spa, but she wouldn't be able to maintain a respectable distance if she did.

"No, I think I'll go out and explore. U—unless you want me to join you?" Her heart pounded in her chest.

"No… no. I'm fine on my own. Relaxing."

Red graced Arabella's cheeks.

Good, I'm not the only one struggling with this, Rebecca thought.

"Those beignets were great. I might have them for dinner, too," Rebecca joked to break the tension.

"You'll need another seat on the plane home if you do," Arabella replied.

"Totally worth it." Rebecca licked her finger and dipped it into the powdered sugar.

Arabella rolled her eyes and shook her head. "Such a child," she mumbled playfully.

5

FINE SHOES

JENN WAITED PATIENTLY for the traffic lights to change so she could walk across the busy road towards the famous Basin Street Station. The large building had been built at the turn of the twentieth century, and the frontage of red brick and large glass windows looked just as impressive today as it must have done back then.

The station building had become a hub, with the open-top double-decker tourist bus stopping on one side of the building and the famous St. Louis Cemetery Number One on the other. Inside the station was a large and grand marble-floored lobby where the tourism officers sat behind large wooden desks and handed out maps and information.

Beyond the lobby was the old station's waiting room which had been restored and contained glass display cases with historical documents and items from days gone by, when the building had been a working railway station. Jenn often spent time in the waiting room looking at the old timetables, maps, and trinkets that were on display.

A recent addition to the building was a shop that had been set up within the old ticket office selling New Orleans merchandise, most of which was overpriced and seemingly pointless, but the tourists loved it.

The traffic light changed, and Jenn hurried across the road and into the tourist office where she was immediately greeted by Miss Mae, a rotund black lady in her seventies. Miss Mae knew everything there was to know about everything. She sat, as always, in her large, worn leather chair.

"Hey, sweetie," Miss Mae greeted her.

Jenn exhaustedly smiled back at Miss Mae. "Hey. Gosh, it's hot out there today!"

Miss Mae laughed. "Oh, you ain't seen nothing, dove."

"Yeah, yeah." Jenn chuckled. "You've seen it hot enough to melt parked cars, I know."

She placed her green high-visibility vest back in the first aid bag behind one of the large desks and walked over to the water cooler where she started to fill a paper cone with ice cold water.

"By the way," Jenn said in between sips, "did a snooty-looking brunette come in here?"

Miss Mae smiled knowingly. "Oh, yeah, we saw her in here." She shook her head and chuckled as Jenn downed the rest of the water. "In her fine shoes."

"Yeah, that's the one." Jenn nodded.

"She didn't like the bus." Miss Mae pointed out of the window at the open-top bus, which was about to depart on a tour of the city.

Jenn frowned. "Why not?"

Miss Mae shrugged. "I didn't ask. She didn't seem to like much."

"No, she doesn't," Jenn agreed.

"She took a map and a few leaflets. Said she'd go and look at the cemetery."

"She paid for a tour?" Jenn questioned with surprise.

Kathryn didn't seem like the kind of person who would want to go on a tour of the cemetery. Jenn would have bet money down at Harrah's Casino that Kathryn would have gone straight to the art museum.

"Yep." Miss Mae released a long and tired sigh and closed her eyes for a moment before looking up at Jenn. "How do you know her, dove?"

"She came into CeeCee's," Jenn said. She poured herself some more cold water. Little and often, that was the key. "Then I saw her at the parade. She wanted directions to here."

"She on vacation?" Miss Mae frowned.

"Kinda, yeah."

"She don't look like she on vacation."

"No, I think it was kind of a last-minute thing," Jenn admitted. She decided not to mention the conversation she'd overheard. It was really none of her business. Moreover, if Kathryn ever found out that anyone else knew about that conversation, she'd know who to blame. Jenn didn't want to be on the receiving end of her anger.

"She's troubled," Miss Mae said with a small shake of her head.

"She's trouble," Jenn enunciated.

"No, troubled," Miss Mae pressed. "Those big old brown eyes of hers, she seemed haunted somehow."

Jenn finished her water and threw the empty cone into the recycling bin. She rolled her eyes. Not a day went by when Miss Mae didn't use her supposed voodoo sixth sense to identify some sort of pain or suffering in a stranger passing through the tourist office.

"Nothing a vacation can't fix, I'm sure," Jenn said.

She tidied some of the leaflets that lined the desks. It didn't need doing, but she liked to keep busy.

"Are you going to be at Jack's tonight?" Miss Mae asked.

"No, I'm on the streetcar tonight," Jenn replied.

Miss Mae shook her head. "I don't know why you still do that job, dove."

Jenn shrugged. "It's fun, you meet lots of interesting people on the streetcar."

Miss Mae sneered with obvious disagreement. "But working the nightshift as a conductor on those street-cars... no, no, no."

Jenn smiled at the maternal head-shaking Miss Mae was offering her from her beaten-up chair.

"It's not as bad as you think," she placated. "Most people are just fine. Besides, it's no worse than working on Bourbon Street in the evening, and you don't mind me doing that."

"At least then I can keep an eye on ya!" Miss Mae laughed loudly.

Miss Mae might have been an older lady, but that did not stop her from getting right in the thick of things when it came to a good party. Jenn had met Miss Mae for the first time when the older woman was entertaining a large crowd at a karaoke bar on Bourbon Street.

Jenn had still been getting used to the novelty of being able to carry around an alcoholic drink and was walking up Bourbon Street sipping on a frozen daiquiri from a plastic cup when she heard the most amazing sound.

Utter silence.

She had been passing a bar with all the doors and windows thrown wide open. The place was packed with people but completely silent. While all of the other bars pumped out loud music and the sound of people talking and laughing turned into an incomprehensible rumbling over the top, this bar was quiet with expectation.

Jenn stopped and looked into the building from the road. Then suddenly a deep and beautiful female voice floated over a loudspeaker. The voice was singing a song that Jenn didn't know the words to, but that didn't stop her from feeling immediately captivated. She found her feet walking towards the bar without a second thought.

The room was small and crowded, but Jenn managed to navigate her way to the stage and was surprised to see that the owner of the voice was a woman in her twilight years. She sat on a well-worn, high-backed chair. It looked out of place in the bar, almost like she had brought it with her from her own living room.

At the end of her first song the bar exploded into whoops and cheers, applause and whistles, and the woman gave the slightest nod of gratitude before moving straight into the next song. She sang five songs in a row before leaving the stage and heading into a dressing room in the back. Jenn asked a member of the bar staff who she was and, before long, she was being introduced to Miss Mae in person.

Miss Mae took an immediate liking to Jenn and explained to her that if she wanted to listen to real jazz and hang out in the best bars, then she needed to head towards Frenchmen Street. Miss Mae scrawled some directions onto a napkin along with the names of bars with days and times scribbled beside them.

Over the next month, Jenn saw Miss Mae perform many times in many different venues, and they struck up a close friendship. Before long, Miss Mae was introducing Jenn to Mr Webb, her boss at the tourist office, and telling the man that he had to hire Jenn.

"Why don't you go on home?" Miss Mae said. She looked around the empty office lobby with her eyebrow raised in amusement. "I think I can manage all these folks."

"Are you sure?" Jenn asked, a smile drifting across her lips.

Miss Mae chuckled. "Go on, before I change my mind."

"You're the best," Jenn said. She gave the woman a quick embrace before grabbing her rucksack that she'd left behind the desk.

"I know." Miss Mae nodded. "Repay me. Come and see me one night, maybe at The Cat?"

"Sure, I'll be there," Jenn promised.

She looped her arms into the rucksack straps, tightening them as she walked through the old waiting room. She took one last deep breath of air-conditioned air before heading out into the stifling heat.

She walked up the sidewalk beside the cemetery and almost immediately let out a groan.

Kathryn was straight in front of her. She was pensively chewing her lip as she leaned against the stark white, crumbling wall that surrounded the cemetery.

Jenn quickly decided that she'd come too far up the sidewalk to turn around. Besides, the road was too busy to cross. She was going to have to head straight towards the prickly woman.

She put her best customer-facing smile on and approached.

"Hello again," she said.

Kathryn frowned at her, seemingly disorientated. A few seconds passed before recognition washed over her face.

"Oh, it's you."

"Yes, me again."

"Are you following me?"

"What?" Jenn blinked. "No, you're the one who keeps bumping into me!"

Kathryn didn't seem to be listening. She heaved herself away from the wall, and Jenn noted that her silk blouse clung to her skin and her face was covered with a sheen of sweat.

"Regretting your outfit yet?" she smirked.

"Can you imagine being buried in one of these wall vaults?" Kathryn asked, ignoring her question and placing her hand on the thick wall.

"Alive? No."

"At all," Kathryn clarified. "Being slid into a hole in the wall like... like an envelope in a desk drawer."

"Well, it's not quite like that," Jenn argued.

"And then... after a year and a day," Kathryn continued, "they scrape out whatever might be left of you and put someone else in instead."

Jenn looked closely at the woman in front of her to try to ascertain if these were serious words or the ramblings brought on from some kind of heatstroke.

"It's the way it's done here," she explained softly. "It's tradition, religion."

"My father died six months ago." Kathryn stared at her hand pressed against the cemetery wall.

"I'm sorry to hear that," Jenn replied. Kathryn may have been a rude, entitled pain in the backside, but Jenn was still sincere in her condolences. Family was important.

"He was buried," Kathryn said. "In the ground. And I visit him as often as I can, but it doesn't feel like it's enough. What about these people? What if they want to visit their loved ones, but someone else is in there?"

Jenn shrugged off her rucksack and knelt down. She unzipped her bag and grabbed a bottle of water. She stood again and grabbed Kathryn's hand, wrapping it around the bottle.

"I think you need to drink something. It's very hot out here."

Kathryn absentmindedly took the bottle. She gave Jenn a serious look. "Do you believe in an afterlife?"

"Not really," Jenn said.

"Not at all? You think we just, what, rot?"

Jenn pinched the bridge of her nose and took a deep breath. "Look, it's Kathryn, right?"

Kathryn nodded.

"Kathryn, I really think you need to get back to your

hotel and lie down for a while. The heat can kinda creep up on you, and—"

"I'm fine," Kathryn argued.

"Humour me." Jenn looked at the bottle of water meaningfully. "It's sealed."

Kathryn twisted the plastic cap off and took a few delicate sips of water.

"Look, I'm heading back to town," Jenn explained. "Maybe I can walk you back to your hotel?"

Kathryn shrugged and gestured for Jenn to lead the way. Jenn was relieved that she didn't put up a fight; she didn't feel like she could cope with that right now.

They walked side by side along the street.

Kathryn sighed and ran the back of her hand across her clammy forehead. "So, you live here?"

"Yep." Jenn nodded. "Five years now."

"Five years." Kathryn paused. "Why?"

Jenn laughed. "Wow. You're really rude, aren't you?"

"Just honest."

"It's a fine line," Jenn said. She pressed the button at the crosswalk. "I moved here because I wanted something different. I'd just graduated in Boston."

"Boston?" Kathryn frowned. "Well, you certainly succeeded in finding something different. What made you stay?"

The light changed, bringing the traffic to a stop. They crossed the road, Jenn leading the way.

"Probably the same reasons that makes you hate it," she admitted. "It's fun, disorganised, full of life, unexplainable."

Kathryn let out a rich, throaty laugh. "So, you have me pegged already?"

"Oh, I think you've been quite clear on your preferences. New Orleans is not one of them."

The walked down a narrow road with abandoned buildings on either side of the street. Kathryn continued to sip from the bottle of water. Jenn continued to wonder if Kathryn was suffering from the heat.

"I suppose," Kathryn said thoughtfully, "I suppose I just don't get *it*."

"Get *what*?"

"It," Kathryn repeated. She waved her hand at their surroundings. "It. New Orleans. The… I don't know, the culture, I guess? It's foreign to me. I feel like I'm out of my comfort zone."

Jenn could understand how the city could easily be outside Kathryn's comfort zone. She knew that New Orleans wasn't for everyone, but she also thought that most people could find something for them in the diverse environment, if only they gave it a chance.

"I think that's what I like about it," Jenn confessed. "I'm constantly surprised by things. I never feel like I've seen it all. It's an adventure."

"I'm too old for adventure."

Jenn laughed. "Oh, come on, you're not that old."

"Not as young as you," Kathryn said, dragging her eyes over Jenn's body.

Jenn shivered at the attention. "Not that old," she repeated.

She glanced at Kathryn. She was very attractive, something that Jenn had only recognised now that Kathryn wasn't being a massive pain. But now the woman was softening, Jenn could appreciate it.

"Too old for adventure," Kathryn repeated before sipping some more water.

Jenn regarded the brunette with a critical eye. "I'm good at this, I think you're... thirty... five?"

Kathryn stopped dead and stared at Jenn in surprise. "How on earth did you know that?"

Jenn stopped and turned back to look at her. "I told you, I'm good at that."

Kathryn shook her head and started walking again. "Well, anyway, too old for adventure."

"You're never too old for adventure. I think if you gave New Orleans a chance, you might even find you like it here."

Kathryn laughed. "Oh, I don't think so."

"Look, I'm not suggesting a cocktail run on Bourbon Street to get wasted. New Orleans has something for everyone, I can guarantee there will be something here for you to enjoy."

"I'm pretty sure there isn't anything here for me," Kathryn argued.

"I'm pretty sure you're wrong."

"Why do you care so much whether *I* like it here or not?"

Jenn opened her mouth to reply, but the truth was, she didn't know why she cared. Kathryn had been an annoyance to her ever since she arrived, but for some reason Jenn felt compelled to make sure she left New Orleans having enjoyed her vacation. Even if it was an enforced vacation which she clearly intended to hate every minute of. For some reason, it was important that she reverse Kathryn's view of her adopted hometown.

"Because I love New Orleans," Jenn finally said, "and I honestly believe that it's rich enough and diverse enough that there will be something you'll enjoy. I work for the tourist office, it's like my mission to make people love it here."

"Hold on." Kathryn paused and placed her hand on Jenn's arm to stop her from walking. "You work at the bar, you work as a marshal at the parade, *and* you work for the tourist office?"

"Yep." Jenn looked at the manicured fingers that briefly touched her arm before fading away again. She instantly missed the sensation.

"Any other jobs I should know about? Will you be serving me breakfast in the morning?" Kathryn chuckled.

"No, but I do run a water aerobics class in your hotel on Thursday," Jenn confessed. She started walking again. Kathryn quickly joined her.

"Water aerobics instructor," Kathryn said disbelievingly. "So, a bartender, a marshal, tour guide, and a water aerobics instructor?"

Jenn bit her lip and looked down at the cracked sidewalk.

"Oh my god, there's more." Kathryn laughed.

"Technically the first aid job is part of the tourist office," Jenn explained.

"Uh-huh." Kathryn nodded with a smug smile.

"I work on the streetcars," Jenn admitted. "As a conductor."

"The trams?" Kathryn frowned.

"Streetcars," Jenn corrected. "Yeah, I'm working tonight. You should come."

"Why would I want to do that?"

"Because the streetcars are a part of New Orleans history! The Saint Charles line is the oldest continuously operating streetcar line in the world, running since 1835. In 2014, it was listed by the National Park Service as a historic landmark."

Kathryn's shoulders shook with barely contained laughter. Jenn looked up to see the woman biting her lip.

She rolled her eyes. "Okay, so that is the exact speech I give at the tourist office, but I mean every word of it. And it's accurate."

"I'm sure it is," Kathryn said with clear amusement. "It's adorable."

"And," Jenn continued, on a roll now, "we've bumped into each other three times today already, so it's obviously fate that I'm supposed to show you how wrong you are about New Orleans."

She didn't know why she was suddenly offering to show the woman around her hometown. She told herself it was in defence. She wanted to hear Kathryn take back the words 'sordid hellhole'.

They arrived at the revolving doors to Kathryn's hotel. Kathryn started to hand back the half-drunk bottle of water.

"Keep it," Jenn instructed. "And make sure you carry a bottle with you in the future. The sun can be fierce, and I can't always be here to save you from dehydration."

"Yes, ma'am." Kathryn gave Jenn a small salute.

"So, what do you say? Want to see the streetcars?"

Kathryn considered the question for a few seconds before nodding. "Well, I don't have any other plans. And, as you say, we seem destined to bump into each other anyway."

"Great." Jenn pointed towards Canal Street. "Meet you by the stop up there at nine minutes past eight."

"Very precise," Kathryn commented.

"It may be the Big Easy, but the streetcars run on time."

"Impressive." Kathryn smiled. "Thank you for the water. I do think I was beginning to feel the sun a little."

"You're welcome."

Kathryn frowned. "I've just realised, I don't even know your name."

"Jenn," she said.

"Jenn," Kathryn repeated with a smile that set Jenn's heart racing. "Well, Jenn, I'll see you tonight at nine minutes past eight."

Kathryn turned and nodded to the doorman before disappearing into the hotel lobby. Jenn watched her leave, wondering what on earth she was getting herself into.

6

STREETCAR NAMED DESIRE

JENN NERVOUSLY PACED up and down the streetcar stop in her work outfit of black trousers, a short-sleeved white shirt, and a black tie. She was waiting for the streetcar to arrive so they could do a quick turnaround and begin the journey back down Saint Charles Avenue.

She knew exactly why she was nervous; she had spent the last couple of hours going over every single element of the interactions she'd had with Kathryn that day. The woman had undergone a miraculous transformation from rude to enigmatic in a short space of time.

As Jenn had eaten her evening meal, she stared blankly at the television in her small apartment. Mentally she was picking over every segment of the conversation they had shared during the walk from the cemetery to the hotel.

She was convinced that Kathryn had been flirting with her. So convinced that after her shower, she had spent a little extra time curling her long blonde hair and had applied a touch more makeup than she usually did for an evening on the streetcars.

She didn't know exactly what to make of Kathryn. She had been rude and abrasive at first, but she'd also been dumped in the middle of town and clearly didn't want to be there. That would have distressed anyone, surely? Later Kathryn had showed another side to her personality. She had a streak of humour, and Jenn wondered what else was buried under the harsh shell. Maybe she'd been wrong to write Kathryn off so quickly?

Jenn's famously poor gaydar was more confused than ever. During her detailed analysis of the conversation, she'd managed to confuse herself even further. At first, she was convinced that Kathryn had been mildly flirting with her. But as doubts began to assert themselves, Jenn worried that she had read too much into things.

Luckily, the two-hour streetcar journey would give her plenty more time to analyse the situation and learn more about her new companion.

The rumbling sound indicated that the streetcar was approaching. Jenn stopped her pacing and waited for the vintage army-green vehicle to arrive at the station stop. The streetcars that ran the Saint Charles Avenue line were the original vehicles, each of them considered a heritage piece in their own right, having been built in the 1920s.

Each streetcar was beautifully maintained. The simple driver's seat at the front of the vehicle was a high wooden swivel chair with space to stand in front. The controls were heavy metal levers. The floor, walls, and window frames were all constructed from wood, and the wooden benches were all restored originals. The only modern items were the glass windows which were reinforced and could be opened to allow airflow on hot days.

Once the doors swung open, Jenn climbed on board and quickly spoke with her co-worker who was relieved to be going home after a long day of driving. Jenn's shift was thankfully a lot shorter and took in two round trips of the line, which took just over four hours to complete. The line was open practically twenty-four hours a day in the summer, but Jenn only ever worked up until midnight.

She placed her rucksack in the corner and began to change the overhead display to show the new destination of the streetcar.

"You're *driving*?!"

Jenn looked down and through the open door to Kathryn, who was looking up at her with an astonished face.

"Yep." Jenn smiled as she noted Kathryn had changed into a black tank top and khaki-coloured cargo trousers.

"I thought you said conductor?" Kathryn asked. She regarded the antiquated vehicle with a frown.

"Same thing." Jenn shrugged. She sat on the driver's seat. "So, what do you say? Trust me?"

Kathryn paused for a moment before climbing up the steep steps and into the vehicle. Jenn watched as she looked at the empty carriage with captivation.

"Is this an original vehicle?"

"Yep." She swivelled her chair around, watching as Kathryn walked down the middle of the carriage. "There are about thirty of them on the line."

Kathryn examined the features with a smile on her face. "Amazing," she breathed.

"Well, look at that, we found something about New Orleans that you like."

Kathryn rolled her eyes playfully. "If you're going to be like that I could leave again."

Jenn reached behind her and pulled a lever which caused the doors to heavily slam shut.

Kathryn stood in the centre of the carriage regarding Jenn with a smirk. She put her hands on her hips and drawled, "Really?"

Jenn swallowed thickly and released the door again. Confident Kathryn was all kinds of scary and hot. Jenn found herself flustered as she turned back to the control panel and mindlessly fiddled with some of the switches.

Kathryn walked back towards the driver's seat and looked at the controls with interest. "So, where are we going?"

"Saint Charles Avenue, all the way to South Carrollton Avenue, then up to South Claiborne and then we turn around and head back again."

Kathryn shrugged disinterestedly as if the street names meant little to her.

"I should warn you the whole trip takes around two hours," Jenn admitted. She hoped the long journey wouldn't put Kathryn off.

Kathryn looked around the carriage, her gaze settling on a wooden bench at the front that ran against the wall. It was the closest to the driver's seat and opposite the door.

"I guess I'll sit here?" she said.

Jenn looked up as Kathryn sat herself down. She placed her arm along the back of the bench and looked out of the window.

She looks like a film star, Jenn thought.

"S—sure," Jenn said out loud. She mentally kicked herself, wondering what on earth had gotten into her.

Other passengers started to approach the streetcar. Jenn greeted them warmly as they made their way down the carriage and took their seats. Jenn looked at the old-fashioned clock on the wall. She reached up and pulled the wire that in turn rang the bell to indicate the vehicle was going to start moving.

The streetcar rattled its way down Canal Street, the open windows of the vehicle providing a nice through-breeze. Jenn could feel Kathryn's eyes upon her and focused intensely on driving. They turned onto Saint Charles Avenue and passed through the edge of the Business District.

They frequently stopped, and passengers got on and off. Jenn used the opportunity to glance back at Kathryn. She could tell that she was unimpressed with the start of the journey, presumably she had already seen the Business District and its standard metropolitan style.

Jenn smiled to herself as she remembered the first time that she had taken the streetcar to see what all the fuss was about. She had also found it boring until farther down the famous Saint Charles Avenue, where she was suddenly awestruck by the buildings and architecture. She hoped Kathryn would feel the same.

They passed through a roundabout, went under the expressway, and Jenn adjusted one of her many rearview mirrors so she could see Kathryn's bored expression without turning around. In the Business District there were no real sights to speak of, but the streetcar was now off of the road and onto a private central reservation which made driving a lot easier.

The traffic thinned out, the Business District faded away, and the Garden District took its place. Large trees began to frame the street, and slowly but surely the landscape started to change. The streetcar rattled along, occasionally stopping to let passengers on and off.

Jenn risked a glance at Kathryn. She was staring out of the open window, enthralled by the sight of the boulevard. Exquisite mansions with porches and balconies lined either side of the street; the trees and gardens were all perfectly landscaped. Churches, university buildings, stylish restaurants, and more went by, and every time Jenn turned to look at Kathryn she was relieved to see her smiling as she took everything in.

At one stop an elderly lady with a cane was waiting. Jenn stopped the streetcar and eagerly hopped down from the vehicle to assist the woman up the steep stairs. Jenn walked the woman to a seat and took her fare money. As she walked back towards the driver's seat, she bent down towards Kathryn and pointed up and out of the vehicle.

"If you look in the trees you can still see the Mardi Gras beads," Jenn told her with a grin. Kathryn looked up at spotted a few of the brightly coloured beads—tossed there back in February—and smiled.

Jenn took her seat again and rang the bell. They moved farther down Saint Charles Avenue. It was a very long road, and by the end of it there were only a couple of passengers still on the streetcar.

Kathryn got up and stood by Jenn at the driver's podium. "May I stand with you?"

"Sure," Jenn replied, "just hold on."

Kathryn nodded and held onto a grab-bar by the door. She watched with interest as Jenn drove the streetcar across Saint Charles and onto South Carrollton Avenue. Kathryn looked out of the front windows with awe as they passed by more beautiful houses, churches, schools, and parks.

"Thank you," she said softly.

"What for?" Jenn asked with a frown as she focused on the road in front of her.

"For showing me this," Kathryn replied.

"Thank you for coming, it's nice to share the journey with someone," Jenn said.

Kathryn chuckled. "Don't you always share the journey with someone? Nearly fifty other someones?"

"You know what I mean. A certain someone." She felt the blush touch her cheeks and quickly turned her attention towards the road.

"So, you drive up here and then what? Do you turn around?"

"Well, we do, but the streetcar doesn't," Jenn said.

She hooked her thumb towards the other end of the vehicle. Kathryn looked over her shoulder towards the identical driver's console at the other end of the carriage.

"Oh, I see. Very clever."

"There's a ten-minute stop when we get there," Jenn told her. "There's a shop if you want to get a drink or something."

"Sounds good." Kathryn nodded her head. "I owe you a drink or two by now."

They stopped at the end terminus, and Kathryn headed over to the shop. Jenn said good night to the departing passengers before closing down her driver's panel and walking up the carriage to the other one.

The sun had started to set, and Jenn knew that the route back would alternate between darkness and beautifully lit buildings. She hoped that Kathryn would enjoy the sight as much as she did. She smiled at the feeling that New Orleans was doing its bit to turn Kathryn's opinions around.

Kathryn returned with a large paper bag. Jenn raised her eyebrow.

"I bought snacks," Kathryn announced. "But then I realised I didn't know what you liked so I got a selection."

Kathryn climbed the steps and balanced the bag on the driver's console. She opened the bag and Jenn peered inside. There were chips, chocolate, and a large bag of marshmallow treats.

"You did good," Jenn said in a serious tone. "I think I'll keep you."

"Best news I've had all day," Kathryn said. "Literally."

Jenn plucked a chocolate bar from the bag. Kathryn took out a bottle of apple juice.

"So, I know I'm still technically a stranger," Jenn said, "but why did your sister dump you here?"

Kathryn let out a sigh and leaned against the wall of the carriage. She absentmindedly picked at the label on the drink bottle.

"Erica and I are very different. She's… she's fun, and I'm not. I take things more seriously, and everything is a joke to her. Let's just say that she thinks that everything can be solved with alcohol and a party mentality."

Jenn didn't have to ask if Kathryn thought the opposite. That much was obvious.

"So, she thinks that... whatever's bothering you... will be solved by partying it up in NOLA?"

"Apparently," Kathryn admitted. "That and there's an important deal being signed right now, and she wants me out of the way."

Jenn quirked an eyebrow. "You work together?"

"Yes, Erica, myself, and our mother set up a PR business after I graduated from college. With my knowledge, Erica's personality, and our mother's capital investment, it's gone from strength to strength."

"And now some deal is going down and they want you out of the way?" Jenn fished. Something didn't make sense. She remembered Erica mentioning a name that had Kathryn launching herself towards her sister in a murderous rage.

Addison, she remembered. *That was it.*

There was clearly a big piece of this puzzle that she was missing out on.

"Yes, they—" Kathryn paused as she noticed other passengers approaching the streetcar.

Jenn resisted the urge to slam the door closed in their faces. Kathryn wandered towards the front bench and took her seat.

Jenn welcomed the passengers on board and took their fares. The opportunity was lost, but the evening was going so well that Jenn hoped she would have another chance to find out what had happened.

A few minutes passed, and more passengers climbed aboard. As the minute hand swept onto the departure time, Jenn closed the door and they were underway again. As soon as they started to move, Kathryn stood up and took her place beside Jenn again.

Kathryn asked questions about the buildings they passed, and Jenn answered as best she could, thankful for her near-encyclopaedic knowledge of her city.

Now and then the streetcar would jolt a little and Kathryn would almost fall into Jenn with a surprised giggle.

Jenn was amazed and mesmerised by the change in the woman. She wondered if Erica was maybe right, that Kathryn was just desperately in need of a vacation. The person who had fumed in the middle of Bourbon Street and the woman whose eyes sparkled with the fairy lights that adorned the passing houses were two different species.

They made small talk, taking the cues from their surroundings. It was never awkward, and the silences were always comfortable. By the end of the hour-long journey back, it seemed as if they had talked about everything and nothing all at once.

It was quarter past ten in the evening when the streetcar came to a stop at Canal Street. Jenn waved goodbye to the departing passengers as they filed off the streetcar.

"That was wonderful." Kathryn beamed as she turned to face Jenn. "I had no idea a simple tram journey could be so much fun."

"Streetcar," Jenn corrected as she shut down the driver's panel.

"Of course. Thank you, again. I know our first meeting was—"

"In the past." Jenn looked up. "You were having a bad day."

Kathryn smiled gratefully before looking around the streetcar. "So, what happens now? Does someone take over from you?"

"I have another journey to do." Jenn indicated the direction of travel with her thumb. "I turn around and do it all again."

"Oh." Kathryn looked around the empty carriage pensively. "Would you... would you like some more company? Or have I bored you enough for one day?"

Jenn felt her eyes light up at the prospect. "I'd love some company! Are you sure, though? It's another two-hour trip."

"Sounds good to me," Kathryn said. "We were talking so much during the journey back that the time just flew by. And the streets look so pretty in the dark with all the lights."

"Great!" Jenn hadn't realised how sad she was at the prospect of Kathryn's departure until she realised she'd be staying. Now, the long shift into the evening was looking much brighter.

7

HUNGER STRIKES

REBECCA KNELT DOWN and angled her camera up, trying to capture the beauty of St Louis Cathedral. The sun was beginning to set, turning the sky a deep purple colour. The white building with three tall, grey spires was offset by the bright background. She knew it was a shot she'd never get again.

Part of the allure of photography was capturing those moments that only came around once. She leaned down a little lower, trying to force the perspective of the towering building. She took a couple of shots and rocked back on her heels as she looked at the screen to see how the pictures had come out.

Perfect, she thought. *Might add that to iStock.*

She looked around and saw Arabella strolling through the pathways of nearby Jackson Square. She took a couple of quick shots of Arabella while she was unaware. In the distance, she heard jazz drifting through the air. She wasn't entirely sure where it was coming from, but that didn't seem to be unusual in New Orleans. An impromptu concert could be set up anywhere, at any time.

She stood up, slung her bag over her shoulder, and walked over to Arabella.

"Capture the perfect shot?" Arabella asked when she approached.

"I did," Rebecca said, thinking about the candid photographs she had taken of Arabella.

"Maybe we should find somewhere to eat dinner?" Arabella suggested.

Rebecca quickly put the lens cap on her camera and put it back into her bag. She'd suggested they eat dinner hours earlier, but Arabella wasn't feeling hungry. Which was unusual because Arabella's eating schedule was regimented.

"Sure." Rebecca looked around the square at the restaurants in sight. "Do you have any idea what you want to eat?"

"Food. Soon."

Rebecca nodded. It seemed Arabella had sailed past hungry and into starving, something that was easy to do when your body was out of sorts after a day of travel. She gestured towards a café in the distance. It looked in good condition, had a glass of wine as a logo, and was close.

When they got there, Rebecca paused to look at the menu. It was the kind of place that did everything. She was about to ask Arabella what she thought when she passed her by and addressed the waitress, asking for a table for two.

She wondered how long Arabella had been suffering in

silence with hunger pangs so Rebecca could get the shot she wanted.

They were quickly seated, and Rebecca ordered a bread basket before the waitress left. She didn't know if one would have arrived anyway, but she didn't wish to leave it to chance. Arabella looked at her gratefully.

"Why didn't you tell me you were starving?"

"You were being artsy."

Rebecca laughed. "Artsy?"

"Yes, you get this faraway look, your eyes glaze over, and you drift off to take pictures." Arabella turned the page of her menu. "I don't want to get in the way."

"You don't get in the way," Rebecca said quickly. "If you're hungry in the future, tell me."

Arabella glanced up from her menu and slightly nodded her head.

"Promise me," Rebecca pressed. She wasn't accepting a half-hearted nod.

"Fine, fine," Arabella agreed.

Rebecca made a mental note to keep an eye on her. She didn't believe for one moment that Arabella would tell her if she was feeling hungry in the future. The woman was one of the most stubborn people she'd ever met.

The waitress placed a bread basket on the table and Rebecca quickly pushed it towards Arabella.

"I know white bread is a sin but eat something before you chew on the menu."

Arabella picked up a piece of bread and immediately started to eat it.

"No butter?" Rebecca asked.

One look told her that white bread and real butter

would be a step too far. She picked up a slice of bread, opened a pot of butter, and started to slather it on.

"It's a crime that you can look the way you do and eat the way you do," Arabella muttered.

"It'll catch up with me," Rebecca said.

"I gleefully await the day." Arabella closed the menu. "In the meantime, I'm having a salad."

Rebecca raised her eyebrow. "A salad? You're on holiday."

"Fat grams don't identify holidays."

Rebecca knew she was onto a losing battle and decided to save the topic for another day. The waitress returned, Arabella ordered salad and sparkling water, and Rebecca ordered a burger and a beer.

"What do you think of New Orleans so far?" Rebecca asked.

"It's certainly different to anything I've seen before," Arabella replied. She picked up another piece of bread. Rebecca knew better than to mention it.

"Is that a good thing or a bad thing?"

Arabella chuckled. "I'm not sure yet. It's very vibrant and different from what I'm used to. I don't think I'm going to be out on Bourbon Street at eleven o'clock this evening. But I'll certainly enjoy a glass of wine at an outdoor café and listen to the jazz one evening."

"Sounds like a great idea, we'll have to schedule that in. Maybe tomorrow, after your spa day and before we meet up with Jenn for dinner?" Rebecca suggested. She was looking forward to a more relaxed Arabella after the spa treatments.

"Maybe. I'm sure I'll fall asleep during the massage."

Arabella sat up straight and twisted her head from side to side to loosen the tight muscles. "They are going to use a new kind of body butter, it firms and smooths."

Rebecca had to stop herself before she claimed that Arabella didn't need such a thing. That road led to a lot of uncomfortable admissions about having watched Arabella closely enough to know.

"Sounds great. Good to know you're not completely anti-butter."

Arabella rolled her eyes and looked away.

The waitress delivered their drinks and Rebecca thanked her. She poured her beer into the glass provided, having learnt that Arabella wasn't a fan of anyone drinking directly from the bottle if a glass was offered.

She noticed Arabella was looking out of the restaurant windows to the seating area outside. She leaned forward and saw a female couple. They were holding hands, leaning in close, and deep in conversation.

"Cute couple," Rebecca said.

Arabella looked away, a light blush on her cheeks.

Rebecca wasn't about to let the subject drop. She continued watching the pair.

"Do you think they've been together long? Maybe this is a first date?"

Arabella sipped her water, her eyes flickering over to the window to assess the women outside.

"I don't think it's a first date, they are very touchy-feely," Arabella said.

Rebecca was about to point out that things way beyond touchy-feely often happened on first dates but thought better of it.

"Maybe," she said. "They make a good couple, though."

"We shouldn't stare," Arabella said. She turned back to face the table and looked down at her drink.

Rebecca sipped her beer. She wanted to press the point, to open a discussion about romantically involved women. But then she knew not to push an already stressed, and clearly very hungry, Arabella. It wasn't the right time.

"I suppose you think I'm a prude?" Arabella asked. "I'm not."

"I didn't say a word."

"Your silence speaks volumes."

"Silence, by virtue of being silent, speaks nothing."

Arabella opened her mouth to reply and then stopped. She closed her mouth, her lips tightening to form a thin line. "Let's talk about something else," she all but demanded.

I hope that massage tomorrow relaxes her, Rebecca thought. "Sure, what would you like to talk about?"

"Your plans for tomorrow," Arabella said quickly, clearly having grasped the first safe subject that had sprung to her mind.

Rebecca nodded. She listed the things she had in mind to do the next day. She hadn't made any firm plans yet, but she had some ideas. As she spoke, Arabella visibly relaxed.

That masseuse is going to earn their money tomorrow, Rebecca mused.

8

MALFUNCTIONING GAYDAR

Jenn waited for the lights to change. Out of the corner of her eye she watched Kathryn leaning against the wall of the streetcar. She'd just finished explaining all of the training she had gone through in order to become a qualified streetcar operator. Kathryn seemed suitably impressed.

The lights changed, and they started moving again. A couple of drunk young men wolf-whistled at them as the streetcar rattled by. Jenn shook her head and chuckled at their childishness.

"You have to admit, this city is obsessed with alcohol." Kathryn grinned. She'd been playfully trying to poke holes in Jenn's love affair with New Orleans for a while now.

"No more so than other places, we just have more relaxed rules." Jenn shrugged.

"But those slushie machines…" Kathryn laughed.

Jenn smiled. "Hey, it gets hot, what can I say? Some people just feel more refreshed after a frozen mojito!"

"Uh-huh."

"Don't knock it until you've tried one." Jenn gently elbowed Kathryn.

The streetcar came to a stop in front of another set of traffic lights. The junction was particularly busy, so Jenn picked up her water bottle and took a few long sips.

She felt Kathryn tapping her on the shoulder.

"Open the door," she commanded.

"What?" Jenn frowned.

"Open the door," Kathryn repeated.

Jenn turned to see Kathryn engaged in some silent conversation through hand gestures with a bartender in a run-down old bar across the street.

She laughed and opened the door. "I won't wait for you," she warned.

Kathryn took off quickly across the thankfully empty road. The bartender was already pouring her an alcoholic slushie as Kathryn waved some dollar bills in his direction.

Jenn's eyes switched from the red light in front of her to the exchange taking place at the bar. She watched as Kathryn looked both ways before running back towards the streetcar. She jumped up the steps just as the lights changed to green.

Jenn burst out laughing and closed the doors. She pulled the bell and took off the brake, causing the streetcar to start moving again. The passengers who had been watching Kathryn's alcohol dash burst into spontaneous applause. Kathryn curtsied and held her drink aloft to them.

"I would have got you one, but you're driving," Kathryn explained. "And I was against the clock."

"No problem," Jenn said. "What did you get?"

Kathryn regarded the icy drink with a frown before sniffing the top. "Red?"

Jenn kept an eye on the road as she reached up and pulled Kathryn's hand down. She took a small sip of the drink through the bright green straw.

"Mmm, strawberry daiquiri! Good choice!"

Kathryn took a sip herself and winced. "Ugh, sugar and food colouring."

"Yeah, never seen a strawberry in its life," Jenn admitted.

The trip raced by and Jenn found herself hoping more passengers wanted to board on the journey back towards Canal Street, just so they could spend some more time together. They laughed until they cried, and Jenn felt her breath restrict in her throat each time Kathryn placed her hand on her arm or shoulder when she spoke.

"Is that a casino down there?" Kathryn asked as they turned back onto Canal Street.

"Yep." Jenn nodded as she carefully navigated around the traffic and tourists on the busy street.

"Suppose you work there, too?" Kathryn laughed at her joke.

Jenn remained silent. She knew a blush was taking over her cheeks.

Kathryn stared at her. "Seriously? How many jobs do you have?"

"A few." Jenn shrugged.

"But you *do* work at the casino?" Kathryn pressed.

"Yeah, I'm not on shift for another week, though."

"Okay, I've consumed half of the world's worst strawberry daiquiri, so you'll have to bear with me here."

Kathryn placed her arm around Jenn's shoulder as she drove up the busy street. "A bartender, a marshal, a tour guide, a streetcar driver, a water aerobics instructor, *and* a casino employee?"

Jenn chuckled. It was amusing to listen to Kathryn listing the jobs she knew about on her fingers.

"Yep, there's more, but you'll have to wait to see what they are," she added flirtatiously.

"Oh, will I now?" Kathryn laughed.

A few short minutes later and the journey and Jenn's shift were finished. Jenn picked up her rucksack and handed the streetcar over to her co-worker. Both she and Kathryn exited the streetcar and stood in the large central reservation on Canal Street, the streetcar tracks on either side of them and the main road on either side of that.

"I had a great time this evening," Jenn said. She leaned casually against a lamppost.

"So did I," Kathryn confessed. "Except that drink. I thought this place was famous for its cocktails?"

"You need to let *me* make you one," Jenn explained. "Not buy one for three bucks."

"Oh, do you charge more?" Kathryn raised her eyebrow.

"I think you can afford me," Jenn said. She quickly took a step forward to place a kiss on Kathryn's lips.

Kathryn jumped back, startled. "What are you doing?!"

Jenn's eyes widened as she took in Kathryn's shocked and horrified expression. Her hand covered her mouth. "Oh my god, I'm so, so sorry."

"I'm not gay!" Kathryn hissed at her. She looked

around to see if anyone had been watching the scene unfold. "What… why… why did you kiss me?"

"Well… duh," Jenn said. She immediately wished she had come up with something better.

"You're… oh…" Kathryn took a deep breath. "I'm… flattered, really I am, but I'm straight. I'm sorry if I gave you the wrong impression."

Jenn swallowed. She attempted to look casual as she shook her head and held up a hand.

"It's fine, no problem… I'm the one who's sorry."

Kathryn stared wordlessly at her before finally nodding her head. "Thank you… for a lovely evening. I really did enjoy the sights. I'll… well… I… should be going."

Jenn nodded. "Okay, do you know your way back?"

Kathryn nodded, the earlier smile gone from her face and replaced with a serious expression. "I do. Good night, Jenn."

"'Night, Kathryn," Jenn said as she watched her turn and walk away.

She watched until Kathryn was out of sight and then leaned back against the lamppost and sighed to herself.

"Jenn, you idiot…"

9

LOOKING GAY

Dinner had been a tense affair. Rebecca was relieved when Arabella said she wanted to head back to the hotel and go to bed.

Clearly Arabella wasn't ready to talk about same-sex relationships and was also embarrassed by her reaction to the start of the conversation. Rebecca knew that Arabella's embarrassment often presented as anger, so they'd eaten in silence save for the odd observational comment about the restaurant's interior decoration.

They walked the short distance back to the Royale, passing crowds of people laughing, drinking, and generally celebrating. Rebecca suddenly felt like she didn't want the evening to be over, she wanted to stay up a while longer and experience a little more of New Orleans.

When they entered the lobby, Rebecca paused. She turned to face Arabella.

"I'm going to have a drink in the bar, so I'll say good-night." She deliberately didn't extend the invitation. She felt guilty for doing so, but she just needed some time to herself. If she was going to pretend that Arabella's reticence to acknowledge anything gay wasn't killing her inside, she needed some time to herself.

"Oh." Arabella seemed at a loss as she peered into the bar. "Okay, well, goodnight."

"See you at breakfast." Rebecca smiled as she passed her and entered the bar. She looked around and saw that many of the chairs and tables were taken, but there were a couple of free spaces at the bar. She approached the closest available barstool and sat down.

The bartender greeted her immediately.

"Hey, can I have a..." Rebecca scanned the optics, debating how much she wanted to forget the events of dinner versus how much of a hangover she wanted the next day. "Jack Daniels and Coke."

A napkin appeared in front of her, and, a moment later, her drink was served. The joy of a hotel bar was that service was always super speedy.

She took a sip before letting out a long sigh.

"Excuse me?"

She turned to acknowledge the brunette beside her. "Yes?"

"I'm so sorry, but I was wondering if I could ask you a question?"

The woman appeared to be drinking whisky, a couple of empty glasses lingered in front of her. Rebecca imagined that was down to the speed of intake rather than the slowness of the bar staff.

"Sure?" she said.

The woman pointed to the rainbow lapel pin that

Rebecca wore on her collar. "Forgive me if I'm being rude, but I'm guessing you identify as… gay?"

Rebecca smiled. This was one of the weirdest come-ons she'd experience in a while.

"Yeah, I'm gay. But I go by Rebecca." She held out her hand.

The woman smiled and shook her hand. "Kathryn."

"Nice to meet you, Kathryn." She took another sip of her drink. "Was that your question?"

"Not exactly."

"Then how can I help?"

Kathryn turned to face her head on. "Do I… look gay?" She gestured to her face and body with both hands.

Rebecca blinked.

Oh, boy, should have gone to bed.

She looked at Kathryn. She was smartly dressed, with mid-length, perfectly styled brown hair. There was nothing about her that screamed gay, she looked… average. Striking, but she'd fit into a crowd easily.

"Well, that's a hard question to answer," Rebecca admitted. "Gay comes in lots of different shapes and sizes. Sometimes it's easy to identify someone's sexuality, but many times it isn't. I wouldn't say you're giving off any obvious indicators of being gay. But, I'm guessing that if you hadn't seen my badge, you wouldn't have guessed my orientation either?"

"That's true," Kathryn allowed. She turned back to the bar.

"Are you?" Rebecca asked.

"Am I?"

"Gay… are you gay?"

"No." Kathryn sipped her drink.

Okay, maybe not a strange come-on, Rebecca decided. "May I ask why you asked if you look gay?"

Kathryn turned back to face her. She leaned in a little closer, as if about to divulge some enormous secret. "A woman… kissed me." She nodded sagely and sat back up. She pinned Rebecca with a knowing look, a 'Well, what do you say about *that*?' kind of look.

"Okay…" Rebecca really wished she had gone to bed instead of heading to the bar for a drink. "So, do you know why she kissed you? Do you know her well?"

"No, I met her today. Today!" Kathryn gestured to the bartender for another drink. "We spent the evening together, and then she kissed me."

"You spent the evening together?" Rebecca quizzed. "Like a date?"

"No… no. Like, she's… well. She works on the trams, and I was with her while she worked. She drives the tram."

"Streetcar," Rebecca corrected.

"Yes, that. Anyway. We did a couple of journeys up and down the route and then she kissed me."

"Why were you with her on the streetcar?"

Kathryn knocked back the last of her whisky as the bartender placed a fresh drink on a napkin in front of her. "She asked. I'm new to the city, she wanted to show me around."

Rebecca massaged her temple. "So, correct me if I'm wrong at any point here…"

Kathryn nodded eagerly.

"You're new to town. Meet this woman. She tells you that she works as a driver on the streetcars and invites you along. You go, you spend the evening together. Right?"

"Yes, all accurate."

"Do you talk on the streetcar?"

"Yes, she told me about her life here, I told her a little about me. Nothing much, small talk mainly. We laughed and joked. Shared some food."

"This is sounding very much like a date," Rebecca pointed out.

Kathryn scrunched her face up in thought. She turned back towards the bar and leaned her head into her hand.

"Maybe she thought it was," she admitted. "You're right, it does sound like a date. But I'm straight... so, I'm drawn back to my original question: do I look gay?"

"And back to my original answer, it's hard to say. Some people dress and style themselves so they stand out as obviously gay, and some people don't. It's impossible to know who is straight and who isn't just by looking at them these days." Rebecca tapped her badge. "Remember, we're only having this conversation because I happen to be wearing this."

"True," Kathryn agreed.

"She was being a bit presumptuous," Rebecca confessed. "I always double-check, you never know when you're misreading signals."

"Oh, it was just a peck," Kathryn said. "I won't be filing charges."

Rebecca smiled and returned her attention to her drink. She wondered what it was about women in their late thirties and older who were so confused by sexual identities. Kathryn seemed to think that she must have been inadvertently wearing a rainbow flag for a woman to have kissed her. Arabella couldn't even look at a female couple without her cheeks reddening.

Times had clearly changed a lot, people were talking more about their sexuality. People of Rebecca's generation rarely had an issue with the subject. Now Rebecca spent her time trying to reassure hot, older women.

"So, are you here with your girlfriend?" Kathryn asked.

Rebecca laughed. "No… not exactly."

Kathryn looked at her with a grin. "Not exactly; that sounds interesting."

Rebecca bit her lip and shook her head. She had come into the bar to wrap her mind around what was happening with Arabella. Who better to talk to about the matter than someone who seemed to be having similar issues.

"We met just before Christmas," Rebecca explained. "Hate at first sight."

Kathryn laughed.

"We were kind of forced to share a car journey home. I swear, at first, I wanted to leave her by the road-side in Spain. But we sort of came together. I saw another side of her. Then she helped me with some things after and we stayed in touch. We're friends. Good friends."

"Just friends?" Kathryn pressed.

"She… she was engaged to be married, but she realised she didn't love him. Soon after we got back, she broke off the engagement. We got closer and…" She blew out a breath and ran a hand through her hair. "I thought we were getting somewhere. But then it kind of morphed back into friendship. We're travelling together and I'm hoping I'll get some kind of answer as to if we're friends, or possibly more."

"You want to be more than friends?"

Rebecca nodded. "Yes, I'll take friendship. But when she said she had feelings for me, and the chance of being more than friends was presented… I knew that was what I wanted."

"She said she has feelings for you?" Kathryn sipped at her drink.

"Yes, well, it's complicated. She needed time to figure out her feelings. I gave her time and space and… maybe I shouldn't have given her so much time and space."

Kathryn patted her on the shoulder. "I think you did the right thing. Very chivalrous of you. Or whatever that word would be for a woman. Respectful?"

Rebecca laughed bitterly. Yes, she'd been very respectful. But a part of her wondered what might have happened if she had been a little pushier. Would she be in a relationship with Arabella? Or just friends and happy in the knowledge that nothing more would come of it? That would free her up to date rather than keeping herself in suspended animation.

Not that she was in any sort of hurry. Arabella was worth waiting for. She just wished she had a timeline to work to. Some indication on whether or not anything would change, and if so, when?

"I suppose I was respectful," Rebecca finally agreed. "But now I'm kind of lost. I don't know if I should ask or leave it alone. Give her time to come to me or not. And I know she's struggling with it, too. But I don't know why. She's not great at opening up."

She sat in silence for a few seconds before she realised Kathryn wasn't saying anything. She turned to look at her.

Kathryn shrugged her shoulders. "I don't know what to tell you. I thought I'd had a rough night, but it wasn't that bad. I overreacted. At the end of the day, someone found me attractive and that's a nice thing to happen. You clearly have it much worse than I do, I feel like a fraud for complaining." She smiled kindly. "I'm really sorry. I hope you and your friend manage to figure everything out."

"Thanks, me too." Rebecca let out a breath she'd been holding and relaxed her shoulders. It felt good to speak to someone, even if it didn't resolve the issue.

She knocked back the rest of her drink. "I think I'm going to head to bed; thanks for listening," she said.

"No problem. I really do hope things work out." Kathryn raised her glass to her lips. She paused and looked at the liquid woozily before putting the glass back down. "I think I better call it a night as well."

Arabella stared up at the ceiling. Her hotel room was beautiful, with original plasterwork features on the ceiling, a picture rail around the walls, and a chandelier light fitting. The bed was divine, a firm but forgiving mattress, soft pillows, and bedding that was crisp and clean yet welcoming.

But she couldn't sleep.

She'd love to say it was jetlag, or the excitement of the day, or the distant sounds of a city that definitely never slept. The truth was, it wasn't any of those things. She had been lying awake for the last three-quarters of an hour because she felt guilty.

She'd ruined dinner with Rebecca. A sudden downturn in her blood sugar levels, coupled with the embarrassment of Rebecca catching her watching a young, female couple, had caused her to become tetchy.

Once she became embarrassed, it was hard for her to snap out of it. Then she started to feel guilty for her behaviour and the whole thing escalated from there.

It wasn't until she'd returned to the hotel room, angrily scrubbed the makeup from her face, and prepared for bed that she realised she could have solved it all with a simple apology. Rebecca was infinitely understanding of her mood swings.

But Arabella felt terrible for putting her through them. It wasn't Rebecca's fault that she was a mess.

She couldn't blame Rebecca for wanting to have a drink in the hotel bar. If their positions were reversed, she'd probably want to drink away any memory of the evening, too.

She turned over and grabbed the unused pillow from the other side of the bed and hugged it to her chest. She knew she was running from her feelings. Certainly, running from something. Every time she started to even consider her feelings for Rebecca, or her thoughts towards homosexuality, her brain shut down.

It was impossible to come to any conclusions if any time you thought about something, your mind went blank.

She heard a muted clicking sound. She turned her head and listened carefully. A moment later, she heard a door closing. Rebecca had returned to her room next door.

She stared at the interconnecting door.

The need to apologise clawed at her.

She didn't quite know what to say. But she had to say something. She hugged the pillow closer to her chest as she tried to think of how to word it. She was torn between a blanket apology and an explanation. Not that she had an explanation as such.

She sat up and kicked the sheets away. She rubbed at her face and debated putting a light amount of foundation on. It was ridiculous, but she knew she was that vain. And she knew Rebecca would see right through it.

She got up and walked into the bathroom. She turned on the bright lights that surrounded the mirror. Leaning in, she looked at her reflection and tilted her head from side to side. She looked tired. But then she had been in bed for a while, of course she would look tired.

"Pull yourself together," she muttered. "Just... say sorry. End of story."

She pushed herself away from the counter and turned off the light. She checked her silk pyjamas were in order, with no undone buttons, and then walked towards the connecting door.

Before she had a chance to connect her shaking knuckles to the wood, she heard Rebecca's door open and close again.

Rebecca had gone out.

She took a few steps back. Her jaw dropped as she stared at the door in horror.

Rebecca had gone *out*.

It was the middle of the night, so it was clear to her where Rebecca was going. To see someone. Probably someone she had just met in the bar. It was the only possible explanation.

She put some distance between herself and the door. She climbed into bed and wrapped the now-cool sheets around her.

She didn't own Rebecca, and Rebecca certainly didn't owe her any explanations. She slowly lowered herself back down to the mattress. She knew sleep wouldn't come easily that night.

10

ANSWERS

ARABELLA LOOKED at her reflection in the mirror of her hotel bathroom. She leaned in close and used her finger to smooth out a stray piece of lipstick. She took a step back and fluffed up her hair.

She rolled her eyes at her behaviour and grabbed her clutch bag from the counter. She picked up her keycard and left the room, walking quickly towards the elevators.

When she'd woken up, she noticed she had a text message from Rebecca saying that she'd meet her downstairs in the restaurant for breakfast.

She'd wondered if Rebecca had knocked to try to wake her that morning. The previous evening, she'd resorted to the sleeping pills she had been saving for the flight home in order to finally get to sleep. Her mind had been spinning up until that point, and she knew sleep wouldn't come without medical intervention.

The morning sun hadn't been welcome, but she'd decided to do her best to try to turn events around. And that started with breakfast—and with trying to not feel like she had a knife in her chest while asking how Rebecca's evening had gone.

She approached the restaurant manager and gave him her name and room number. "My companion should already be here, Rebecca Edwards?"

He checked his list and nodded. "Ah, of course. If you'll join me please, Miss Henley." He snatched a menu from his podium and led her through the large dining room.

She saw Rebecca sitting in a booth by the window, watching the world go by while holding a mug of what she guessed was hot coffee. She turned and saw Arabella approaching and smiled in greeting.

"Hey, good morning."

"Good morning." Arabella took her seat.

"Can I get you some tea or coffee?" the manager asked.

"Coffee, please."

"And some more for me, please," Rebecca asked.

He opened the menu and handed it to Arabella. "I'll be back with coffee in a moment."

"So, wow, those beds are something, right?" Rebecca asked.

Arabella gripped the menu tightly. "Yes, very comfortable."

"It was like heaven," Rebecca added.

Arabella stared at the breakfast menu with an intensity that caused her to fear it might spontaneously combust in her hands. Was she really expected to discuss Rebecca's...

what? Conquest? She hadn't signed up to that. She wouldn't do it.

"I don't think I've had a better night's sleep in ages," Rebecca continued on.

Arabella's jaw was so tight she wondered if she'd ever be able to unlatch it to eat her breakfast. Her eyes turned to look at the oatmeal, minimal chewing required.

"Two pots of coffee." The restaurant manager returned and placed the two silver pots on the table. "Are you ready to order?"

"I am, I'm famished," Rebecca said. She immediately ordered a plate of pancakes with fresh fruit, as well as a side plate of bacon.

Arabella lowered her menu and looked at Rebecca in disgust. Famished. She shivered at the suggestion.

Rebecca frowned. "What? Pancakes and bacon are a breakfast thing here."

"Unbelievable," she muttered and quickly glanced at her menu again. "Eggs benedict, please." Diet be damned,

The manager took their menus and departed again.

Rebecca looked at her with a confused expression. "Is everything okay?"

"Why wouldn't it be?" Arabella asked. She swiped the fabric napkin from the table and unfolded it, placing it on her lap.

"I don't know, you seem a little off…" Rebecca trailed off as her eyes drifted behind Arabella.

"Good morning!" she called out suddenly.

Arabella turned around in the booth and saw a woman walking towards them. She was in her mid-thirties, wore far too much makeup, and hadn't bothered to do anything with her brown locks.

Ah, the conquest.

"Hi there!" the slattern said. "How are you this morning?"

Arabella rolled her eyes and returned her attention to pouring some coffee. She couldn't deal with that awful American accent before she'd ingested some caffeine.

"I'm good, how are you? Headache?" Rebecca asked with a chuckle.

"Yes, a little. This must be your friend?"

"Yes, this is Arabella. Arabella, this is Kathryn. I met her at the bar last night."

Kathryn stuck her hand out and Arabella gave it the minutest of shakes.

"She wouldn't stop talking about you," Kathryn said.

Arabella raised her eyebrow. She didn't think that statement was entirely appropriate considering the circumstances.

"You have a great friend in this one," Kathryn said, jutting a thumb towards Rebecca.

Rebecca blushed and waved Kathryn away. "Go and have your breakfast, you'll need it to soak up all that alcohol," she laughed.

"You're right, you're absolutely right. Have a good day, hope to catch up with you both later."

"Good to know I'm a topic of conversation," Arabella said after Kathryn left.

Rebecca's blushed deepened. "Well, she was talking a lot, and I felt I needed to say something. She'd had a lot to drink."

"So I gather."

Arabella was reeling. Knowing that Rebecca was off having late-night trysts was one thing. Having to discuss them the next morning over stainless-steel kitchenware was another matter. And the drunken woman involved in the whole debacle wanting to greet her and shake her hand… it was more than she could take.

She was fuming. How dare Rebecca drag her all this way and then behave like that. Okay, so maybe she *was* a prude. But it just wasn't acceptable.

"You know, Rebecca—" Arabella started.

"One second…" Rebecca gestured towards the restaurant manager as he was passing. "Excuse me, I was wondering if you could organise a new room keycard for me? I went to the gym late last night, and I had to try several times before it let me in. When I got back to my room it was the same thing."

He looked apologetic. "Of course, miss. I'll get reception to get a new card for you, and I'll deliver it with your breakfast."

"Thank you, I thought I better ask now before I forget and get locked out of my room entirely!"

He nodded politely before leaving. Rebecca turned back to Arabella. "Sorry about that, I wanted to catch him before I forgot again. You were saying?"

"Y—you went to the gym last night?" Arabella asked.

"Yes, I had a quick drink in the bar, chatted with Kathryn for a bit, and then decided to go to bed. But on the way back to my room I realised how wired I was and thought I'd take advantage of the twenty-four-hour gym.

They weren't kidding about the views, you'll love it up there."

Arabella felt faint with relief. She slumped back into her chair and stared at the tablecloth.

"Wow, are you okay?" Rebecca was out of her seat and next to her in a few short seconds. "You've gone really pale."

"Fine, fine." Arabella tried to sit up. She realised her hands were shaking slightly, so she clasped them in her lap. "I took a couple of sleeping pills to get to sleep last night; I think I just need to eat something."

"Are you sure?" Rebecca placed her hand on Arabella's shoulder and looked at her seriously.

She took a deep breath and nodded her head. The shock was starting to dissipate, and she was feeling better already. Rebecca hadn't gone off with some woman. She'd just gone to the gym, all perfectly reasonable. She wondered why she hadn't even considered it before.

She tried to push down the reason why she was so relieved. It was another thing she wasn't quite ready to acknowledge. Something she knew she would have to recognise sooner rather than later.

Rebecca's hand still rested on her shoulder. Arabella looked up and met her eyes.

"I'm okay, sorry if I scared you… As I say, just tired. And probably the pills. Some breakfast will do me a world of good."

Rebecca lowered her hand but continued to watch Arabella as if afraid she might shatter at any moment.

"Maybe I should stay behind today?"

"No, I don't want you to change your plans. And I'll

be here at the hotel. If anything happens—which it won't—I'll be in good hands."

Rebecca didn't look fully convinced, but she slowly nodded. "Okay, but if you feel unwell again, I want you to text me and I'll come straight back."

"Agreed. But seriously, I'm fine." Arabella took a sip of coffee. Luckily her shaking hands were back under control. "Tell me what you're planning to do today again?"

Rebecca reached across the table and pulled her coffee cup closer, having apparently decided to relocate to sit beside Arabella.

She started talking about her plans. She'd already decided to head out with her camera and explore the French Quarter some more.

Arabella tuned out the details, too consumed with the happiness she felt at knowing that Rebecca hadn't hooked up with some stranger the night before.

She couldn't wait any longer, she had to figure out her feelings and take action. Rebecca was a catch, and if she didn't hurry up and make up her mind, she might lose her.

Luckily, she had an entire day relaxing at the spa to think things through and decide what she wanted.

11

STARTING OVER

JENN SLOWLY OPENED the door from her apartment building to the street. She looked in both directions, trying to determine if it was safe or not. She had half expected to see Kathryn standing right outside her building, such was the frequency of their bumping into each other the previous day.

Thankfully, there was no sign of her.

She stepped outside and hurried along the street towards her third favourite coffee shop. She decided on that one as she considered it to be the least touristy and therefore the one with the smallest chance of attracting someone new to the city. Someone like Kathryn.

After she grabbed a coffee to go, she took the long route down to the Mississippi River. She was thankfully early for her afternoon shift on one of the few remaining steamboats that took passengers out on trips up and down the river.

Not only was it a job she enjoyed, but it would give

her the opportunity to take her mind off of the ill-fated kiss from the previous evening. Since it had happened, her brain had unhelpfully replayed the kiss over and over again.

Distraction would be welcome, and an afternoon on the river was perfect for that. It was hard to be caught up in your own troubles when you were sailing along the Mississippi, regaling tourists with stories of times gone by and listening to the sounds of the live jazz band aboard.

All the stresses and worries of the day seemed to disappear when she was on the river. The gentle sway of the boat knocked them overboard, and the paddlewheel washed them away.

In the years since Jenn first started working on the steamboat, she'd taken on most jobs at some point. Now she'd progressed to the role of host, which was more of a pleasure than a job.

Being a host involved greeting people as they queued on the dockside while they waited for the ship to be prepared. She also helped them to board, and then walked around the boat during the cruise and answered questions.

She'd once joked with her boss that she was literally paid to chat with passengers. He'd quickly gotten his phone and showed her some of the online reviews the company had received. All of the reviews were extremely positive. Many mentioned Jenn personally and thanked her for her time.

The positive publicity was worth its weight in gold. And it was definitely worth the company's time to pay Jenn to chat with the passengers.

Jenn loved to chat, and most of the part-time jobs she had enabled her to speak with people from all walks of life. No matter what was happening in her own world, she knew she would be able to surround herself with people and pass the time of day with some small talk.

Now thoughts of the miscalculated kiss were rushing through her mind, and Jenn knew that she was in desperate need of some distraction. But her first job was to walk the long way around to the dock. The long way because she didn't want to bump into Kathryn as she had so many times the day before.

So, she walked out and around the tourist areas of the French Quarter before walking back along the riverside road towards the dock.

Unfortunately, there was only one way into the dock, through a paved plaza with a number of popular cafes on either side. Chairs and tables were scattered across the paved area, giving tourists the best view of the river and the ships.

She turned into the plaza and immediately came to a dead stop.

"You have *got* to be kidding me," she mumbled.

Kathryn sat at a table with a glass of water and a cup of what she guessed was coffee in front of her. She was facing away from Jenn, looking towards the river through large, dark sunglasses.

Jenn took in the scene and calculated a way around Kathryn without being seen. She knew there was an alleyway where the trash was kept—she sighed. She couldn't justify climbing over bags of trash just to avoid Kathryn. And what would she do for the next thirteen days of Kathryn's stay in the city? It would be impossible to avoid her.

The kiss had been an honest mistake, and the best way to clear the air was to apologise and try to move forward.

She took a deep breath and walked over to Kathryn's table.

Standing in front of Kathryn, she offered a shy smile.

"Hi, I'm Jenn Cook. I'm gay with the worst gaydar on the planet. I sometimes mistakenly kiss straight women, but I promise it's not a regular occurrence. And, when I do, I'm very sorry."

The sunglasses made Kathryn's eyes unreadable. Luckily, a smile crept onto her lips and after a few short moments, Kathryn raised her hand.

"Kathryn Foster. Pleasure to meet you, Miss Cook."

Jenn shook Kathryn's proffered hand. "I'm so sorry. I —I just…"

"Don't mention it." Kathryn shook her head softly. "It was a stressful day for me yesterday. You'd been very kind, and I'm sorry I reacted in the way I did."

Jenn let out a relieved breath and finally lowered her shoulders away from her ears. She couldn't believe that Kathryn was being so forgiving. After her outburst yesterday, Jenn was sure Kathryn would be livid.

She wondered again if the first impressions she'd had of her were entirely wrong. Maybe her sister Erica was right, she thought again; maybe Kathryn was stressed beyond all reason and a vacation was exactly what she needed.

"So, we're good?" Jenn confirmed. "I don't have to sneak around the city in case I bump into you?"

"Were you?"

Jenn smiled at Kathryn's raised eyebrow that appeared from under the sunglasses. "I might have been."

"Well, you're doing a terrible job." Kathryn gestured to herself.

"Yeah, seems like fate keeps throwing us together," Jenn pointed out.

"Indeed it does. Are you going to the casino today? Or are you driving streetcars?" Kathryn took a sip of coffee. "Or maybe the tourist office?"

Jenn rubbed the back of her neck. "Um, no, not any of them."

"Day off?" Kathryn enquired with a surprised tone.

"Nope." Jenn grinned.

"Oh my god, you're going to yet another job, aren't you?"

Jenn chuckled and nodded.

"Are you trying for some kind of record?" Kathryn deadpanned. "Is someone following you and taking notes?"

"Ha-ha. No, I just like change," Jenn explained.

"I see. So, what is it today? Lion tamer? Trainee astronaut?"

"Nah, that's Monday," Jenn joked.

Even with the dark glasses, she could tell Kathryn was rolling her eyes.

"Actually, I'm working there for the afternoon," Jenn said, pointing towards the steamboat at the dock.

Kathryn turned to look in the direction she pointed. "Where?"

"The steamboat," Jenn clarified.

"Wait, don't tell me." She pretended to size Jenn up. "You're the captain?"

Jenn laughed. "No, I'm a host."

"Host? What does a host do?" Kathryn enquired with a smile.

"Help people aboard, make sure everyone is happy, point out interesting sights along the river," Jenn answered.

"Sounds like fun," Kathryn commented.

Before Jenn knew what she was saying, an invitation spilled from her lips. "Would you like to come?"

"Me?" Kathryn looked confused.

"Yes, you. Consider it our second non-date. It's a lot of fun, and a great way to see the city. I still want you to love New Orleans."

Kathryn removed her sunglasses and regarded the ship with interest. "How long is this trip?"

"Three hours. There's food included." Jenn didn't know why she was inviting Kathryn. It was as if she were a glutton for punishment.

"Maybe." Kathryn sighed and looked away from the steamboat and up at Jenn. "I wouldn't want to get in the way. In *your* way."

Jenn nodded. "I understand. It's a large boat, but I understand if you have other plans."

A waitress appeared and placed a Caesar salad on the table in front of Kathryn. Kathryn thanked her, the waitress nodded and left them alone again.

"I'll leave you to your lunch," Jenn said. "Seriously, though, if you're at a loose end you should come along. We depart at two, and I guarantee you'll enjoy it. I'll leave a ticket for you at check-in, in case you decide to come along."

"Thank you." Kathryn nodded politely. "I'll think about it."

Jenn nodded and gave an awkward wave goodbye before walking towards the dock. As she walked, she rolled her eyes at herself. What was she thinking inviting Kathryn on board? And why did she *wave* goodbye?

On the bright side, Kathryn didn't seem to hate her, and all was forgiven. That knowledge alone added a spring to her step.

ALL ABOARD

JENN WALKED along the dockside while the boat was being prepared for the upcoming cruise. Passengers were starting to gather and wait to board, so she approached them and asked about their hometowns, vacation plans, and offered suggestions for restaurants and where to find the best jazz in town.

She was asked many of the same questions time and again. Best gumbo, best jazz, best beignets. She mixed it up a bit, she didn't want to sound like she had a favourite or was driving customers to a certain establishment.

It also meant she had to ensure she was up to date with what was going on in New Orleans. She didn't want to recommend somewhere that had closed a month ago. It was another reason why the job was a pleasure and a challenge.

She looked up at the gathering crowd, trying to see if she could spot Kathryn. When she didn't see her, she found she was torn between relief and disappointment.

"Jenn!"

She spun around at the sound of her name. Her English friend Rebecca ran to meet her, and they collided in a messy hug.

"Bex!" She sprinted over and held out her arms. "It's so good to see you!"

"So good to see you, too!" Rebecca greeted her.

Jenn took a step back and looked at her friend. It had been years since they'd seen each other.

"You haven't changed a bit," Jenn said.

"Neither have you! Well, more tanned."

"And you're just as pale as ever."

"Guilty, trying to fix that, though," Rebecca said.

Jenn looked around. "Where's your girlfriend?"

Rebecca chuckled. "I told you, Arabella is not my girlfriend. Just… a friend. Who I'm travelling with."

"Right." Jenn clucked her tongue.

Rebecca playfully elbowed her in the ribs. "Hey, I'm not saying I wouldn't be happy—ecstatic, even—if it happened. It's just not happening yet."

"I hear you. So, where is your not-girlfriend?"

"Chilling at the hotel spa. She's been majorly stressed with work, so she's taking a day out to relax. She's joining us for dinner, though. She's looking forward to meeting you."

"I'm looking forward to meeting her. You don't talk about anyone else lately," Jenn joked.

Rebecca's cheeks started to redden. It was true, though; most of Rebecca's recent communications had included mentions of the mysterious Arabella. Ever since they had shared a journey over Christmas. It was clear that Rebecca was head over heels for the woman.

Jenn had tried to ferret out more information, but Rebecca had been reticent. Finally, she promised that she would dish the dirt when they met up in the summer.

"Yeah, yeah, whatever," Rebecca now sidestepped the subject. "When's this boat get moving?"

"You're coming along?" Jenn asked.

"Of course! You said I had to see it, so I here I am."

"That's great! I thought you might be jetlagged."

"I can sleep when I die," Rebecca joked. She pulled a leaflet out of her shorts pocket and opened it up. "Besides, I'm looking forward to listening to 'soothing jazz' while eating 'world-class food'."

Jenn laughed. "Hey, I didn't write that. But the jazz is soothing. And the food... well, it's not going to hurt you. Too bad."

Her walkie-talkie sprang to life, and the captain gave the all-clear for passengers to begin boarding. Jenn looked apologetically at Rebecca.

"Hey, it's fine, I knew you'd be working. I'll just hang around and entertain myself, no problem," Rebecca reassured her.

"We'll catch up later," Jenn promised.

She started the passenger boarding process, beginning by assisting a wheelchair-bound passenger up the ramp and onto the boat. She positioned the passenger and her family at the back of the boat with the best view of the enormous paddlewheel.

She watched as other customers boarded and started to make their way around the ship, seeking out the best views and the most comfortable seats. She walked around and greeted people, introducing herself and answering still more questions.

The jazz ensemble gathered in the central room in the middle of the boat, and the sound of music swept over the entire ship through its speakers. It was looking to be another wonderful day on the Mississippi.

The steamboat's whistle loudly sounded, and the ropes were untied from the dock. The large paddlewheel slowly came to life, manoeuvring the boat onto the river.

Everyone's attention was diverted to the iconic wheel as it carved its way through the water. Jenn took the opportunity to go down towards the engine room and crew area to grab a drink.

The boat was a maze of levels and stairwells. After grabbing a bottle of water, Jenn navigated her way along the boat, taking five different sets of stairs to get to the front of the ship.

The front of the boat was always empty at the start of the cruise, as passengers made a beeline for the large wheel at the back, so Jenn was surprised when she arrived on the prow's lower deck and saw someone sitting at a table reading a book. Her surprise increased as she realised that someone was Kathryn.

"You came." Jenn smiled and looked at the book Kathryn was absorbed in. "And you're reading about the streetcars?"

"Yes, on both counts," Kathryn agreed. She glanced at the front of the book. "I met someone with a passion for the streetcars, and she made them sound so fascinating I had to learn more."

Jenn smiled at the compliment. "You're missing the wheel."

"The wind is coming from the east," Kathryn pointed out. "As delightful as the river is, I don't want to be covered in it. I'll take a look at it once we turn around."

"Okay, well, I'll leave you to your book and the river. I hope you have a nice and relaxing cruise. I'll see you around."

Jenn passed Kathryn to make her way towards the rear of the boat.

"Jenn?"

She paused and turned to see Kathryn looking at her.

"Thank you for inviting me," Kathryn said, smiling.

"You're welcome."

"Hello again!" Jenn turned to see Rebecca approaching them, but she wasn't greeting her. For some reason, she was speaking to Kathryn.

"Small world," Kathryn said, and she closed her book.

"You—you know each other?" Jenn stammered.

"Yep, we're staying in the same hotel," Rebecca said. "We met last night at the bar."

Kathryn gestured to the chair beside her. "Would you like to join me?"

"Sounds great." Rebecca dropped herself into the chair. "What are you reading?"

Jenn heard someone call her name, she was needed elsewhere. She looked at her friend and her crush and realised they were in their own world, talking to each other, completely unaware of her.

She turned and hurried away. Now she was regretting inviting Kathryn on board. How did she know

Rebecca? A chat at the hotel bar? What had they discussed?

She took a deep breath to calm herself. Rebecca was a friend, and she was in love with Arabella. And Kathryn was very, very straight. The worst that could happen was some mild discomfort if Rebecca told Kathryn an embarrassing story. Or if Kathryn told Rebecca about the kiss.

She stopped walking and let out a groan. Why did they have to know each other? And why did she have to fall for straight girls?

13

REALISATION

ARABELLA LET OUT A LONG SIGH. The spa was pure bliss. Her back had been pummelled by her technician, Dhia, for sixty minutes. Now she was relaxing on a comfortable bed, her hair wrapped in a towel, her face covered in some anti-ageing, collagen-infused product that left her skin tingling.

To say she was relaxed would be an understatement. The hotel fire alarm could sound, and she would wave it away and tell the flames she'd be out in another ten minutes. There was a fresh smell in the air. It smelt like the mountains without all the fuss and bother of travelling. And she could hear wind chimes, not annoying ones, just the occasional chime, as well as the sound of a babbling brook.

"Everything okay, Miss Henley?" Dhia asked.

"Perfection," Arabella replied.

Her eyes were closed and all the stresses that had laid so heavily on her just an hour ago seemed to be inconsequential. For the first time in a long time, she felt like she had clarity in her life. Like she had time to stop and think.

There were no clients on the telephone, no junior agent who needed to be trained, no receptionist who hung up while transferring every single important call.

It was just her.

A smile caused her lips to curl slightly beneath the mask. She missed Rebecca. While that wouldn't ordinarily be a thing to smile about, it gave her a clarity that had been absent recently.

The previous night she had been devastated at the idea of Rebecca being with another woman. She had almost fainted at breakfast when she realised that Rebecca had innocently spent the early hours of the morning in the gym.

She obviously had feelings for Rebecca. Feelings that she had never quite managed to explain. She'd spent the last few months trying to decide what she was, attempting to put an exact label on what she wanted her relationship with Rebecca to be.

When she had asked Rebecca to give her time, she had naively expected to be able to return at a later date with the exact parameters of their new relationship. She anticipated that she'd be able to tie it all up in a nice bow, place a label on it, and move on with her life.

Except that never happened. She never found a label. She could never decide what she was, or what she wanted. Half of the time, just thinking about it sent her into a panicked spiral. She wondered if her whole life had been a lie. She'd been engaged to be married to a man. Had she ever loved him? Did she know what love was? Was she even capable of love?

It was only now, in the calmness of the spa, that she realised she had missed a huge piece of the jigsaw puzzle. At no point had she spoken to Rebecca and asked for her help and guidance on her newly discovered feelings.

Instead, she'd spent most of her time avoiding Rebecca, or worse, snapping at her while her brain did somersaults trying to come to a conclusion.

Rebecca was the one person she knew who could help her figure out her feelings. Of course, Rebecca had at some point realised her own sexuality, and she seemed very comfortable with that. Arabella couldn't imagine that had been easy, and she would bet that Rebecca had assistance in finding her way.

Of course, it was very important to her that she didn't lead Rebecca on. Whether Rebecca was a close friend, or something more intimate, she was important to Arabella. If possible, Arabella wanted to remain on good terms with her.

But she needed to talk to her. As uncomfortable as that conversation might be. As embarrassing as it could end up. She needed to tell Rebecca what was going on in her mind and ask for Rebecca's help in finding her way.

She'd asked for space and Rebecca had given her oceans of it. She'd been more patient and understanding than Arabella ever would have been. Now it was time to come clean and be open with her, to tell her what little she had worked out for herself and ask for help with the rest of it.

She'd been blinded by jealousy the previous evening,

suffocated by it as she tried to sleep. Eventually, she'd had to take medication to get the mental images out of her mind.

It was time to speak to Rebecca, before she lost her to someone else.

14

WOMAN OVERBOARD

KATHRYN LOWERED her book and looked out at the river. She had to admit, it was a peaceful feeling to be sailing up the river on an original steamboat.

She regarded the woman beside her. Rebecca was taking photographs with what looked like an extremely expensive camera.

It seemed that New Orleans was a very small city, or at least the part of it that she had toured was. First, she was constantly bumping into Jenn, now Rebecca as well. She smiled to herself as she remembered Jenn's panicked look when she realised that she and Rebecca knew each other. That was definitely something to explore.

"Photographer?" Kathryn enquired casually.

"Yes. Well, freelance," Rebecca replied. "But when you work for yourself like that, work and social life kind of drift into one."

"I can imagine. It must be hard to turn off."

"Impossible," Rebecca agreed. "But it's okay, I'm doing something I love."

Rebecca replaced her lens cap and put the camera on the table between them. She looked at the book in Kathryn's lap.

"Streetcars?"

"Mmm. It was in the hotel lobby, so I thought I'd borrow it."

Rebecca nodded. "So, the kissing conductor was... Jenn?"

"It was," Kathryn confirmed. "I must thank you for your words of wisdom last night, you certainly put things into context for me."

"I'm glad." Rebecca smiled.

Kathryn leaned forward. "So, how do you know Jenn?"

"We've known each other for years," Rebecca replied. "We met when we were both visiting New York. We sat next to each other on an open-top bus tour. Been friends ever since."

Kathryn nodded. She remained silent for a moment, in the hope that Rebecca would choose to share more information. She wanted to know if Jenn had spoken about her, if the two had ever been more than just friends, everything. Suddenly, with no work to occupy her mind, this was at the forefront of her brain.

Rebecca continued to look out at the river.

Kathryn rolled her eyes. She would have to prompt the woman, it seemed. "Did she... say anything to you?"

"About you?" Rebecca asked.

"Yes, about last night."

Rebecca shook her head. "Nothing. I arrived yesterday, today was the first time we've spoken, and we haven't had much time to catch up."

Kathryn let out a small sigh of relief. The last thing she wanted was to be the butt of some joke between the two.

"But," Rebecca continued, "now I know that it was Jenn that kissed you, I can honestly say that she's probably just as mortified about the mistake as you were."

"I wasn't mortified," Kathryn defended.

Rebecca gave her a look.

"Okay, I was… well, I overreacted," Kathryn admitted. "But I've calmed down now, and I realise it was all a big misunderstanding. I saw Jenn at lunchtime, and she apologised and invited me here. So, it's all been ironed out."

"I'm glad to hear that, Jenn's a great person. And if you're visiting New Orleans then there is no one better to show you around."

"Will she be showing you around, too? And your friend I met at breakfast?" Kathryn asked.

Rebecca smothered a small cough and returned her attention to the view. She was clearly regretting her decision to tell Kathryn about her unrequited love for her traveling companion, though Kathryn wasn't sure what Rebecca saw in the uptight and rude English woman she had been introduced to that morning.

"Y—yeah, she will," Rebecca answered. "We're having dinner tonight."

"I hope you have a nice time, and I hope you manage to figure things out with your friend… Arabella, was it?" Kathryn asked. She didn't want Rebecca to be nervous that she would blurt out her secret and cause problems for her.

Rebecca's calm and collected thoughts from the previous evening had managed to cut through the drunken fear and settle her mind.

She'd overreacted to the kiss, pure and simple. The stress of the day, and the past few months, had built up and she'd lashed out unexpectedly.

"Yeah." Rebecca nodded.

"Doesn't she like cruises?" Kathryn asked.

"She's having a spa day. She's had a rough few weeks," Rebecca explained. "First day of holiday, so she wanted to relax in the spa and meet up later."

She looked like she could use some unwinding, Kathryn thought. *And get the stick surgically removed from her ass.*

"Sounds like a good idea," she said aloud. "I browsed through the spa brochure myself, but I couldn't resist heading out for a coffee. I'm still not sure New Orleans is the place for me, but they do make great coffee."

Rebecca looked surprised. "You don't like New Orleans?"

Kathryn shrugged. "It's not really my kind of place." She held up her hand to ward off Rebecca's next question. "It wasn't exactly my choice to come here, long story."

Rebecca blinked. "Right... so, you're here on holiday, but you never chose to come here?"

"Essentially, yes. If I had my choice, New Orleans wouldn't be somewhere I would come and visit."

Rebecca chuckled. "No wonder Jenn took you on the streetcars. She loves New Orleans and will do anything to help people see it through her eyes."

"So I've noticed. And she's everywhere! Seriously, how many jobs does she have?"

Rebecca shrugged. "I lost count. She likes doing a bit of this and a bit of that."

"She's everywhere," Kathryn repeated incredulously.

Rebecca smiled. "She likes to work. When she first arrived here, she struggled to find a job in the city, so she came to the French Quarter and took on a few part-time jobs. She enjoyed them so much that she never left most of them, and now she likes the variation."

Kathryn couldn't imagine what Jenn's schedule must look like. She couldn't imagine not knowing where she'd be from one day to the next, or one week to the next. She liked having her own desk, her own belongings surrounding her.

"I'm sorry, I can't stand it any longer," Rebecca announced. "Why are you here if you don't want to be here?" She threw up her hands. "I don't get it."

Kathryn smiled. "I was visiting the business quarter for a conference with my sister, we run a PR company together. I thought we were driving home, but she'd booked me into the hotel without telling me and was planning to abandon me here. An enforced vacation."

"Wow, wish I had a sister who would book me into a swanky hotel and force me to have a vacation," Rebecca said.

Kathryn laughed. "Well, let's just say I've been difficult to work with for a while. There's been a lot of family stress lately."

"I'm sorry to hear that."

"It's okay, I wasn't dealing with it very well. Erica decided to kill two birds with one stone. Keep me out of the way while a big deal is being signed in the office and force me to take a break." Kathryn stretched her legs out and rested them on a metal railing. "I hate to admit it, but I think she was right. As much as I hated being dropped here—and I really did hate that—I'm feeling a little better. I'm itching to check my email, but waking up this morning with no obligations was a very new feeling. A nice feeling."

"Sounds like you needed a holiday," Rebecca said.

"I did. So, as I said, I wouldn't have chosen New Orleans, but I'm learning to co-exist with it."

Rebecca opened her mouth to reply, but before she could formulate any words, a shout and then a splash sounded from the side of the ship.

Kathryn spun her head around. "Was that… someone going in?"

Rebecca was on her feet and rushing to the railing to see what was going on. "There's a man in the water!"

Kathryn stood beside her. They were on the bottom deck, only inches from the water due to the uniquely flat design of the steamboat. She spotted a man spluttering in the river. People were screaming from one of the top decks.

"Did he fall?" Kathryn asked.

"He looks plastered, I think he might have fallen," Rebecca replied.

A flash of movement from the back of the boat caught Kathryn's eye. Jenn was on the lower deck, looking out at the river. A moment later, she had climbed the railing and was in the water, too.

"What the hell is she doing?" Kathryn cried.

Rebecca pointed to the water where the man had

vanished. "He went under."

"Shouldn't she throw a preserver to him or something?" Kathryn demanded. "Not go in there herself!"

"Did you see how uncoordinated he was? He wouldn't have caught or held onto a life ring." Rebecca moved along the deck to get a better view of what was going on. Kathryn was right beside her.

"Why isn't anyone else going in?" Kathryn asked. She looked around, hoping to spot another member of staff.

Rebecca took off her sunglasses and handed them to Kathryn. She started to climb the railing.

"Ma'am!"

Rebecca paused. A member of the crew was running towards her.

"Ma'am, step off the railing, please. We need to keep the number of people in the water to a minimum."

Kathryn looked over to where Jenn was struggling with the man, trying to pull him up so he could breath. Every now and then both their heads disappeared beneath the water line.

"She needs help!" Kathryn shouted.

"Ma'am, she is fully trained to deal with these situations. Please, let her do her job."

Kathryn wanted to punch the woman. She wanted to jump in herself, except that she knew that she wasn't a strong enough swimmer to save herself, never mind two other people.

Rebecca climbed down, but she was clutching onto the railing and staring helplessly into the water.

"How long do we wait before we do something?" she demanded.

An alarm was blaring across the ship. Kathryn had been so caught up with the drama that she hadn't even heard it begin. A few more members of the crew were gathering at the back of the ship now, pulling on ropes and preparing a lifebuoy.

She looked back out into the water. Her breath caught in her throat when she couldn't see either Jenn or the drunken man. For a brief second, they both completely vanished from sight, as if they had never been there at all.

Ice cold fear washed over Kathryn. She felt as if she were the one drowning.

Suddenly Jenn spluttered to the surface. A determined look fixed on her face, she waved over to her crew mates, and a rope was thrown into the murky water.

Kathryn gripped onto the handrail as if it were her own lifeline. She watched as Jenn caught the rope and expertly weaved it around herself, all while keeping her charge safe and above the water.

The alarm blared all around her. People on the decks above were screaming and crying, but everything faded as Kathryn focused on Jenn, willing her to get back to the safety of the ship.

It was agonisingly slow going, but, eventually, Jenn was secured to the rope and her colleagues pulled her in. Kathryn hurried towards the aft of the ship but was stopped by the crew member who had stopped Rebecca from jumping in the water.

"Sorry, ma'am, I'm going to have to ask you to remain here."

Kathryn paused. She stood on her tiptoes to look over the woman and watched as Jenn was dragged aboard.

15

ANGRY CONCERN

Jenn thought back to every time she had ever complained about the stifling heat of a summer in New Orleans and wished she could feel like that again. Her teeth wouldn't stop chattering. The thick blanket that had been wrapped around her shoulders seemed to be doing no good at all.

The sensible thing to do would be to go up on deck and sit in the sun, but she needed some time to herself, away from the passengers. Not to mention no one wanted to smell her at the moment.

As soon as she had been pulled aboard, she was dragged to the calm of the staff room, a room in the middle of the ship with no windows.

She was checked over by the only other person on the ship who had a first aid certificate and was deemed to simply need to rest. This was her assessment, too. The drama quickly died down, and her colleagues quickly went back to work to leave her to recover.

She realised she was being watched and looked up. In the doorway, arms folded and with a furious expression, was Kathryn.

Jenn didn't say anything. She looked back down at the large pool of water that was forming below the wooden bench she was sitting on.

"I thought you were dead," Kathryn angrily informed her.

Jenn frowned. "You were worried about me?"

"Of course I was!"

"You seem kinda angry," Jenn pointed out, still staring at the floor.

She heard Kathryn let out a deep breath.

"It all happened so fast," Kathryn said, her tone softer now. She sat on a bench opposite Jenn.

Jenn wanted to point out that it had happened a hell of a lot faster from her perspective but figured now wasn't the time to be arguing.

She shivered again, curling into herself even more tensely and gripping the blanket tightly. When her eyes closed, she could see the entire thing as if it were happening again.

The guy was in his late thirties and had obviously been appreciating New Orleans freely available alcohol for some time before he boarded the steamboat.

The moment she spotted him, she had made a mental note to keep an eye on him. Years of working in bars had provided her with a sixth sense when it came to identifying troublemakers.

It wasn't long before he was standing on the railing,

arms stretched, releasing his inner Kate Winslet. In a flash, he lost his footing and plunged into the water.

Jenn knew that he was too drunk to be able to swim, and probably too gone to even catch the lifebuoy. She radioed the incident into the captain, pulled the alarm, and ran down the steps to the lower deck before plunging into the murky water.

The water had been freezing cold, especially when she dove under to bring the drunken idiot back to the surface. It took a few attempts to grab hold of him, she had to resort to using touch as the muddy water meant visibility was practically zero.

She knew she was racing against the clock. Not only was she getting colder by the second, but in the back of her mind she knew how notoriously difficult it was to slow or manoeuvre a steamboat. The longer she was in the water, the farther the boat would be from her, and the harder it would be to get back aboard.

It had been less than ten minutes between her jumping into the river and being pulled back on the boat. The passenger was being taken care of in the first aid room. Jenn was thankful to be away from him.

The silence was becoming thick. She could feel Kathryn's eyes boring into the top of her head, but no words were coming.

"I'm fine," Jenn finally said.

"That remains to be seen," Kathryn huffed.

Jenn let out a small chuckle. "Seriously, I'm just a bit cold, I'll warm up in no time." As if to prove her point, her body involuntarily shuddered again.

She heard Kathryn get up. A moment later she felt the

woman take a seat beside her and wrap her arm around Jenn's blanket-covered shoulder. Kathryn pulled her close in a futile attempt to help warm her.

"Thank you," Jenn mumbled.

"You were under the water for so long and no one was doing anything."

"Standard procedure," Jenn admitted quietly. "Once someone has gone in, you have to wait before anyone else goes in after them or there'll be more crew in the water than on the boat."

"I thought you were dead," Kathryn repeated. The arm around her shoulder tightened.

"Jenn, are you okay?"

She looked up to see Rebecca rushing into the staff room. She had a takeaway mug of coffee in one hand and another blanket in the other. Kathryn stood up and took the blanket from Rebecca and proceeded to wrap Jenn up in it.

Jenn poked a hand through a gap and gratefully took the mug.

"I'm fine."

"She's not fine," Kathryn argued. "As you can see, she's chilled to the bone."

"I'm fine," Jenn repeated. It was becoming a mantra.

"Can I get you anything else?" Rebecca asked. She sat on the bench opposite.

Jenn took a sip of the drink. Coffee, milky and sweet, just as she liked it.

"No, I'm good. Welcome to New Orleans," Jenn joked.

Rebecca laughed. "Yeah, non-stop entertainment."

Jenn shrugged. "We try to keep people happy. And alive."

"He better thank you for saving his drunken ass," Kathryn said. She took her seat beside Jenn and placed a hand on her back.

Jenn wished the blankets weren't so thick. She would have been cold, but at least she would have been able to feel Kathryn's hand more easily.

She suddenly remembered that she was due for a short shift in CeeCee's later. There was no way she could go there covered in Mississippi mud, and it would take her too much time to head home to shower and then head out again.

Rebecca saw her panic. "What's up?"

"I need to call CeeCee's and tell them I can't make it later. I'm due to work for a couple of hours before we meet up for dinner," Jenn explained.

"Where's your phone?" Rebecca stood up.

Jenn thought for a moment. "I left my bag behind the bar on the top deck."

"No problem, I'll grab it. Back in a few."

Jenn watched Rebecca leave. She sipped at the coffee again, relishing the warmth it brought her, even if it was temporary.

"You don't have to sit here," she said to Kathryn. "I'm okay. You should go back to the cruise. The gumbo is really good. And the jazz band, you should go listen to them play."

"Would you say it's the best gumbo and jazz in New Orleans?"

Jenn turned to looked at Kathryn curiously. "What do you mean?"

"Is the gumbo the best I will taste in New Orleans? Is the band the best I will hear?" Kathryn repeated.

"Well, no. But they—"

"Then I'm fine here. Unless you want to be alone?"

"No. I just—"

"Then I'm fine here," Kathryn insisted. "We'll just sit together, and maybe you can tell me where I can find the best gumbo?"

Jenn smiled and nodded. "Sure, I can suggest a few places. You should try Mama Dee's, great food there. And ambiance, in fact—"

"I kind of hoped you'd *show* me the best places," Kathryn hinted. "As friends, of course."

Jenn felt her eyes widen. "Oh, okay. Yes, that sounds great."

Kathryn chuckled. She reached into her bag and pulled out a small notepad and a pen. She flipped the pad open and wrote down a number before tearing the sheet of paper out and handing it to Jenn.

"The hotel number, and my room number. Maybe you could give me a call when you have a ten-minute window between your numerous jobs."

"How about tonight?" Rebecca asked as she walked back into the staff room. "We can all have dinner together. Arabella won't mind."

Jenn was so relieved that Rebecca had offered. She'd wanted to immediately invite Kathryn out that evening, not wanting to miss an opportunity. But she didn't want to sound overly eager, nor did she want to cancel on Rebecca and Arabella.

Kathryn looked from Rebecca to Jenn and smiled. "That sounds great." She stood up and pointed towards the door. "I'll leave you to make your call and freshen up. Call me and let me know where and when to meet." She walked towards the door and paused. "As friends."

"As friends." Jenn nodded quickly.

Kathryn looked Jenn up and down one last time before leaving the staff room. She left, and Jenn listened to the sound of her walking down the narrow, echoing corridor. Once she was sure that Kathryn could no longer hear her, she turned to Rebecca and beamed happily.

"Thank you!"

"No problem," Rebecca said. She held out Jenn's bag for her. "I heard the end of the conversation—you couldn't let an opportunity like that go. I can see the way you look at her."

"Yeah, but it won't go anywhere," Jenn said. "She's straight. But she's cool, when you get to know her."

"She told me about what happened last night," Rebecca said.

Jenn felt her cheeks burn with embarrassment.

"She was at the bar, a bit tipsy. She saw my rainbow flag badge and wanted to know if she looked gay," Rebecca explained.

Jenn snorted a laugh. "What did you say?"

Rebecca sat down and shrugged. "Who looks gay these days?"

"True. You sure you don't mind inviting her to dinner with us? Will Arabella mind?"

"She'll be fine," Rebecca reassured her. "But do I need to give you the standard warning about falling for a straight woman?"

Jenn laughed. "No, I'm okay, I promise. Yeah, I have a thing for her, but she's fun to be friends with. Just… enjoying my life."

Rebecca looked at her for a moment before finally nodding her head. "As long as you know what you're doing," she said.

"I do. Well, I think I do," Jenn replied. "What's the worst that can happen?"

"Broken heart?" Rebecca suggested.

Jenn bit her lip. Rebecca was right. It wasn't fun and games to pine over someone you couldn't have. Even if she convinced herself that she was just friends with Kathryn, in the back of her mind she knew that she wanted more. And Rebecca was suffering through the same issues. She'd have to get the gossip on what was happening with her and Arabella. Later, when she'd stopped shivering.

16

PROFESSIONAL PAIN IN MY ARSE

ARABELLA HEARD Rebecca's hotel door closing. She marked her place in her book and set it to one side. She sat on the bed, able to see her reflection in the large mirror on the opposite wall. She looked nervous.

She took a deep breath before shuffling off the sumptuously soft bed. Crossing to the mirror, she looked at her reflection again and adjusted her hair a little.

She'd made the decision to speak with Rebecca as soon as she returned. No more beating around the bush, no more silent treatment, no more flares of anger. They were both grown-ups and could handle adult conversations.

Leaning in close to the mirror, she checked her mascara and then straightened the collar on her short-sleeved blouse.

An excited knock on the door sounded through the room.

"Arabella? You in there?"

Her eyes widened in shock. She hadn't expected

Rebecca to call on her so suddenly. She looked around the room, checking that everything was in place.

"Arabella?" Rebecca called again.

"Coming," Arabella replied. She lunged for her book and shoved it in the drawer of the bedside table. She didn't need Rebecca knowing that she was reading a self-help book about how to empower her subconscious brain.

She took a deep breath and opened the door. Rebecca rushed into the room a second later.

"Oh my god, you will not believe what you missed today," Rebecca announced.

Arabella smiled as Rebecca plonked herself down on the edge of the bed and leaned back onto her hands.

"Jenn dove into the Mississippi River and saved a drunk man. And, let me tell you, that river ain't clean." Rebecca made a face.

"Is she okay?" Arabella asked. She pulled out the chair at the desk and sat down.

"Yes, she's fine. I was just sitting there chatting with Kathryn and then splash—"

"Kathryn?" Arabella interrupted. She felt her nails dig into the upholstered arm of the chair.

"Yes, we met her at breakfast this morning," Rebecca reminded her.

As if she needed reminding.

"So… you arranged to meet her today?" Arabella asked.

"No, I think Jenn invited her," Rebecca said. She sat up. "Anyway, I heard this splash and we looked over—"

"Jenn knows her?" Arabella asked.

"Yeah, they met yesterday. We're having dinner with

them both tonight," Rebecca said quickly, clearly wanting to get onto the next part of her story. "Anyway… splash."

"Splash," Arabella agreed. She wasn't going to get anything else out of Rebecca until she'd told her story.

"Right." Rebecca's eyes flashed with excitement. "So, there's this man in the water. Drunk as a skunk. No way he's rescuing himself. Then the alarm is blaring, and people are screaming. And Jenn just jumps in after him."

Rebecca jumped to her feet and walked over to the window to start pacing. "So, Kathryn and I are watching and they both keep going under the water. And the crew are gathering at the back of the boat, but no one is doing anything. So, I climb up onto the railing—"

"Don't you dare tell me you jumped in," Arabella demanded. She looked Rebecca over critically. She didn't look like someone who had taken an unscheduled swim in the toxic-looking river. But there was always the chance she'd done so and then had a shower and cleaned up. Not that a shower would protect her from the untold nastiness that was obviously lurking in the murky waterway.

"No, this woman stopped me before I had the chance."

"Good!" Arabella felt her hand shake at the thought of Rebecca diving into the water. Even though she knew she was safe and well, the terror of what might have happened was palpable.

"Anyway, eventually they got their act together and threw her a rope. It was a mess. Kathryn was livid." Rebecca looked out of the window, peering down at the street below.

Kathryn again. Arabella pursed her lips and turned

away. "I thought we were only meeting up with Jenn for dinner?"

"We were," Rebecca replied distractedly. Something at street level had caught her attention. "But Kathryn invited Jenn out, so I thought I'd ask her to come and join us tonight."

Arabella frowned. She couldn't fathom the connections. "Can you please explain to me who Kathryn is, how she knows Jenn, how she knows you, and why I'm suddenly having dinner with her?"

So much for no flares of anger.

Rebecca turned around, confusion clear on her face. "I didn't think you would mind. I… I can cancel?"

"Who. Is. Kathryn?"

"She's just someone on holiday," Rebecca explained. "She came to the city yesterday and bumped into Jenn. Then they arranged to meet up later that evening. Jenn thought it was a date, but Kathryn's straight—"

Thank you, lord, Arabella thought.

"Jenn tried to kiss her at the end of the not-date. Kathryn came back to the hotel to have a drink, I bumped into her and she asked me if she looked gay. She saw my rainbow badge. Anyway… Jenn saw her this morning and apologised and invited her to go on the cruise."

Arabella could feel her heart rate returning to normal. Kathryn was straight. And Jenn was interested in her. No messy spanners in the works.

"Kathryn realised she overreacted after the kiss and wants to apologise to Jenn. Jenn is crazy about her, I think. Kathryn wanted to have dinner with Jenn one night while she's in town, so I invited her along with us tonight.

That way Jenn can still meet up with us and see Kathryn at the same time. And I can keep an eye on Jenn."

"Keep an eye on her?" Arabella asked.

"She's got a classic crush on a straight woman, I need to make sure she doesn't get hurt," Rebecca answered.

Arabella bristled a little. Had she hurt Rebecca by not being honest about her feelings? Was this a thing in the lesbian community? Accidentally falling for straight women and having your heart broken?

"Do you mind having dinner, all four of us?" Rebecca sought clarification.

"No, the more the merrier." Of course, Arabella wasn't over the moon about spending more time with Kathryn, but at least Jenn would be there to keep her occupied.

"I think you'll like her, you're a lot alike."

Arabella flared her nostrils. "Oh, really? And what, pray tell, do we have in common?"

No more being nice, she wasn't standing for being compared to some drunken barfly with gay panic and a terrible accent.

"Um." Rebecca's eyes widened in panic. "Well, you... she works in PR."

"P. R." Arabella raised her eyebrow. "And what, precisely, does PR have to do with me?"

"I mean she's a professional," Rebecca said. Her tongue darted out and licked her lips.

Professional pain in my arse.

"Like, she... owns skirt suits and works in an office," Rebecca continued.

Arabella stared at her. "Owns suits... and works in an office. I see. I'm glad you have such a thorough understanding of the complexities of our individual personalities to know that we'll be best friends based upon your uncanny observations of our practically identical lifestyles."

She stood up and stalked into the bathroom. She picked up her makeup bag and tossed it carelessly onto the counter. She shook her head and turned on her heel and entered the main room again.

"It's because I'm old, isn't it? She's old, I'm old. Boom. We'll do cross-stitch together. As long as our eyesight doesn't go first." She folded her arms and glared at Rebecca.

"Old? She's not—I mean **you're** not old. Neither of you are old. I mean, I don't even know how old you are!" Rebecca's eyes flicked between her and the open interconnecting door, clearly wanting to escape before she buried her leg in her mouth up to the kneecap.

Arabella shook her head and walked back into the bathroom. She angrily unzipped her makeup bag. The copious bottles of lotions and potions stared back at her mockingly.

She let out a sigh and leaned heavily on the sink. She closed her eyes and hung her head in shame.

17

OLD

REBECCA LET out the breath that had been trapped in her throat since a furious Arabella had demanded to know, essentially, if she was considered old. She knew that Arabella was insecure about her age and her looks. A few days after she first met Arabella, she had discovered that the woman travelled with a *case* of makeup.

Since then, Rebecca had noticed that Arabella never let anyone see her unless she was perfectly presented. Her hair, makeup, and clothes were always fussed to faultlessness.

Rebecca took a deep inhale of air-conditioned goodness and approached the open bathroom door. Arabella stood in front of the sink, bracing herself for impact against the white porcelain. Eyes closed, head slung dejectedly downwards.

She opened her mouth to speak when she heard Arabella mumble something. It was so quiet that it was lost immediately in the space between them.

"I didn't hear that," Rebecca said.

"Forty-three."

Rebecca swallowed. She had gotten the impression that Arabella only mentioned her age to people she had power over, or those she would soon be murdering. And she knew that now was definitely not the time to mention that she suspected that Kathryn was considerably younger than Arabella.

Arabella stood up and turned towards Rebecca with a solemn expression.

"Now you know."

Rebecca brought her hand up to her mouth in a pathetic attempt to cover her smile.

Arabella frowned. "You're... laughing at me?"

"I'm sorry, it's just you've said your age in the same way some people deliver news of a death." She couldn't help but let out a small snort. "Doctor, will he be okay? I'm terribly sorry, miss, he's forty-three."

Arabella stared at her, blinking a few times. "This isn't a laughing matter."

"I beg to disagree, it's hysterical," Rebecca said as she fought to hold back giggles. "You sound like you're telling a child that you killed their puppy."

Arabella opened her mouth, and Rebecca knew that whatever was about to come out wouldn't be pleasant. She quickly walked forward and cupped her hand over Arabella's open mouth.

"You're not old. You're not even middle-aged. Forty-three is nothing. Nothing at all. I know people say it all the time, but it's true; you're as young as you feel. And I know you worry about your looks... but you're beautiful.

With and without makeup. Like, seriously… breathtakingly beautiful."

She felt her cheeks begin to heat up and realised that this was the exact opposite of giving Arabella the space she had requested. She looked up into Arabella's shocked eyes and took a hesitant step back, removing her hand from her mouth.

"Sorry." She gestured to her hand. "Didn't mean to… silence you like that. I just wanted you to really hear what I was saying."

"You don't think I'm old?" Arabella asked, almost breathlessly.

"No, not at all. Forty-three isn't old, not these days. And you look after yourself, you eat well, you exercise…" Rebecca waved her hand towards Arabella's body. "You look amazing. Definitely not old."

"I'm fat," Arabella said as if she were stating that fire was hot.

It was Rebecca's turn to blink silently for a few seconds. "Excuse me?"

Arabella gestured towards her hips, and then her torso. "Fat. And the wrinkles around my eyes."

"Has someone told you that you're fat?" Rebecca demanded. Suddenly she wanted to board a flight back to Heathrow and throttle Alastair. She was sure it was that brainless numbskull.

Arabella looked shocked at Rebecca's harsh tone and took a tiny step back.

"Well, I am…" She gestured again to her body.

Rebecca turned around and presented Arabella with her back for a couple of moments while she let the rage pass over her. Once she was calm enough that she didn't think she would throw something, she turned back again.

"You are *not* fat. No, you're not skin and bone either. You have *curves*, which women are allowed to have. In fact, many people, myself included, think that some curves on a woman are incredibly sexy. And as for wrinkles… it happens when you live your life. You smile and you get lines, you frown and you get lines. It means you've lived your life and experienced things, and nothing is more attractive than that."

Rebecca could feel herself vibrating with anger. She couldn't believe that Arabella felt this way about herself. Sure, she knew she was insecure, but this was more than she'd suspected. How could anyone have ever said anything negative about her? They should have worshipped her, not put her down.

Arabella looked like she was caught between embarrassment and shy gratitude.

"I'm going to go and start to get ready for dinner. I need to shower and stuff," Rebecca said. She needed to get out of the small space with such a vulnerable-looking Arabella before she said something she'd regret.

Give her space, give her space, Rebecca chanted her mantra to herself.

Arabella nodded. "Meet you downstairs?"

"Sure, meet you in the lobby at seven," Rebecca said.

18

CRUISING TOWARDS A BROKEN HEART

JENN STEPPED INTO THE SHOWER, relieved when the hot water hit her skin and started to wash off the grimy dirt from the river. She looked at the floor of the shower and grimaced at the dirty water flowing towards the drain.

The thought of a fantastic evening of great food, entertainment, and friendship helped to shake off the residual effects of the biting cold Mississippi that still plagued her.

She'd stayed in the staff room for the rest of the trip, not wanting any of the passengers to catch sight of her looking like the proverbial drowned rat. And definitely not wanting to speak to the man she had rescued. She had very little to say to him that would keep her in employment.

She spent the time thinking about places to eat and things to do that evening. She wanted it to be perfect. Everyone was new to New Orleans and she wanted to show them the very best it had to offer. Especially if that meant that she might be able to win Kathryn over a little.

Within ten minutes, she had called in some favours and booked a table at her favourite restaurant.

Kathryn had very clearly stated that dinner wasn't a date, but that didn't stop Jenn from wanting to go all out when it came to getting ready. There was nothing wrong with getting dressed up, especially after swimming in a river so dirty that you feared you'd never get the smell out of your hair again.

As she poured shampoo into her hand, she thought about Kathryn and all the interactions they'd had to date. To say that she was confused by Kathryn was an understatement. From being convinced that she was a terrible, stuck-up snob, to thinking she was one of the most enigmatic and interesting people she'd met in just a few hours.

And then from the kiss to the realisation of the enormous mistake she'd made. Jenn had run through a ton of emotions in record time.

She lathered the shampoo and worked it into her long hair, letting out a sigh at the knowledge that she'd soon feel more like herself.

She couldn't get the kiss out of her head. It had seemed so perfect. The warm evening air, the sound of the streetcars rumbling along the road, the twinkling lights from the old-fashioned lampposts.

And then there was Kathryn's angry face. Closely followed by the cold wave of dread and panic that hit Jenn like a truck. She turned the temperature of the water up a little to counteract the shiver that ran down her spine.

Jenn didn't like labels, primarily because she didn't know which one to put on herself. She'd started her sexual life being straight, then thinking she might be bisexual, then lesbian, then pansexual. She hadn't dated a man in years, but she still found some attractive. So, pansexual, if she was pushed to put a label on herself. Not that she entirely understood the need for labels.

As terrible as her gaydar had always been, she still couldn't believe how badly she had misread the signals she thought she'd been receiving from Kathryn. It wasn't like Jenn to go in for a kiss at the end of a date unless she was absolutely certain about things.

She wondered if maybe Kathryn wasn't 100% straight. Maybe, buried deeply within her, lay someone who wasn't sure. That had certainly been the case with Jenn.

Her own first experience with a woman had been with someone who was very comfortable in their sexuality and certainly not new to the idea of a female lover, as Jenn had been. Since then, Jenn's misfiring gaydar had always directed her towards women either as experienced as her or more so.

Jenn had never been anyone's first, and she certainly had no idea about guiding a gay awakening in a supposedly straight woman. Not to mention the fact that Kathryn could actually be straight, despite some of the evidence to the contrary.

She sighed and rinsed the shampoo out of her hair.

Rebecca was right, she might be cruising straight for a broken heart. It was a dangerous game. On one hand, she'd enjoyed her time with Kathryn so much that she wanted to hang out with her more. On the other, she was deeply attracted to Kathryn and hoped for more than just friendship. But could she separate the two?

If Kathryn was absolutely straight and had no interest

in Jenn, how would Jenn feel? Especially if they spent more time together. There was a real danger that the more time Jenn spent with Kathryn, the more she would fall for the woman. And that road led to a lot of emotional pain, pain that Jenn desperately wanted to avoid.

She'd always been told that she was a sensitive soul, and it was true. Jenn wore her heart on her sleeve. It had caused her many problems over the years, from falling in love with the wrong person to having people take advantage of her sweet nature.

She closed her eyes and tilted her face towards the water spray.

Why does it have to be so complicated? She wondered.

In the distance she heard her phone beep, signalling that she had forty-five minutes before she had to leave. Her phone was the only reason she ever arrived anywhere on time. She reached for the bottle of conditioner and started to pick up the pace. She had a dinner to get to.

19

EVENING RENDEZVOUS

KATHRYN SAT in the lobby of the Royale and looked around the lavish space. Understated, it was not. But at least it wasn't as tacky as most of the rest of New Orleans. No, that was unfair. Much of New Orleans was very pretty. It was Bourbon Street and some of the offshoots that were filled with seedy establishments and the people who frequented them.

Jenn had proved to her yesterday that New Orleans was also a place of calm boulevards with timeless charm and beautiful architecture. And the steamboat on the Mississippi had been breathtakingly enchanting, up until the moment where she felt for certain she was about to witness Jenn's demise.

She shuddered, gripping the plush sofa below her fingers to ground herself. She tried to ignore the feeling of dread that had clawed at her as she watched Jenn's head dip below the water. And she definitely ignored the fact that she had no such concerns for the drunken man who was just as close to perishing. He'd gotten himself into the situation by being drunk and acting the fool.

Natural selection, she mused.

She heard someone walking across the lobby and looked up to see Arabella. She resisted the urge to roll her eyes. Dinner with Jenn was something she was looking forward to, and having Rebecca join them would certainly be enjoyable. But Arabella's stuck-up attitude at breakfast wasn't something she relished sitting through again.

Arabella was thrusting her hand towards her. "Hi, Arabella Henley. I just wanted to apologise for this morning. I'd had a terrible night and I'd yet to have coffee, so I'm afraid I was awful."

Kathryn felt her eyebrow raise off her face. Were her emotions that transparent? "That's... perfectly fine." She shook the offered hand. "I was hardly at my best either. Kathryn Foster, by the way."

Arabella smiled kindly. "Then it's a great chance to start again."

Kathryn gestured to the space beside her on the sofa, and Arabella sat down. Kathryn noted that she was wearing a simple white blouse and a draped skirt that fell just below the knees. It was a print that Kathryn recognised; she owned a similar garment.

Having been dumped in New Orleans without the opportunity to pack correctly, Kathryn wore a tight navy-blue dress that she had worn one evening at the conference. It was a little more corporate than she would have liked.

Her sister Erica had taken the opportunity to hide some T-shirts and shorts in her suitcase, but they weren't suitable for dinner. It added to her feeling of insecurity, being incorrectly dressed, in a place that didn't quite suit her.

Arabella glanced at her watch. She rolled her eyes. "Rebecca is always late," she said good-humouredly.

"Sounds like my sister," Kathryn said. "She operates in her own time zone." She paused. "Correction, more like her own planet."

Arabella chuckled. "Family… what's the saying? Can't live with them, can't live without them?"

"You have no idea." Kathryn shook her head. She wasn't about to explain her family situation to a complete stranger, but she felt for sure that whatever difficulties Arabella had with her family, Kathryn could top them and then some.

She noticed Arabella straighten slightly, her gaze captured by someone exiting the elevators. Without even turning, she knew that Rebecca had arrived.

Arabella stood up and smiled. "You look wonderful," she greeted Rebecca. She gestured to Kathryn. "And look who I found."

Rebecca was wearing a wine-red summer dress. It was lacy around the capped sleeves and stopped just above the knees. It was a complete contrast to what Kathryn had previously seen Rebecca in, but then Rebecca did seem to be a mass of contradictions, and very much her own person.

"You look stunning," Rebecca told Arabella. She quickly looked at Kathryn. "I mean, you both look stunning." Panic settled into Rebecca's eyes, and she looked back at Arabella in fear. Kathryn detected a hint of jealousy from Arabella, or maybe it was just concern on Rebecca's part that Arabella would misinterpret the compliment.

"Everyone's stunning," Kathryn said, trying to defuse what had suddenly become a tense situation. She turned away from the two women who were now shyly looking at each other.

Ridiculous, Kathryn thought. *Why are these two not together? They're obviously interested in one another.*

She turned away, and her breath instantly caught in her chest. Jenn was walking in through the main entrance of the hotel. She was wearing a simple, white, summer dress. For someone who'd been in the river just a few hours ago, she looked ready to be part of a fashion show. To say it wasn't what Kathryn had expected would be an understatement.

Jenn walked towards them, grinning happily.

"Well, you clean up nicely," Kathryn announced.

"I try my best." Jenn winked.

"Jenn, this is Arabella," Rebecca introduced the two.

Kathryn watched as Arabella and Jenn greeted each other. She swallowed hard, bringing some much-needed moisture to her throat. She didn't know what it was about Jenn, but she was strangely drawn to her.

She'd never had any feelings towards women at all. She wasn't a homophobe, but she knew her own mind and her own desires. Clearly, there was something about Jenn that she found fascinating. Surely that could be the case without her being *attracted* to Jenn. Couldn't it?

Jenn turned to face Kathryn. She frowned. "When are you going to get changed?"

Kathryn paused for a split second until she noticed the twinkle in Jenn's eyes. "Rude!" She tapped Jenn's arm with her clutch bag.

"You look great." Jenn smiled.

"I wasn't sure how to dress," Kathryn admitted. "I didn't know if we'd be going to a nice restaurant or if the best gumbo in New Orleans was served through a hole in a wall."

"If it is, then I need to get changed," Arabella joked.

Jenn laughed. "Well, the guidebooks would probably send you to some dirty little café downtown, but don't worry—I know somewhere perfect. It has seats and everything."

"Seats?" Rebecca gushed. "You spoil us."

"Sure do, stick with me. You can trust your local guide," Jenn said.

"I do," Kathryn confessed. "My tour guide is a life-saving, first aid-giving, streetcar-driving, water aerobics instructor."

"Sounds like a fascinating person," Jenn quipped. She gestured for Kathryn to take her arm.

"She certainly is." Kathryn took Jenn's arm and allowed herself to be led out of the lobby and into the city at night.

A HIDDEN OASIS

ARABELLA AND REBECCA walked a little way behind Jenn and Kathryn. Arabella could have quite happily ditched the idea of dinner altogether. She was ready to talk to Rebecca. Even more so after her impassioned speech in Arabella's bathroom.

She'd kept her age a secret from most people her entire life. She'd attended a small private school, and most of her classmates had resembled greyhounds being released from a racetrack gate upon graduation day. They'd been so eager to be successes that they had all sprinted off to make their fortunes and hadn't spoken to each other since.

Following university, she'd been given a prestigious role within the family business. She'd lied about her age, attempting to appear older than she was in order to fit in with the other executives.

But time moved on, and one day she realised that she was employing executives younger than she was. She'd stared at the dates of birth on employment applications, wondering if there'd been a typo, thinking that surely someone born in that year should still be in high school. She'd gotten old.

That had happened a few years ago, and now every passing year felt like a large, rusty cog hammering itself into place in an old-fashioned clock. Moving her ever closer to old age, wrinkles, and the scrap heap.

Lying about her age had become second nature, or at least keeping it a closely guarded secret had. And keeping up the illusion required many hours in front of the mirror with enough make-up to give Donald Trump a new career as a runway model. Okay, maybe not *that* much make-up.

"You okay?" Rebecca asked. "You look miles away."

Rebecca had hidden away in her room after her declaration that Arabella was foolish to worry about her age. Arabella knew why, she was giving her time. Sweet, wonderful Rebecca who put everyone else's feelings in front of her own was, yet again, doing just that.

Arabella had wanted to burst into her room. She had wanted to explain what had been going through her mind and announce that she was fed up with hiding how she felt. But this evening wasn't about her, it was about Rebecca meeting up with a dear friend. Dropping a ton of emotional baggage on Rebecca before they went to dinner would have been unfair.

She reached out and took Rebecca's hand in hers. "I'm good, really good."

Rebecca looked in surprise at their joined hands. "G—great."

"Thank you, for what you said earlier," Arabella added. "It meant a lot to me."

"I meant every word," Rebecca promised.

"I know."

They walked in silence for a few more minutes, following Jenn as she expertly navigated the traffic. They turned into a side street and found a small courtyard with cobbles on the ground and trees and ivy interlaced into a canopy above them. Fairy lights twinkled in the foliage.

Rebecca's mouth fell open, and she stared at the surroundings.

Arabella squeezed her hand. "You'll have to come back here with your camera," she suggested.

Rebecca silently nodded, still taking in the beautiful square.

Arabella could practically see the photographer considering angles and lighting, figuring out the best way to frame the shots and the ideal time of day to do so.

Jenn turned around and smiled at Rebecca's awestruck expression. "Thought you might like this place," she said.

Rebecca looked at the doorway they'd come through in confusion. "I passed this road earlier, I had no idea this was here."

"Local knowledge." Jenn tapped the side of her head. "This place has great food, and there's a jazz club in the backroom. I got all of us tickets for the show tonight."

"Jazz in the backroom?" Kathryn asked with a grin. "This place feels like a movie."

"What can I say? We inspired Hollywood," Jenn said. "Shall we head inside?"

Everyone agreed. Jenn led them further into the courtyard and through a set of wooden doors. She spoke with the waiter and soon they were walking up a set of marble steps to the second floor and onto a terrace surrounded with an ornate balcony.

Arabella looked over the balcony and down onto the busy street below. She could see tourists snapping pictures or looking at maps on their phones. On the street corner, one of the many impromptu jazz bands had set up and was playing some of the classics. It was a postcard-perfect scene.

She turned and took her seat at the stunning cast-iron table. Jenn and Kathryn were examining the menu, and Rebecca was sipping from a freshly poured glass of water.

"Rebecca?" Arabella said softly.

Rebecca looked at her from over the edge of her glass.

"I'm very glad we came here."

Rebecca looked at her strangely, happy but obviously wondering what alien shape-shifter had taken the place of her friend.

"After dinner, maybe we could have drinks in the hotel bar?" Arabella suggested. "Just the two of us."

"S—sure," Rebecca stammered. She shakily placed her glass back on the table.

"Nothing bad," Arabella reassured. "Hopefully, quite the opposite."

Rebecca's eyes sparkled. She nodded her head and grabbed for a menu.

"Let's eat," Rebecca announced to the table.

21

SOMETHING IN THE AIR

JENN NOTICED REBECCA BLUSHING SLIGHTLY, and she wondered what she had missed between her friend and Arabella. She'd been so wrapped up in pointing out interesting dishes to Kathryn that she'd not looked up at the other couple until Rebecca had spoken.

She'd clearly overlooked something, but she wasn't sure what it was. She glanced over the top of her menu towards Arabella. She seemed nice. She was attractive and seemed to be very smart. Jenn could totally see what Rebecca saw in her.

On top of that, Arabella looked at Rebecca like she was ice cream on a hot day. How they had still not quite managed to get together was beyond her. Unless something had recently happened to move the process along? She decided that she'd grill Rebecca about it the next day. For now, she wanted to focus on Kathryn.

She noticed Kathryn's fingers were tapping away on

the back of her menu, in time with the lively beat of the jazz being played in the street.

"You like jazz?" Jenn asked.

"I never really listened to it before coming here," Kathryn said.

Jenn's mouth dropped open. She stared at Kathryn, incredulous.

"You've *never* listened to jazz?"

"Nope. Not my style."

"Seems to be your style." Jenn pointed to Kathryn's tapping fingers.

Kathryn paused and looked at her traitorous fingers. "It's catchy. Let's say it's growing on me."

"I love the music here," Rebecca said. "It really brings everything to life, it's so vibrant."

"Yes," Arabella agreed, "and you're extremely lucky that all of your bands appear to be very good. Not like some of the buskers you see in London. You know, I once saw a man playing a road construction cone like a kazoo. I believe it was 'Sweet Home Alabama', but it's hard to tell at a railway station."

"I've seen him!" Rebecca exclaimed. "Victoria Station, right?"

Arabella nodded. "Don't tell me… you thought he was marvellous?"

"I did! He has some lungs to keep that up for the whole of rush hour. I gave him five quid," Rebecca said.

Arabella rolled her eyes. "It's people like you who encourage people like them."

She said it kindly, but it was obvious she meant it.

"Exactly," Kathryn agreed. She gestured towards the

band on the street corner. "They have real talent, I'd happily pay them for their time. But why people insist on giving money to people who have no musical talent is beyond me. Like your construction cone gentleman."

Arabella nodded readily, happy to have an ally.

"I don't give him money because I think he's a genius musician," Rebecca explained. "I give him money because he is probably homeless and needs the money."

Arabella opened her mouth, presumably to argue. Rebecca quickly placed a finger on Arabella's lips to silence her.

"No, we're not talking about this now. We can debate whether or not homeless people buy bread or crack with the money I give them *another* day."

Arabella looked suitably chastised and quickly nodded. Rebecca lowered her hand and continued to examine her menu. Jenn smiled to herself. She could see what Rebecca meant when she'd explained how Arabella could sometimes be a little opinionated. Rebecca had joked that she was still training her.

Jenn plucked the drinks menu from the table. "Well, you can't visit New Orleans without having a real cocktail made by a professional bartender. Anyone want a drink?"

"I'd love a Bellini," Arabella said.

"That sounds perfect. Refreshing and not too sweet," Kathryn agreed.

Jenn looked at Rebecca who nodded her agreement. She turned around and gestured to the waiter. "Can we have four Bellinis, please?"

He nodded and turned to place the order with the bar.

"I'm assuming it won't arrive in an icy slush?" Kathryn joked.

"Nope. You'll even get it in the right glass," Jenn replied.

"My, how refined!" Kathryn affected a Southern belle accent and placed her hand on her chest.

Over the course of the next two hours, the four women dined on exquisite traditional Cajun food while listening to the band play a selection of jazz classics. It was a better evening than Jenn could have ever hoped for.

Arabella and Kathryn seemed to hit it off. Once conversation started to flow, it became clear that they had quite a lot in common. Jenn was grateful for Arabella's expert conversational skills. It had led her to discover that Kathryn had been born in Brazil but had lived in New York her entire adult life.

She worked in public relations with her sister and her mother. The darkness that flashed through her eyes at the mere mention of her mother indicated to Jenn that it was best to avoid the subject altogether.

Though it was becoming clear that Jenn and Kathryn had literally nothing in common, their conversation flowed easily. A perfect example of opposites attracting, which did nothing to keep Jenn's crush from growing with each passing minute. She felt proud to be out on the town with someone like Kathryn.

The sun had set. The glow from the streetlights and the soft, glimmering lights that were wrapped around the balcony balustrades were all that illuminated them. Jenn never wanted the night to end.

Apparently, Rebecca didn't share her desire. She

watched as her friend downed the last of her wine and let out a big, fake yawn. Jenn smiled to herself. She didn't know if Rebecca wanted to make herself scarce to give her some alone time with Kathryn, or if there was something else going on.

There had definitely been something strange in the air between Rebecca and Arabella all night. If Jenn hadn't been told that they weren't a couple, she would have bet money that they were. Another example of her misfiring gaydar. She slumped a little in her seat, remembering that Kathryn was oh so straight. She wished it wasn't the case, but, perfect night out or not, she was.

She realised that she had been foolish to think she could socialise with Kathryn and not get caught up in her web. Of course she'd fall for her. She'd already fallen during the streetcar trip.

"I'm so sorry, but I think I'm going to have to call it an early night," Rebecca said.

"Same for me, I think I'm starting to feel the jetlag," Arabella added.

"Oh, that's a shame," Kathryn said. "I thought you'd both be joining us for the jazz?"

Rebecca looked at Jenn, clearly having forgotten all about the show they were supposed to listen to after the meal.

Jenn waved her hand distractedly. "It's fine, I just called in a couple of favours for the tickets... I can easily move them to another night when you're not feeling so tired."

"Are you sure?" Rebecca asked.

Jenn could tell that Rebecca really wanted to leave but didn't want to cause her any difficulties.

"Absolutely," she said. "Text me in the morning and we can make other arrangements."

"You're a star." Rebecca stood and gave Jenn a hug. "Sorry, I'm just shattered."

"Yeah, right," Jenn mumbled in her ear. "I'll want all the gossip later."

Red appeared on Rebecca's cheeks, and she softly nodded her agreement. She handed her some money to pay for their dinner, despite Jenn having asked her not to. Shortly after, Arabella and Rebecca said their farewells and hurried from the restaurant.

"Jetlag can be rough," Kathryn said.

"Yeah, it can be," Jenn agreed. She didn't bother mentioning that she was pretty sure jetlag had nothing to do with their sudden disappearance.

22

THE EX, THE JAZZ, AND THE ALCOHOL

KATHRYN SIPPED wine from her glass. Jenn had chosen a wonderful vintage. She wondered where Jenn had acquired that knowledge from. She couldn't imagine it was from that awful bar where she had first met her. Everything in there was fluorescent and mixed with ice.

All in all, she was having a surprisingly fun evening. The restaurant was perfection. Not only was the food, drink, and service exceptional, but it also looked like it was a movie set. They were a stone's throw from busy Bourbon Street, littered with drunks, but it felt like they were miles away.

It was the kind of restaurant that was reviewed in magazines but rarely found in the real world. Charm and sophistication, but with all the convenience of modern-day dining.

And the company had been more than she could have hoped for. Arabella was witty and fun once you got to know her. Rebecca was delightful, and Jenn… *Jenn*. She gazed at her dinner companion, who stood at the balustrade looking down at the jazz band on the corner.

Jenn was more than she had ever expected. They'd had a great time on the streetcars the night before, but she'd really shone over dinner. She was very intelligent, funny, and kinder than anyone Kathryn had ever met before.

She didn't think she was guilty of judging books by their covers, but she'd definitely done so when she'd first met Jenn. To Kathryn, she was a bartender in a tank top and ripped denim shorts. Nothing more. Probably uneducated, definitely not someone she'd cast a second look at.

She couldn't have been more wrong. Jenn was not only educated, she was *smart*. Kathryn had met many people with qualifications coming out of their backside, but they could still be dumb as a box of rocks. Jenn had a natural curiosity about the world which had developed into a keen intellect.

The dinner invitation had originally been to reassure herself that Jenn was safe and well after the river incident. Maybe to try to apologise for her reaction to the kiss. Much to her surprise, it had turned into one of the most pleasant dinners she'd attended in a number of years.

She took another sip of wine. As she looked up again, she realised that a tall blonde woman was walking straight towards Jenn. Not towards the balustrade to look at the band, but towards Jenn.

"Grace!" Jenn announced happily when she noticed the woman beside her.

"Jenn, I thought it was you!"

The two women embraced. Kathryn narrowed her eyes, wondering who the interloper was. Didn't they know it was rude to interrupt someone's meal? Even if the food had been consumed long ago.

"Wow, it's been... what? Three years?" Jenn asked as they pulled away from the hug.

Grace nodded. "Yep. I just got back in town a couple of days ago. I was going to call you, but I've been so busy. Then I was having dinner with my girlfriend and I looked out here and there you were."

"Here I am." Jenn smiled from ear to ear.

Kathryn watched the two of them, wondering who on earth Grace was. She found herself hoping it was a co-worker from one of Jenn's many jobs. She didn't want to reflect on why that mattered to her.

"Oh, Grace," Jenn said, as she seemed to suddenly remember who she was with. She gestured toward Kathryn. "This is Kathryn, she's on vacation here."

Kathryn offered her hand. "Pleasure to meet you."

"Likewise." Grace smiled as she shook Kathryn's hand. "Anyway, I'll let you get back to your dinner. I just had to come over and say hello."

"I'm so glad you did, it's great to see you," Jenn said.

Grace pulled Jenn into another hug, placing a kiss on her cheek. "I'll call you, we'll catch up."

They exchanged farewells and Grace walked away. Jenn took her seat at the table again, watching as Grace walked away.

Eventually, the silence had dragged on too long for Kathryn.

"So..." she said.

"She's my ex. We dated for a while," Jenn admitted.

"Oh." Kathryn looked up to catch another glimpse of

the blonde who had now taken her seat inside the restaurant. "Didn't work out?"

"No." Jenn shook her head. "But we're still friends. I think we were always better friends than lovers."

Kathryn could feel a blush flare on her cheeks. She didn't want to appear to have a problem with same-sex relationships; she didn't. Even if her reaction to the kiss might have been interpreted otherwise.

"I see." She forced a wide smile. "It's nice that you're still friendly."

"Life's too short. We all need friends, right?"

Kathryn chuckled. Jenn raised a questioning eyebrow at her unexpected response.

"Some of us clearly find it easier to make friends," Kathryn said by way of explanation.

Sadness flashed across Jenn's face before she quickly masked it again. She looked at her watch. "Wow, look at the time. We better get moving if we're going to catch the show."

Kathryn gestured to the band on the street. "We've seen a show."

"Oh, they're good, but this show is better," Jenn promised.

She turned around and gestured for the waiter to bring the bill.

"Obviously, I'll be paying for dinner," Kathryn said, already sliding her credit card from its compartment in her phone case.

"No, you won't," Jenn argued.

Kathryn raised her eyebrow. "Oh, no?"

"No, this is my treat." Jenn handed the waiter some

cash the moment the bill landed on the table. "You can get the next one."

Kathryn decided not to dispute the matter, especially as she knew she'd rather enjoy another night of Jenn's company.

Once the bill was settled, they walked back downstairs and through a small door into a backroom that she never would have known about if she hadn't been following Jenn. The room was small but well decorated. There was a tiny raised stage at one end of the room. The rest of the room was filled with small round tables and mismatched chairs. Most notably, the room was completely empty.

"Where would you like to sit?" Jenn grinned.

"Are you sure it's tonight?" Kathryn looked at her watch and then around the empty room. "It's due to start in eleven minutes."

"This is New Orleans. It won't start on time, and people will arrive about thirty seconds before."

Kathryn smiled. "This takes some getting used to," she said.

"It's worth it," Jenn promised her.

Kathryn's smile bloomed into a laugh. She pointed to a table near the front but off to the side. They both sat down, and a waiter approached them almost immediately. Kathryn wondered if the service was always this good or if Jenn had called in a couple of favours.

"What do you think?" Jenn asked. "More cocktails?"

Kathryn bit her lip and nodded. "I'll have one if you do."

"Bellini?"

Kathryn nodded again.

"Two Bellinis," Jenn ordered.

They were soon alone again. A question had been gnawing at Kathryn's brain for a while, something she desperately wanted to know.

"This may be completely inappropriate," she started. "So, don't feel obligated to answer."

"Okay," Jenn replied, seemingly unfazed.

"How did you know you were gay?"

"Well, just to clarify, technically I identify as pansexual," Jenn explained.

"Wait, hold on." Kathryn sat up as she thought about the term. "I know this one."

Jenn laughed.

"Shh, shh." Kathryn waved her hand to silence Jenn's laughter, it was hard to think when someone was guffawing all over the place. "Oh, yeah, it's like bisexual, but..." She trailed off, not remembering exactly what it was.

"It means attraction to someone else, regardless of gender," Jenn explained.

Kathryn frowned.

"The dictionary defines bisexual as someone attracted to either men or women, although some people question that definition. Either way, pan is more inclusive because it includes people who are genderfluid."

Kathryn sat back and considered that. "That's fascinating. I rarely hear about pansexuality."

"A lot of the rainbow community is still discovering terms that they are comfortable with," Jenn explained. "But, to answer your question, I had my first non-straight thought when I was about thirteen and I saw two women kissing in the grocery store. I couldn't get the image out of my head, it was so different and kinda forbidden. A couple of years later, I was dared to kiss a girl at my school, so I did. I'm pansexual, but I favour relationships with women."

"Which would make you a le—"

Jenn put her hand up. "No. That wouldn't make me a lesbian. It would make me a pansexual in a relationship with a woman."

Kathryn could detect a little anger from Jenn. Clearly, she had misspoken. She decided to drop the subject for now. She needed to research these terms further.

The waiter placed two Bellinis on the table.

Once he had left, Jenn leaned forward. "Can I ask you a question?"

Kathryn felt her heart skip a beat. Jenn was about to ask her about her own sexuality. And she'd no doubt say the wrong thing and ruin the evening.

"Sure," she replied.

"Was that the best gumbo you ever ate?"

Kathryn let out a sigh and quickly nodded. "Absolutely delicious. The entire dinner was amazing."

Jenn opened her mouth to reply but paused when she noticed people entering the room. Kathryn turned around and saw Grace and her girlfriend walking in and taking a seat.

"We can go if you like," Kathryn offered. She wouldn't like to see her ex when she was out trying to have a good time, she wondered if Jenn felt the same way.

"No, it's fine," Jenn replied. "We're good."

"May I ask why you broke up?" Kathryn asked as she

watched Grace and her girlfriend take a seat and look at the drinks menu.

"We just drifted apart," Jenn admitted wistfully. "Mind-blowing sex can't sustain a relationship forever."

Kathryn was glad she hadn't been sipping her Bellini when those words fell from Jenn's mouth.

"No, I suppose not," she managed in a whisper. She found herself looking towards Grace with a curious gaze.

They sat in silence, watching as the room filled with people. After a few minutes the room was packed, and the atmosphere was electrifying.

Kathryn noticed Grace and her girlfriend had started making out while they waited for the band to arrive. She couldn't tear her eyes away, despite really wanting to. Jenn caught her staring and looked highly amused. Kathryn made a concerted effort to angle her head down towards the table so she didn't feel tempted to snoop. She decided that the Bellinis and the wine had gone to her head.

Luckily the band soon arrived. The lead saxophonist introduced his fellow musicians, and they began to play soulful and lively jazz tunes. Kathryn had never really cared for jazz, but she had to admit that it was very enjoyable to listen to. Her eyes kept getting drawn to the back of the room where Grace was still making out with her girlfriend.

Halfway through the set the waiter took more orders, and before Jenn had a chance to speak Kathryn had ordered two more Bellinis for them.

23

READY

THE WALK from the restaurant to the hotel had been made in silence. Rebecca casually glanced at Arabella as they'd walked, noting that she seemed to be getting more nervous as they got closer to the hotel. Closer to talking.

Rebecca was just as nervous. Arabella had told her she wanted to talk. She had added that it wasn't bad, but Rebecca didn't know if Arabella's concept of a positive conversation was the same as hers.

She didn't want to talk. Talking could end everything they had. Admittedly, it wasn't much, but it was friendship with a hint of something more to come. Rebecca didn't know if she could cope with the loss of the possibility of them being something more.

At first, she had taken Arabella's words and actions to mean a positive development, but it wasn't long before negative thoughts and anxiety had turned that around. Before she'd finished her main course, she was convinced of the worse.

They walked into the hotel bar, which was thankfully quiet. Arabella pointed to a table and high-backed leather chairs in the corner. "Take a seat, what would you like to drink?"

"Just water," Rebecca replied.

Arabella raised her eyebrow. "Just water? Seriously?"

"Fine, apple juice."

Arabella looked at her for a moment, as if she wanted to say something. She broke eye contact and walked over to the bar. Rebecca wiped her clammy palms on her dress before taking a seat. Her mind was racing with a hundred different scenarios, considering all the things that Arabella may say and all her possible responses.

Despite the rapid synaptic action, she didn't know what her response would be. When Arabella pulled the plug on the idea of romance, should she look unaffected in order to save the friendship? Or should she be honest and admit how crushed she was?

You shouldn't have said anything in the bathroom, Rebecca chastised herself.

Arabella lowered a glass of apple juice and a glass of red wine to the table. "I can hear you thinking over there."

"Can't help it," Rebecca said. "I don't think I've ever had a good conversation following someone saying, 'nothing bad'."

Arabella sat back in her chair and looked at Rebecca thoughtfully. "I'm ready," she said softly.

"For?" Rebecca was confused.

Arabella chuckled. "Us. Well, exploring whatever this thing between us is."

Rebecca wished she'd ordered something stronger to

drink. She sipped on her apple juice, trying to process what had been said.

"You look like I just shot your childhood pet," Arabella commented with a smile.

"I thought you were breaking up with me! Or putting a stop to the direction we were going in."

"Why on earth would you think that?"

Rebecca stared at Arabella. The woman was unreal.

"I held your hand when we walked to the restaurant," Arabella pointed out, as if that was supposed to clarify everything.

"Jenn and Kathryn were walking arm in arm, I thought you wanted to do something similar." A light bulb went off in Rebecca's head. Understanding hit her like a sonic boom. "Wait, wait… you… us?"

Arabella nodded.

Rebecca reached for Arabella's wine glass and took a long sip of the rich, red liquid.

Arabella watched her with an amused expression. "I wanted to speak with you earlier, but I didn't think it was fair to start to talk about this before dinner. I wanted to ensure that we'd have time to talk after the meal, hence asking you to have drinks here afterwards. I didn't realise you'd panic quite so much about it. I'm sorry, I should have read the situation better."

"An apology, too?" Rebecca widened her eyes and stared at Arabella. "Who are you and where is—"

"Oh, shush," Arabella cut her off. "I'm changing my mind already."

"What did change your mind?" Rebecca had to know

162

where this was coming from. What had led Arabella to her decision?

"Firstly, I want to apologise for how I have treated you," Arabella started. "I'm aware that it must have been hard for you lately, I've been giving you mixed messages and I've been all over the place emotionally."

"It's fine." Rebecca shrugged her shoulders.

"No, it's not."

Rebecca swallowed nervously. Arabella was right, it wasn't fine. She'd been on edge for weeks wondering what they were and where they were going, the mantra of *Give her time* running over and over in her head.

"When we drove home from Portugal, I was a very different person to the person I am today. As I've said to you before, I was on autopilot. Heading towards a life, a marriage, that I was destined to have. I'd never thought once about what I actually wanted in life. It seemed like an irrelevant luxury."

"And then I came along," Rebecca said.

"Quite." Arabella smiled. "And you blew all of that order and predetermined planning out of the water. And thank goodness you did. I was sleepwalking into a nightmare, one which I surely would have woken up from at some point. Probably when it was too late. Realising that I was miserable, and my life had been wasted."

Arabella took a sip of wine. She edged back into the wing-backed chair and looked at the liquid thoughtfully.

"It was an enormous change for me. To go from planning my wedding to a man—to Alastair—and preparing to give up work… to the unknown. You woke me up, reminded me that we only get one life and it's for living the way we want to live it. But, my upbringing meant I'd never really known what I wanted."

Rebecca remembered the heartbreaking moment when Arabella told her she didn't know how to be happy. At first, she'd thought it was a dramatic statement based on some truth blown out of all proportion, but she'd soon discovered that it was true.

Arabella's parents had never been about fun or seeking happiness. They were about duty, building a career, and a family. Arabella had never stopped to look outside of that path, and a child who had never been taught what happiness was couldn't identify it as an adult.

"Going from such a set plan in life to realising you don't know anything…" Arabella shivered slightly. "It's terrifying, Rebecca. Really, it is. My only constant was you. You'd woken me up to see this new world and the possibilities within it."

Rebecca knew that Arabella had struggled with the new 'directionless' life she was living. Another reason why she had given her space. She wanted to be the one person not pushing Arabella into a certain direction.

"When I kissed you, I thought I knew exactly what I wanted. I thought we'd drift into a relationship. Slowly, but surely. But then I started to get cold feet."

Rebecca thought back to the time before their trip to Scotland. They'd shared a few kisses and cuddled a little. It had felt like Arabella was holding back, but Rebecca had just written it off as a new feeling for the previously straight woman.

"And then Scotland…" Arabella trailed off.

Scotland was a topic that Rebecca had learnt to avoid.

Something happened that had nearly ripped them apart, it was just that she didn't know what had happened. So, she avoided the entire subject.

"I owe you an explanation," Arabella said.

"You owe me nothing," Rebecca replied. Sure, she wanted to know, but she didn't want Arabella to feel obligated.

"I panicked. When we realised that our flight would be cancelled, driving all the way to Scotland seemed like a great idea. I realised it would be a lot like our trip from Portugal. Sharing a car journey for so many hours, I thought it would be wonderful. I could even share the driving that time."

"What changed?"

"Realisation and expectation," Arabella said.

"You lost me." Rebecca frowned.

"I realised that we were on our way to Scotland. Our first trip together, a... tester for whether or not we were compatible as travel companions. And maybe more. And then I wondered if the expectation would be that we would... become more in Scotland. And I couldn't get that thought out of my head. I wasn't ready, but we were on the way and I felt trapped. So, when the car broke down, I was relieved."

"Relieved? More like livid," Rebecca pointed out. She'd thought Arabella had been difficult when she'd first met her in Portugal, but that was nothing compared to how she had been when they had broken down on the motorway. She'd gone crazy, and then demanded to go home. The trip was cancelled, and for a while, they didn't even speak.

"I panicked. We'd been driving for three hours, and I was terrified of what expectations you had of me and what expectations I had of myself. It was like driving towards a ticking time bomb. When the car broke down, the dam on my emotions broke with it." Arabella placed her wine glass back on the table.

"There were never any expectations," Rebecca gently said.

"I know. I realised that the moment I got home. By then, it was too late. I'd embarrassed myself, caused a huge scene, and…" She put her head in her hand.

Rebecca grabbed a nearby stool and placed it beside Arabella's chair.

"So, you hid from me for a while?"

"Yes," Arabella admitted. "I was so embarrassed. I realised I should have just spoken to you, but that seemed impossible at the time. It wasn't until later that I realised how stupid I'd been."

"Do you now know that you can talk to me about anything, at any time?" Rebecca asked.

Arabella looked up at her. There were unshed tears in her eyes as she nodded.

"And do you know that I would never have any expectations of you?"

Another nod.

Rebecca let out a sigh of relief. "Good. Because, I've seen you at your worst. And you scare the shit out of me. But you can always, always talk to me. And I'm happy to continue to give you space."

"I don't want any more space," Arabella said.

Rebecca raised her eyebrows.

"I've been using that space to hide. I've been burying my feelings. I'm not training for the London Marathon, I'm running away from my own mind. Every time I close my eyes, or pause working for two seconds, this flood of questions rushes through my brain. And every single time, I bury it."

"Why?"

Arabella shrugged. "Fear of the unknown? I don't know. But I do know that I am sick of that. I can't carry on living my life in this limbo. I've changed as a person, I'm probably still changing. I told myself I didn't want to start a relationship with you because I didn't know if I felt romantic feelings towards you, or if you were just the best friend I ever had."

Rebecca was still terrified of where this conversation was heading. She wanted to give Arabella the chance to figure things out for herself, she didn't want to push her. But she felt like there was an axe over their heads, waiting to drop.

"A—and?"

"I realised it can be both," Arabella said. "I'm still not ready. But I'm not prepared to hold you at arm's length any more either. I'm hoping to figure this out on my own, and I realise that I can't do that. I need your help. But I understand if you don't want to do tha—"

"I'll help," Rebecca said quickly.

"I may end up hurting you."

"I'll take the risk." Rebecca put her hand on Arabella's. "I know there is something between us, I feel it all the time. I hoped that you would feel it, too. But I know that it's really hard to deal with it all on your own."

"It is," Arabella agreed. "I've been holding back—burying my feelings—to try to protect us both. But all I've done is made things even harder for us. I suppose I thought I could figure it all out and then come to with a decision. As clear cut as that."

"But it's not that easy?" Rebecca guessed.

"No, it's really not that easy." Arabella smiled at her. "Help me?"

Rebecca grinned. "I'd like that. But you have to start talking to me and telling me what's going on in your brain."

"I know, I'm going to make a concerted effort to do just that."

"Good, because it won't work unless you do," Rebecca admitted. She needed Arabella to understand that she needed to start to open up. Even if it was hard, and sometimes embarrassing.

"I've been thinking about it a lot over the past couple of days. I'm fed up with being scared. I want to move on. Someone very wise told me I needed to live my life and fill it with love and happiness."

Rebecca could feel her cheeks hurting as her grin grew impossibly wide. She'd patiently waited for Arabella to come to some kind of decision, hoping for this but fearing and preparing for worse. Now she couldn't believe that her patience had paid off.

"Are you *sure* about this?" Rebecca checked.

Arabella lifted her hand and cupped Rebecca's cheek. She leaned forward and looked into her eyes.

"Very sure. I've done a lot of soul-searching, and I realise... I need you in my life. The very thought of you being with someone else…" Jealousy flashed in Arabella's eyes.

Rebecca closed the gap between them and pressed her lips to Arabella's. They shared a chaste kiss, considering they were still sitting in a public hotel bar. When Rebecca withdrew she brought her own hand up to Arabella's cheek.

"No chance of me being with someone else. I've only been able to think of you for some time now," she confessed.

Arabella smiled. "Good. I feel the same. And I am so sorry I've been up and down lately. I'm going to try my best to stop that. And obviously I'll talk to you when I feel nervous."

Rebecca lowered her hand and reached over to sip her apple juice. The adrenaline was wearing off, and she was suddenly exhausted, having been in a state of near-panic for so long.

"Are you okay?" Arabella asked.

"Yeah, just… happy," Rebecca admitted. "Really happy. And no idea what to do with myself." She laughed.

Arabella tilted her head for a moment as she considered it. "I'm happy, too. There you go… it seems I'm already learning."

24

PDA

Jenn and Kathryn walked arm in arm down Royal Street towards the hotel, discussing the jazz set they had just listened to. Jenn was relieved that Kathryn had apparently had such a good night. She was animated and clearly excited as she spoke about the musicians and her favourite pieces of music.

It was night and day from the person who had loudly slated the entirety of New Orleans in the middle of Bourbon Street just a couple of days before.

Jenn was more confused than ever. The glances, the licking of her lips, the body language... everything pointed to a woman who wasn't 100% straight.

It didn't help that there seemed to be an abnormally high number of kissing women around them that evening. First, there had been Grace and her new girlfriend making out at the back of the jazz venue. Now, they were following another female couple who were holding hands and sneaking kisses occasionally.

"There's a lot of that around here." Kathryn gestured to the couple in front of them.

"Love?" Jenn questioned.

"Public displays of it, yes."

"Does that make you uncomfortable?"

"I'm not used to it," Kathryn admitted.

"Like jazz?" Jenn chuckled.

The couple in front of them suddenly stopped and pulled each other into a passionate open-mouthed kiss. They stepped around the amorous couple. Jenn noted that Kathryn's eyes nearly bugged out of her head at the sight.

"Like jazz," Kathryn agreed once they had moved further along the street. "Maybe it will grow on me like jazz did."

Jenn swallowed hard. It was comments like this that made Jenn question Kathryn's claim to be straight. She couldn't read the words as anything other than flirtatious.

They walked in silence for the last couple of minutes to the hotel. As they arrived Jenn gestured towards the door.

"Your home, sweet home," she said. "I had a great night."

"So did I." Kathryn swayed slightly.

She'd been doing that a lot since they started to walk home. Jenn had tried to slow her alcohol intake during the music, once she had noticed Kathryn's glazed eyes. But Kathryn wasn't really a person you argued with, and the drinks had continued to flow.

"Wonderful food," Kathryn said. She took a step forward, closer to Jenn. "Wonderful music." She stepped forward again, forcing Jenn to take a step back. She felt the cold stone wall of the hotel behind her.

"Wonderful company."

Jenn saw a glint in Kathryn's eye and knew what was going to happen a split second before it did. But it was a little too late. Kathryn lunged forward and placed a sloppy kiss on her lips.

Jenn ducked away from the kiss.

"Kathryn, you're drunk... and straight, remember?"

Kathryn pouted. "I'm not drunk."

"You are." Jenn caught Kathryn by her upper arms and held her in place. "I'm not going to kiss you while you're drunk. I won't take advantage."

Kathryn smirked. "It's just a friendly goodnight kiss." She winked seductively.

Jenn knew she had to get out of there and fast. It may have been exactly what she wanted, but she knew that Kathryn was in no state to be giving any kind of consent. She placed a swift kiss on Kathryn's cheek.

"Good night, Kathryn."

She gently pushed on Kathryn's upper arms, so she could be free of her. She gestured towards the door to the hotel.

"Good night, dear," Kathryn said. She was still smirking but seemed to understand that she wouldn't be convincing Jenn of anything this evening. She turned around and walked into the hotel.

Jenn watched her walk into the lobby before letting out a long breath. She knew Kathryn would be trouble from the first moment she saw her, but she had no idea just how much trouble that would be.

BOO-BOO

"CAN WE GO TO MY ROOM?" Arabella asked.

Rebecca raised an eyebrow.

"Not like that." Arabella rolled her eyes. She gestured around the bar, which was starting to become a little busier. "I just don't want to be with so many people."

"Sure." Rebecca stood up and held out her hand to Arabella.

Arabella smiled and took the offered hand. "Better get used to this. They'll be a lot of it, dating an older woman."

A shadow passed over Rebecca's face before quickly clearing. "Yes, remember, I told you about my ex?"

Arabella got to her feet. *Oh, yes,* she thought. *The forty-nine-year-old.* She'd almost forgotten that Rebecca's previous partner had been much older than Rebecca. In fact, much older than Arabella also.

She then recalled the reason they broke up. The older woman had let Rebecca go, worried about trapping her in a relationship with someone so much older. And she'd done so after Rebecca had proposed marriage.

Marriage.

Arabella had just gotten out of one engagement. She wasn't ready to dive into another. In fact, the whole debacle had put her off of the idea of marriage entirely. She wondered what Rebecca's thoughts were. And children. She'd not even considered that.

Calm down, she told herself. *There's plenty of time to talk about these things. Get your anxiety under control.*

"You okay?" Rebecca asked at the prolonged silence.

"Yes, sorry, I was just thinking."

"About?" Rebecca pressed. "You did promise you'd tell me what you were worrying about."

"Who says I was worrying?"

Rebecca chuckled and pointed her finger to the centre of Arabella's forehead, right between her eyes. "Worry Central has traffic," she said. She gently poked the crinkled skin.

Arabella relaxed her face. "We are not referring to that part of my face as Worry Central."

Rebecca shrugged her shoulder. "You might not be."

"I'm regretting inviting you to my room," Arabella joked.

"You're not," Rebecca replied, winking as she did.

"No, you're right, I'm not," Arabella said.

She reached down and took Rebecca's hand. They slowly walked through the bar and towards the elevators.

"I'm sorry we had to cut the evening with Jenn short," Arabella said. "I know you've been looking forward to catching up with her. What with her spending half of the afternoon swimming in the river, and then us rushing off after dinner…"

"It's fine. She'll understand." Rebecca pressed the call button for the elevator.

"Oh, so you'll be telling her… about us, I mean?" Arabella asked.

"Hell yes, I will. I'll be telling her the second I see her next. I'll be telling everyone I can. All the time. 'Hello, this is my girlfriend.' And 'Have you met my girlfriend?' That kind of thing."

Arabella sighed. "Must we use the word girlfriend? I feel like I'm too old to be someone's girlfriend."

The elevator arrived, and they stepped inside.

"Partner?" Rebecca suggested, selecting their floor. "Although that does sound very…"

"Very?" she asked.

"Permanent," Rebecca said. A trace of worry passed over her face.

Arabella swallowed. "I… don't want to make any promises. And I certainly don't want to hurt you. But I can't envisage me walking away from this. Not in the near future. You mean too much to me."

Rebecca looked pleased with the comment. She bit her lip. "We can pick an appropriate name for you later," she decided. "Until then, I'm just going to introduce you as my boo-boo."

"It will be the last introduction you ever give," Arabella promised.

The elevator doors opened, and they made their way towards the rooms. For the first time in many years, Arabella felt butterflies careening into her stomach walls.

It was exciting. Nerve-wracking, too. She didn't know what she was doing, or what would happen next. But she did know that felt happiness.

"What do you want to do tonight?" Rebecca asked. "I have cards, we can play a game? Or watch some TV?"

"I'd love to see some of the photos you took today," Arabella replied. "I want to see New Orleans through your eyes."

Rebecca paused by her door. "Really? You're not just saying that?"

"Absolutely not, I love seeing the photos you take. Trying to figure out why a certain scene, or object, caught your eye." It was true. She enjoyed trying to figure out what made Rebecca tick. It was a habit she had begun shortly after they met, and a subject that she didn't think she'd ever fully discover. Rebecca was different from the other people in her life, she was on a completely different path. Her own path, forged by desire, dreams, and determination.

Rebecca opened her room door. "I'll grab my camera and the cables, and I'll come through. Obviously, I won't say no to a cup of tea."

"Says the person who mocked me for bringing a travel kettle," Arabella chuckled. She pulled her room key out of her bag.

"No, I mocked you for bringing three different varieties of tea and around two hundred individual tea bags."

"And now you want one of those tea bags," Arabella pointed out. "Good thing I brought extra."

Rebecca leaned in and kissed Arabella's cheek. "Whatever you say, boo-boo."

26

A LOT TO DRINK

THE DISTANT SOUND of people going about their morning routines eventually woke Kathryn. She flopped over in the king-sized bed to lay on her back.

Her brain thrummed with a post-alcohol haze. She squinted at the ceiling, struggling to piece her memories together.

Where am I? she wondered. *And how much did I drink?*

Suddenly she sat up in bed, clutching the sheet to her naked chest in shock.

"Shit!"

Total recollection of the previous evening came to her like a tsunami crashing against her frontal lobe. She brought her other hand up to hold her head. She winced.

"Shit," she muttered again.

She had kissed Jenn Cook. She'd tried for much more, too. While she had claimed it was intended to be an innocent goodnight kiss, it was anything but.

She swallowed hard. Pain in her head pulsated like a

siren. This wasn't just a hangover, this was a hangover and outright shock.

"What am I doing?" she muttered to herself. "I'm not gay. I'm not."

It even sounded weak to her own ears. She got out of bed and grabbed the white hotel-issued dressing gown and tossed it around her body. She walked over to the mirror and stared at her reflection.

"I am not gay."

She regarded herself in the mirror for a few silent moments before adding, "So why did you kiss a woman?"

Her reflection stared back at her in confusion. "And why can't you get her out of your head?"

She blew out a breath. No answer was forthcoming, because she didn't have one. It was as if she were a completely different person when she was around Jenn.

She tilted her head to one side. "I've... been under a lot of stress."

She walked over to the coffee machine, selected a pod, and placed it in the top of the device. "I'm in a strange city, alone. And lonely." She started the machine and walked into the bathroom, switching on the light.

"I'm confused... and suffering from... from emotional loss." She looked at her reflection, this one less flattering with the bright bathroom lights glaring at her. She blew out a long sigh.

"And I'd had a lot to drink."

She rubbed at her eyes before reaching into her toiletry bag and pulling out a packet of pain medication. She'd been through a lot lately, but that was no reason to take it out on Jenn.

She'd simply had the misfortune of being one of the very few people who had shown Kathryn some kindness lately. And Kathryn had repaid her by getting startlingly drunk and sending the most enormous of mixed signals. She wasn't gay, but for some reason she couldn't be trusted around Jenn Cook.

The coffee machine finished whirring, and she walked back into the main room. She picked up the cup and placed it down on the desk beside the hotel directory.

Panic coursed through her body.

Jenn would be coming to the hotel today to teach a water aerobics class. Kathryn lunged for the directory and hurriedly flipped through the pages. She quickly found the activities list and ran a shaking finger down the page.

Midday.

She turned to look at the alarm clock beside the bed.

Eleven o'clock.

She hurriedly headed for the shower, nearly tripping over the desk chair in her self-imposed rush.

The museum, she thought to herself as she turned on the shower. *I'm a tourist, of course I won't be here. Doesn't mean I'm avoiding her. Just... seeing a museum.*

27

VERY GOOD FRIENDS

REBECCA WALKED out onto the roof terrace of the hotel. She took a deep breath and stretched up to the sky. It was a good day. A great day, in fact, to take a dip in the pool and meet Jenn for some water aerobics before having lunch with her girlfriend.

Girlfriend. She tossed the word over and over in her mind. She smiled.

"There you are," Jenn called out from a storage room at the back of the pool.

"Here I am."

"How am I supposed to get any gossip out of you if you turn up five minutes before the class starts?" Jenn chastised her.

"Sorry, I lost track of time." She held her arms out to the side and pointed to her bikini top and shorts. "Is this suitable for water aerobics? I've never done it, so I didn't know."

Jenn put floatation noodles on the ground and walked

over to her. She was wearing a black swimsuit, something Rebecca wished she had brought. Jenn eyed the bikini top before pulling on the straps a little.

"You'll be fine," she said, satisfied that the material would stay in place. "Now, spill. What was all that about last night? That big fake yawn and a sudden need to leave. You're so obvious."

Rebecca turned around a few times to check they were alone, primarily to be sure that Arabella hadn't suddenly turned up.

"Arabella told me she wanted us to have a drink at the hotel bar after dinner. To talk."

Jenn raised her eyebrow and let out a sigh. "Uh-oh."

"Right?" Rebecca nodded. "Exactly. She told me it was nothing bad, but since when has that ever been a thing?"

"People say it's not bad so that you stay calm up until the moment they drop a ton of bad news on you." Jenn nodded sagely.

"Precisely!"

"So, what was the bad news?"

"It wasn't bad news," Rebecca admitted. A grin crossed her face, she was powerless to stop it. "She wants us to give it a go, you know, being together."

Jenn's eyes widened. "That's great news!"

"I know. I mean, she scared me half to death with all that 'let's talk later' stuff. But we chatted, and she explained a few things, why she's been so up and down with me and that she's come to some realisations. And she explained what happened on the way to Scotland."

Jenn winced. Rebecca had told her about the car trouble on the way to Scotland, Arabella's subsequent explosion and the week of silent treatment. At that point, Jenn had told Rebecca that Arabella was unhinged and to stay away from her.

Not that that was ever an option for Rebecca. The second their lips had touched that first time, she was hooked.

"So, what happened?" Jenn asked.

"She was scared out of her mind. She thought that we were going away to... you know, cement our relationship or something. She worked herself into a state over it. But didn't tell me, obviously. Then, when the car broke down, she saw a way out. She apologised, but that's classic Arabella. Bottle it all up and then explode at a later date."

Jenn chuckled. "And now you're in a relationship with her?"

Rebecca bit her lip and blushed. "Okay, that sounds bad. I didn't mean it like that. I mean, she feels so much, but she's not good at expressing things. I love that about her, she's like this huge ball of emotions, but she's so used to bottling them up... when she lets them out it can be beautiful. It can also be scary as hell, but she's working on it." She sighed. "I'm not explaining this very well."

Jenn put her hand on her shoulder and squeezed. "Are you happy?"

"So happy."

"Then you don't need to explain. As long as you're happy and you think she's the one for you, then I'm happy. She seems great. I had a great time last night."

"We did, too. I'm so sorry we bailed like that, I just had to know."

Jenn laughed. "Yeah, I would have dumped you, too." She looked up. "Speak of the devil."

Rebecca turned around. Her eyes widened, and she felt a lump in her throat. Of course, she knew she'd be seeing Arabella in a swimsuit. But she hadn't actually processed the fact that she'd be seeing Arabella in a swimsuit.

"You're drooling," Jenn whispered.

Rebecca couldn't control her expression. All she could see was long, toned legs that went on and on. Not to mention creamy breasts that were barely covered. They bounced as Arabella walked towards them.

"Morning," Jenn greeted. "Ready to burn some calories?"

"Absolutely," Arabella replied. "I need to after that sumptuous dinner last night. Is that your plan? Take people out for a wonderful, fattening meal, and then get them to come to your aerobics workout the next day?"

"Yep. You got me. I get a cut from the restaurant and from the hotel, it's a great money spinner."

Arabella chuckled and turned to look at Rebecca. She raised an eyebrow and smirked. "Are you okay?"

"Nice suit. Swimming. I mean… nice swimsuit," Rebecca finally said. She winced.

"Smooth," Jenn commented. "Real smooth."

The door from the gym opened, and some more guests walked onto the roof terrace.

"Okay, I better get started." Jenn walked away and greeted the newcomers.

Rebecca's eyes were transfixed on Arabella's long neck. They only broke contact to move down towards her chest.

"I can feel your eyes on me," Arabella whispered.

Rebecca eyes snapped up to Arabella's.

"Sorry," she apologised. "I… just—"

"I didn't say I didn't like it."

Rebecca smiled. She leaned forward and placed a soft kiss on Arabella's lips.

Arabella smiled. "What was that for?"

"Because I can." Rebecca shrugged. "I'm enjoying the fact that I can do that whenever I want."

Arabella returned the kiss.

"Hey, lovebirds, you ready to get started?"

Rebecca jumped a little. She felt herself blush.

"I'm ready," Arabella said as if nothing had happened.

"Great. By the way, it's really nice to see you two together," Jenn said.

Arabella beamed happily. "Thank you, it's nice to be together."

"Don't know why, she's not a great catch," Jenn joked. "If you want an upgrade, let me know and we can hit some of the bars here."

"Hey!" Rebecca complained. "You can't pull us apart. She's my boo-boo."

Arabella rolled her eyes. "I think I might take you up on that offer, Jenn."

"I think you better. No one wants to be called someone's boo-boo."

Arabella gave Rebecca an 'I told you so' look.

"But we should go out to celebrate—damn, I'm working at Façade tonight." Jenn bit her lip thoughtfully as she looked at Rebecca. "You could come down if you like? I can leave tickets at the door?"

Rebecca and Jenn shared a look. Jenn obviously didn't know if Arabella would be comfortable with the idea of going to Façade. Rebecca didn't know either. But she was in the business of stretching Arabella's boundaries and showing her new things.

"Yeah, I think we might," she replied.

"What's Façade?" Arabella asked.

"I'll tell you later," Rebecca said. "Let's get on with the exercise so I can get back to the eating."

28

TIME TO APOLOGISE

FIVE HOURS PASSED. Five hours of Kathryn looking over her shoulder and tiptoeing around establishments in case Jenn worked there. This was the problem when you were trying to avoid someone who appeared to have a million jobs in and around the city.

First, it had been a coffee shop where she'd eaten breakfast, then one of the many museums. Following that was another café, then a small parade which Kathryn had ended up running away from the second she saw it. A while later, it was a restaurant, then the pharmacy, and, finally, a bench by the docks.

Every single location terrified Kathryn. She had been on edge the entire day, and it was starting to take its toll. Jenn was nowhere in sight. Kathryn had a pain in her neck from constantly twisting around to seek out long, blonde curls.

Kathryn remembered when she was a little girl and used to play chasing games with her father. She would run up to him and tap his arm and declare that he was 'it' before turning and running away. As soon as she started to flee, she would be overcome with terror, knowing that her pursuer was faster and stronger than she was.

Almost immediately she would begin to hyperventilate as she heard her father approaching and saying he was coming to get her. She knew her father would never hurt her, but there was something about being chased that she hated.

Now she felt like she was in a giant version of the game. One where Jenn was potentially hiding around any corner. The mere thought had Kathryn's breath quickening. She looked around at the people milling around the docks to assure herself that she was safe.

Five hours was enough. Kathryn knew she couldn't maintain this level of panic any longer. She decided it was up to her to change the rules of the game. If she was going to get any peace, then she needed to take control and confront Jenn.

She wanted to find Jenn and apologise for her behaviour. And, of course, to reiterate that she was not gay. She needed to explain that her actions were simply down to stress, alcohol, and loneliness. Kathryn winced. No, definitely not loneliness, just stress and alcohol. She didn't need to explain her woes to someone she barely knew.

She was not gay, that was the main message she needed to convey.

She needed to find Jenn. She'd spent hours trying to avoid her, now to see if she could find her. She realised that she was just around the corner from the bar where she had first met her. It was as good a place to try as any.

She started walking, considering how convenient it was that everything in the French Quarter was within easy walking distance. She supposed the city did have its charm, despite her first impressions.

As she turned a corner onto Bourbon Street, she mentally gave herself a pat on the back that she had correctly remembered just where the rundown CeeCee's Bar was.

She stepped inside, her heart sinking when a young brunette looked up at her.

"Hey. What can I get you?"

She looked around nervously. Suddenly wondering if her new plan was such a good one. "I was looking for Jenn. Is she not working today?"

The tall, skinny brunette shook her head. "Nope, sorry, not her shift tonight."

"Oh," Kathryn said. "You wouldn't happen to know where I could find her, would you?" She suddenly released how odd it sounded for some random woman to stroll into the bar looking for Jenn. "She, um, left her phone on the table when we were having lunch, and she probably needs it…"

"Oh! Yeah, yeah, of course. Well, she's up at Façade tonight. She should be there now, setting up and stuff."

Kathryn smiled, happy that her ruse had worked. "Wonderful! I'm new in town, where is Façade?"

The young woman indicated down the road with her thumb. "Straight down the street, just beyond Jack's Lobster Bar."

"Thank you so much." Kathryn smiled and quickly left.

Finally, she had a solid plan. One which didn't involve roaming the streets of New Orleans for hours on end.

She was going to go to Façade, whatever that was. And she would tell Jenn in no uncertain terms that her sexuality was not in question. She was most definitely straight. The drunken kiss was just that, a drunken kiss. A mistake. Which she would apologise for.

What could possibly go wrong?

29

GETTING CLOSER

REBECCA SAT on the desk chair in Arabella's hotel room while she waited for Arabella to get ready. They'd had a fantastic day. A leisurely breakfast, water aerobics followed by a swim in the pool, then a visit to the casino—where Arabella had won at nearly every machine or table game she tried, and then a small shopping trip to Canal Place, followed by a quick meal in the hotel's restaurant.

It was the perfect vacation day. Rebecca couldn't have planned anything better if she'd tried. And she knew all of that was down to being with Arabella. She'd always loved spending time with her, it was no exaggeration to say that they had become the best of friends.

But things were different, less than twenty-four hours after Arabella had admitted her feelings. There was a lightness between them now. As if some wall had been knocked down.

"Why won't you tell me where we're going?" Arabella called from the bathroom.

"Because it's a surprise," Rebecca replied. That wasn't entirely true. She wanted to see the surprise on Arabella's face.

Arabella appeared in the doorway, holding a tube of mascara. One eye had been painted to perfection. The other was bare.

"It's not a surprise, it's some kind of joke. I saw the way you and Jenn looked at each other. And then the refusal to tell me exactly what it is. You're messing with me."

"I am," Rebecca confessed. "I'm taking you somewhere that I think you'll like, but honestly I don't know what your reaction will be."

Arabella paused. She narrowed her eyes to regard Rebecca. It was a ridiculous look, considering the mascara situation.

"And, if I don't like it?"

"We'll leave," Rebecca said. "I want you to experience new things, go to places you wouldn't normally go. But I don't want you to have a bad time. If you don't like anything, we'll move on. I promise."

That seemed to calm Arabella's concerns. She nodded and walked back into the bathroom.

Rebecca smiled to herself. Arabella was certainly being more communicative lately, and she welcomed it. She'd spent weeks wondering what was going on inside her head, pondering where a sudden mood swing had come from. She hoped her openness continued.

"If you introduce me as that ridiculous name again, I'll tear you limb from limb," Arabella called from the bathroom.

"Sorry, didn't quite catch that, boo-boo," Rebecca said, barely able to keep a straight face.

Silence.

She wondered if Arabella was ignoring her. A moment later, her question was answered. No, Arabella wasn't ignoring her. She swept out of the bathroom with a murderous look over her face.

"Stop calling me that," she demanded, a glint of humour in her eye.

As she got closer, Rebecca grabbed her by the arm and pulled her onto her lap. She wrapped her arms around Arabella and silenced her with a kiss.

Arabella melted against her, wrapping her arms around Rebecca's shoulders and returning the kiss with enthusiasm.

Rebecca hadn't expected the kiss to take that kind of turn, not that she was complaining. Not at all. In fact, now she found she wanted more. She placed her hands on Arabella's waist and quickly stood up, manoeuvring Arabella onto the desk in front of the chair. She pressed Arabella back against the wall with her own body, never once breaking the kiss.

Arabella's hands started to roam Rebecca's body, working their way down her back and up her sides. Her fingers gripped eagerly, like she couldn't get enough.

Rebecca surged impossibly closer, pressing her front against Arabella's. Her mind was short-circuiting. This was what she had dreamed of and hoped for. She just hadn't expected it right now.

At the back of her mind, a little voice questioned if Arabella was ready for this kind of kiss. She seemed ready, but Rebecca wasn't going to take any risks and ruin the day they'd had.

She broke the kiss and leaned her forehead against Arabella's as she took a couple of deep breaths to calm herself down.

"Well," Arabella said, "that was…"

Rebecca closed her eyes, praying for a positive response.

"Incredible," Arabella finished.

Rebecca smiled. "You're incredible."

"And you're the reason we're going to be late," Arabella told her. She placed a flat palm on Rebecca's chest and pushed her back. She slid from the desk. "I can't believe you hoisted me up there like some…"

"Some?" Rebecca asked. She knew Arabella had enjoyed it, her flushed cheeks gave her away.

"Never mind." Arabella brushed down her dress. She turned around and looked at her reflection.

Rebecca looked over her shoulder. Arabella's lipstick was a mess, her hair was mussed, and some of her mascara that hadn't dried was smudged. She looked a mess. A beautiful mess.

"Your fault we'll be late," Arabella said, her eyes meeting Rebecca's in the reflection.

Rebecca held up her hands. "My fault."

Arabella turned around again. She placed one hand on Rebecca's chin and held her face in place, with a finger from the other hand she cleared away lipstick.

"Leave it," Rebecca suggested. "Let everyone know."

"I didn't know you were such an exhibitionist," Arabella joked. She placed a quick kiss on Rebecca's lips and then walked back into the bathroom to finish getting ready.

Rebecca looked at her reflection. She looked just like someone who had recently been in a passionate lip-lock. While she didn't mind the fact, she thought it best to clean herself up a little.

She walked through the open interconnecting door into her own room, smiling ear to ear as she went.

30

ECHO

KATHRYN WAS so busy mentally preparing her speech that she barely gave the fluorescent sign for Façade a second thought. She walked straight into the building.

She passed a couple of women and entered what looked like a nightclub. A large bar area took up the middle of the room and around the large and dimly lit room were tables and chairs, as well as plush sofas and armchairs. Two large stages on either side of the room were professionally lit.

Kathryn wondered if live jazz was played of an evening. Everywhere in town seemed to advertise live jazz.

She walked over to the bar and nodded at a young woman cleaning some glasses. "Hello, is Jenn here?"

The woman frowned at her. "Well, yeah, she's probably getting ready."

"Could you get her for me?"

The woman looked very uncertain. "She's getting ready."

Kathryn wanted to roll her eyes but decided against it. "I need to speak to her, it's very urgent."

The young woman sighed. She put down the glass and the cloth and walked out of the bar area and across the room.

Kathryn shook her head. *What's her problem? And how much time does Jenn need get ready to pour a few drinks?*

She walked around the bar area for a bit before sitting on a stool. She stared at the enormous range of drinks on offer and wondered how anyone in New Orleans managed to get anything done.

Someone sat down on the stool next to her.

"Decided to get here early and get the good seats, huh? I like that."

Kathryn turned to regard the woman beside her. She was a large lady, probably in her early forties. She wore a white tank top which displayed a variety of tattoos on both her arms. She had short hair which had been gelled into impressive spikes.

"Yes." Kathryn nodded, unsure of what to say. Apparently, there were good seats and bad seats, and somehow, she'd managed to get a good one. Maybe the day wouldn't be a complete waste.

"Well, you picked a good night for it. I hear the show tonight is going to be amazing! I'm Echo, by the way."

Kathryn took the woman's offered hand. Echo shook her hand with a vice-like grip.

"I'm Kathryn. Echo is an interesting name. Is it a nickname?"

"Well, kinda." Echo snorted a laugh. "But I can only tell you about that when we've shared a vodka slammer."

Kathryn smiled. Echo seemed to be yet another of the larger-than-life characters she was meeting on her trip.

"I've never had a vodka slammer, but it sounds like fun."

Echo looked at Kathryn with a knowing grin. "You're not from around here, are you?"

Kathryn shook her head. "No, just visiting."

"Well, if you need anyone to show you around town, I'm your woman," Echo pointed to herself with her thumb. "Really, if you need anything at all."

"Thank you, that's very kind." Kathryn smiled.

"Er, Kathryn?"

Kathryn turned around. Jenn was approaching them, a frown on her face as she looked from Kathryn to Echo.

"Oh, Jenn. There you are." She turned back to Echo. "Excuse me a moment."

"I'll be sure to save your seat," Echo offered.

"That'd be great."

Kathryn lowered herself from the barstool. She gestured for Jenn to follow her out of earshot from her new acquaintance. She didn't want to air too much dirty laundry in front of a stranger.

"What are you doing here? And why are you talking to Echo?" Jenn hissed as soon as they were far enough away.

Kathryn was taken aback by Jenn's attitude. She blinked. "I'm sorry?"

"Why are you here?" Jenn demanded.

Kathryn really didn't appreciate her attitude one bit. Okay, she'd messed up, but Jenn was behaving abysmally.

"What do you mean? I can go wherever I like," Kathryn replied.

"No, really, why are you here? You shouldn't be here."

"Well, I came to *apologise,* but I don't know if I want to anymore!" Kathryn argued.

"What?" Jenn frowned in confusion.

"I came to apologise," Kathryn repeated. "For the kiss," she added in a whisper.

"Oh."

"I wanted to explain that I didn't mean to give you mixed signals. I was very tired and emotional. I'd had too much to drink and I was… well, I shouldn't have kissed you. I'm not gay."

Jenn snorted a laugh.

"Is something funny?" Kathryn demanded. She was apologising, and Jenn was laughing in her face. What had gotten into her?

"Nothing," Jenn said.

"Well, it must be something. I guess you think it's funny that I tried to kiss you despite being straight. But I'm sorry, that's just the way it is. I'm completely straight."

Jenn bit her lip, looking like she was trying to prevent another laugh.

"Really," Kathryn demanded. "What's so funny about that?"

"Nothing at all." Jenn shook her head but was still smiling.

"You think something is amusing," she pointed out. "You know, I don't know if you've had a bad day, but you need an attitude adjustment."

"What?!"

"You heard me." Kathryn folded her arms and stared at Jenn.

"What did I do?"

"Demanding to know why I'm here as if I'm not allowed in some… music… bar… place!" Kathryn replied. "And asking me why I'm talking to my new friend."

"New friend?" Jenn folded her arms and laughed softly. "Okay. Whatever."

"I think that kiss—that drunken kiss, I might add—went to your head. And you think you own me or something." Kathryn laughed derisively.

Jenn held up her hands. "You know what, Kathryn? Fine. I apologise for my behaviour. I was wrong, you were right. Clearly, you are not gay, and I understand that the kiss was just a mistake."

Kathryn hesitated a moment. Something felt off, but she'd triumphed and won the battle of words and so she was satisfied.

"Yes, well… thank you."

"Now," Jenn smiled. "You go and spend some time with your new friend. Don't let me stop you."

Kathryn frowned at Jenn's smile. Something was definitely wrong. Maybe Jenn didn't like Echo. She glanced at the woman at the bar. Yes, she might be perceived as a bit rough around the edges, but Kathryn wasn't going to let stereotypes put her off. Echo seemed perfectly polite and, at the moment, infinitely nicer than Jenn.

"Fine, I will." She nodded her head sharply to emphasise the point.

"Fine," Jenn repeated. She shook her head and chuckled as she turned and walked towards the staff room.

Kathryn frowned. Something was very wrong, but she wasn't going to let Jenn have the upper hand. If Jenn wanted her to leave and not hang out with Echo, then Kathryn would stay and would talk to Echo all damn night.

She returned to the barstool and let out a sigh.

"Problem?" Echo frowned.

"Not really." Kathryn shook her head. "She was being possessive, but I put her in her place."

"Good for you! So, are you and her?" Echo gestured between them with her finger.

Kathryn balked. "Me and Jenn? No, no, nothing there at all."

Echo looked at her for a couple of seconds before grinning. "Kathryn, can I buy you a drink?"

"You know, that sounds like just what I need."

31

FAÇADE

ARABELLA SAW a queue of people at the door to Façade. She looked at the neon flashing lights and frowned. "What is this place?"

"You'll see," Rebecca replied.

She rolled her eyes. Rebecca still refused to tell her anything. Not that she was worried. Rebecca had yet to lead her wrong. She knew Arabella's limits, and while she might push on them a little, she never went beyond them.

They joined the queue, and Arabella realised everyone in the queue was a woman, even the security guard at the door.

Is this a gay bar? she wondered to herself. If it was, she couldn't understand the secrecy. Did Rebecca really think she was such a prude that she wouldn't be able to cope with a gay bar?

The queue moved quickly, and they were soon in the venue. There were stages at each end of the room, a variety of chairs and tables in between, and a large bar in the middle of the room.

Her eyes focused on someone familiar sitting at the bar.

"Is that… Kathryn?" Arabella asked in surprise.

Rebecca followed her gaze. "Yeah, she's looking a bit drunk."

"Seems to be a common theme with her," Arabella pointed out.

"Hey, she's on holiday. Don't judge."

"I thought you hated her for messing your friend around?" Arabella asked.

"No, I hate that she messed my friend around," Rebecca corrected. "But I don't hate *her*."

Arabella smiled at yet another example of Rebecca's compassion. If someone had upset her friend the way they had Jenn, Arabella wouldn't be so generous.

"Do you mind if we go and sit with her?" Rebecca asked.

"If you'd like to…"

"Yeah, I want to know why she's here. And what's going on with her and Jenn."

"Oh, so you want to meddle?" Arabella laughed.

"No." Rebecca smiled. "Just… fish for information."

They approached Kathryn and the woman she was talking with. They were so deep in conversation that they didn't notice Arabella and Rebecca beside them until Rebecca delicately coughed.

Kathryn turned around and beamed when she saw them. "Hi!"

Oh dear, drunk as a skunk, Arabella thought.

"Hi, we didn't expect to see you here," Rebecca said. She gestured to the two stools beside her. "May we join you?"

"Absolutely," Kathryn said. "This is my friend, Echo. Echo, this is Rebecca and Arabella. They're English."

Arabella felt her eyebrow raise in amusement. She didn't think she'd ever been introduced like that before. She shook hands with the interestingly named Echo and took her seat, leaving a space between herself and Kathryn. If Rebecca really wanted to sit with her, she could sit *next* to her.

"Can I get anyone a drink?" Arabella offered.

"That's very kind of you," Echo immediately spoke up. "I'll have another beer."

"White wine would be lovely," Kathryn said.

"Rum and coke for me," Rebecca ordered as she sat down.

Arabella made eye contact with bartender and ordered the drinks, getting herself a white wine as well.

"So, you seen the show before?" Echo asked.

"I have, Arabella hasn't," Rebecca answered.

Arabella looked over to the stages. *Show*, she thought. *Hmm.*

"How about you?" Rebecca asked.

"I have, but this one hasn't," Echo said with a gesture towards Kathryn. "I keep telling her, she's in for a real treat!"

"Yes, you do," Kathryn said. She sounded a little glazed, and Arabella felt sorry for her. She wondered how the woman had found herself in some kind of gay bar with Echo. She couldn't imagine it was planned.

"So, you know what the show is?" Rebecca asked. She sounded cautious.

"No, but Echo says it's amazing," Kathryn said.

The bartender served the drinks, and the conversation ended.

Rebecca leaned in close to Arabella. "Okay, this is weird. Why is she here?"

"I've no idea," Arabella said. "Could Jenn have invited her?"

"I doubt it," Rebecca replied. "I don't see why she'd invite her to—"

Suddenly the lights in the bar dimmed. Music started blaring through wall-mounted speakers.

Arabella looked around the audience, noting that the predominantly female crowd had started clapping loudly and wolf-whistling. She noticed that Kathryn was looking around in confusion as well. Wherever they were, and whatever they were about to see, it was clear that it was only her and Kathryn who were out of the loop.

A single spotlight appeared on the main stage.

Jenn Cook stepped into the light, wearing a tight, floor-length red dress with slits up each leg to her hips.

The crowd roared with excitement as Jenn winked and blew kisses at them.

"It's a burlesque show," Rebecca shouted in Arabella's ear about the din.

Arabella looked at Rebecca in shock, and then leant forward to look at Kathryn. The woman had practically swallowed her own tongue at the sight of Jenn on the stage.

This should be interesting, Arabella thought.

"Are you okay to stay?" Rebecca asked.

"Absolutely," she replied. She wasn't about to miss both shows: the one Jenn was putting on, and Kathryn's reaction to it.

She turned to face the stage and started to applaud with the rest of the audience.

3 2

WHAT A SHOW

THE SHOW ENDED, and the room was soon awash in cheers and applause. Arabella turned to look at Rebecca who was eyeing her curiously.

"What did you think?" Rebecca asked.

"It was amazing," Arabella replied while clapping her appreciation.

Rebecca sagged in relief. Clearly, she'd been concerned that Arabella might not have enjoyed such a risqué art form. She could understand Rebecca not explaining what the show was beforehand, she wasn't sure she would have gone if she had known. But she was so happy that she had.

She'd never seen a burlesque show before, she'd made assumptions about them, but she was pleased to find that —in this case—she was wrong. The show was undeniably naughty but also extremely classy.

It had been a little unsettling at first to watch one of Rebecca's friends as she danced, swivelled, teased, and, ultimately, undressed. But she'd soon got into the show and could appreciate the artistic content, as well as the incredible bodily strength that Jenn possessed. She'd made a mental note to talk to Jenn about her workout routine.

She looked down the bar at Kathryn. Echo was standing above her, applauding so loudly that Arabella was deafened by it. Kathryn wasn't reacting at all. She seemed to be in her own world, staring at the empty stage in a stupor.

Arabella cupped her hand to Rebecca's ear and whispered, "Someone clearly enjoyed the show."

Rebecca cast a casual glance towards Kathryn before turning back to Arabella with a grin.

The applause was starting to die down, and they could hear each other again.

"Man, what a show!" Echo shouted.

"Indeed, it was," Arabella agreed.

Echo ordered another round of drinks. Arabella regarded Kathryn's pale face and thought that the last thing the woman needed was another drink.

Echo put her hand on Kathryn's shoulder. "Man, that show was incredible. You tapped that?"

Kathryn was still staring at the stage, completely unaware of her surroundings.

"Hey, earth to Kathryn?" Echo asked.

Kathryn slowly turned to look at Echo. "Oh, I'm sorry, I was miles away. What did you say?"

Echo smiled. "I asked if you've tapped that?"

Kathryn recoiled. "No! Absolutely not!"

Rebecca looked at Arabella with a raised eyebrow. Arabella unashamedly watched the interaction.

Echo chuckled and held up her hands. "It's okay, I'm not the jealous type. I know how to share my toys."

Arabella almost snorted a laugh. Supposedly straight Kathryn had somehow—and judging by the look on her face, *mistakenly*—found herself in a burlesque lesbian bar. With a new girlfriend called Echo who had been plying her with drinks for some time. She watched Kathryn swallow hard and realised with a chuckle that the same fact was now dawning on Kathryn.

Echo put her arm around Kathryn. "After this, I was wondering if you wanted to go on to Shady's? It's not as classy as it is here. There the girls take it all off, not just down to their panties like they do here."

Arabella covered her mouth to contain her laughter. Yes, Kathryn had got herself into quite the mess.

Kathryn's mouth opened and closed a few times as she struggled to know what to say. Arabella regarded her a little more closely. She nudged Rebecca. "I think she's about to go," she said.

"Go?" Rebecca asked.

She gestured towards Kathryn with her head.

Echo seemed none the wiser in regard to Kathryn's unstable state.

"Unless you want to go back to my place?" Echo suggested. "We could crack open a couple of beers and I can give you a hands-on demonstration of why they call me Echo."

Kathryn's eyes fluttered closed just as Rebecca turned around. A split-second later, Kathryn was out for the count, Rebecca catching her before she fell to the floor.

33

ALL A MISUNDERSTANDING

JENN SAT in her light blue silk kimono, eating potato chips from a large bag on the dressing table in front of her. The air-conditioning unit in her small dressing room was silently blowing out ice-cold air. She watched the rise and fall of Kathryn's chest, strictly for medical reasons, of course.

Five minutes earlier, a quick knock at her door from Monica had informed her that they'd had a 'fainter' in the bar. It wasn't uncommon that the heat, or the excitement during some of the racier shows, would get to one of the audience.

As the dressing room was one of the few places where there was a door, a sofa, and reliable air-conditioning it ended up being the go-to place for any casualties.

Jenn had been surprised when an unconscious Kathryn had been carried in by one of the bouncers, accompanied by Rebecca.

Rebecca had quickly explained that she seemed to just

be overheated and exhausted. Apparently, Echo had been queueing up drinks for her for a while. Rebecca hadn't stayed, wanting to get back to Arabella, and so Jenn had watched and waited for Kathryn to come back to the land of the living.

She didn't have to wait long. Brown eyes fluttered open and looked around the room. Soon, they found Jenn, and terror filled them.

Jenn smiled. "Hey."

"Hey," Kathryn replied softly. "What... what happened?"

"Easy! Go easy sitting up," Jenn said as Kathryn gingerly raised herself up from the couch. "You fainted," she explained. She picked up a glass of cold water from the dressing table and handed it to Kathryn without standing up.

Kathryn gratefully took the glass and drank down some of the liquid. She nervously looked around the room as she did. She had barely finished drinking when she asked, "Where's Echo?"

"Your girlfriend? She went to get you a taxi," Jenn said seriously. Kathryn's eyes widened, and Jenn had to laugh. "I'm kidding, she's gone."

"Oh, thank god," Kathryn sighed in relief.

"Remind me," Jenn drawled. "You originally came here to tell me that you're not gay, right? Before you got yourself a girlfriend and watched my burlesque show at one of the most popular lesbian bars in the city. Right?"

Kathryn looked up at Jenn with an exasperated expression. "It's all a misunderstanding."

"You seem pretty good at them," Jenn commented. She stood up and walked behind a dressing screen.

After a few silent moments Kathryn spoke again. "The show was amazing."

"Thank you," Jenn said simply. She didn't wish to be drawn into any further conversation.

"I'd never seen burlesque before."

Jenn removed her kimono and sighed softly. She leant her head on the wall of the dressing area. Why did Kathryn have to faint? Why was she now trapped with the frustrating woman? She was thankful for the tall dressing screen, which meant she didn't have to see her.

"I didn't think you would have," Jenn replied.

"What made you get into it?"

Jenn started to strip out of her stage outfit. Since she was stuck with Kathryn, she might as well make conversation.

"A couple of years after I came to New Orleans, I saw a show. There are a lot of competitions in the city when it comes to burlesque," Jenn explained. "I'd always been interested in dance and performing, and I decided to go to a class, just for me, you know?"

She pulled on a pair of skinny denim shorts. "My teacher said I was good at it, she wanted me to go on at a talent night. It was the seediest place ever, and I hated every second of it. Men were whistling and leering and throwing money at me. I felt like a stripper, and that wasn't what I was there for. Burlesque is an art form."

Jenn put a white tank top on and walked out from the dressing screen, back towards her dressing table. "But I met a woman who worked here at Façade. She asked me to come down and interview. I do one show a week, and I do it because I enjoy it. It's a nice setup here."

Kathryn nodded.

"And I'm sorry I was short with you earlier," Jenn continued. "It's just I knew you had no idea Façade was a gay bar, and Echo, well, she likes to collect fresh baby-dykes. I wanted to warn you."

Kathryn chuckled. "And then I pissed you off and you threw me to the wolves?"

Jenn laughed. "Yep, pretty much."

Kathryn smiled and took another long gulp of water.

"Are you feeling better? Can I get you more water?" Jenn asked.

"I'm feeling better," Kathryn said. "Just a little over-heated and, well… it doesn't matter now."

"Go on," Jenn gently pressed, even though she wasn't sure she wanted to know.

She'd had a lot of time to think about Kathryn's yo-yoing sexuality, and even though she found Kathryn extremely attractive, she'd decided to keep her distance. The last thing she needed was to get her heart broken by someone who hadn't gotten their act together.

While she didn't believe for one moment that Kathryn was straight, she wasn't ready to be the one who got hurt trying to help the woman see that for herself. No, it had to end now.

Kathryn looked at her nervously. She looked like she was mentally weighing up her options before she finally whispered, "I think I'm… confused."

"Confused?" Jenn frowned.

"Yes, confused." Kathryn nodded. "I've seen a lot of

things since I came to this city and, well, tonight was an eye-opener."

Jenn suddenly understood what she meant. "Ah, confused. What's so bad about feeling confused?"

"I'm straight," Kathryn explained. "I've always been straight, I have never *ever* looked at a woman in... that way. But now I'm, well, I'm seeing things and feeling things I haven't felt before."

Jenn held her breath for a second as she wondered what to do next. After Kathryn's drunken kiss she had stayed awake all night. *Avoidance is the best strategy*, she reminded herself. *Come on, you can do this.*

She'd previously met women visiting New Orleans who were curious and wanted someone to explore with. And on a couple of occasions Jenn had participated in their experiments.

Each had ended disastrously. For Jenn. Usually when the women went back home to their husbands or boyfriends, having managed to scratch the itch and leave it in New Orleans.

Jenn couldn't stand to have her heart broken again.

"Look, Kathryn," she started. She looked down at the floor, choosing her words carefully. "I—I have feelings for you. You've got to know that. You're smart, funny, and—" She looked up and sighed. "Breathtakingly beautiful. But I can't be your experimental toy. I just can't."

Kathryn blushed bright red and broke eye contact. "I'm not asking you to be."

"I think you are, or at least I think you eventually *will*," Jenn admitted quietly. "I've been here before; straight woman comes to the Big Easy and sees the other side of the coin. Wants to experiment. Then they go home, back to their life. But I'm left here."

"I…" Kathryn started. "You kissed *me*, after the tram—"

"Streetcar," Jenn correctly softly.

"After the *streetcar*, you kissed me. You started all of this!" Kathryn pointed out.

"I know, and I apologised," Jenn said. "I shouldn't have kissed you, but I thought you were flirting with me."

"Maybe I was." Kathryn sighed. She put her head in her hands. "I just don't know any more."

Jenn swallowed hard. "I… you… you're just tired and emotional. Like you said to me earlier."

"I suppose," Kathryn muttered. She looked up again.

Jenn took a deep breath. She had to end this here and now. She was already in pain. Prolonging it would just make things worse. "I think it would be best if we avoided each other."

Kathryn paused for a moment, looking at Jenn in hurt and confusion. But the confusion slowly faded, replaced with understanding.

"I agree. I'm sorry… I shouldn't have come here."

"It's fine, I appreciate you coming to apologise. And hey, now you know you like burlesque," Jenn pointed out. "Another thing that New Orleans has taught you about yourself."

Kathryn put the empty glass on the dressing table and stood up and looked nervously at the door.

"Do I want to know how Echo got her nickname?"

Jenn laughed. "Probably not."

Kathryn nodded. "Is there another way out of here?

I'm not sure I want to see her again… I think we're engaged."

Jenn grinned. She'd miss Kathryn's dry wit. "Sure, I'll walk you through to the fire exit."

She grabbed her bags, and they both left the dressing room. They walked down a small hallway, Jenn saying goodbye to a few members of staff as they left.

She pushed the door open and gestured for Kathryn to step out into the warm night air.

"You know," she couldn't help saying. "If you are curious, then Façade is a good place to hang out. It's more upmarket than some of the other bars, if you don't include Echo."

Kathryn shook her head nervously. "I… I don't think I'll come back."

They walked up the empty alleyway.

"If you are curious, then you should probably explore it," Jenn said sympathetically. "The person we end up with is an important factor in our lives. If you maybe are gay, or bi, then you're opening up your possibilities of finding your true love."

Kathryn chuckled lightly. "True love?"

"Yeah." Jenn smiled. "Don't you believe in true love?"

"No," Kathryn said quickly. "I think that's just a fairy tale our parents tell us to protect us from how lonely the world can be. Something to keep people occupied, millions of people seeking out their true love to prevent them from actually seeing how dire their life is. The concept of true love is just a distraction."

Jenn stopped walking and blinked at Kathryn in shock. "Wow."

"What?" Kathryn frowned.

"That's some heavy shit right there." Jenn chuckled. "But seriously, have you ever been in love?"

"Of course I have." Kathryn shrugged. "I just don't think it's this all-encompassing dream state that we're led to believe it is."

"I take it back," Jenn said.

"Take what back?"

"Don't explore your curiosity. Don't go bringing that doom and gloom attitude into the queer community," Jenn laughed.

Kathryn gently slapped the back of Jenn's arm.

They continued up the alleyway towards the busy road ahead.

Kathryn regarded Jenn curiously. "So, you believe in true love?"

"Yep." She smiled. "I think that there is someone, the perfect someone, out there for everyone. And you know what else?"

"What else?" Kathryn smiled.

"I also believe in fate," Jenn confessed. "So, I also believe that fate will push you towards your true love if you let it. I bet you think that's silly, right?"

"Yes," Kathryn said simply. "But I sometimes wish I could believe in that kind of thing, too."

"Too much of a realist, huh?" Jenn asked.

Kathryn nodded. "Something like that."

They approached the end of the alleyway, coming to a stop before they joined the bustle of the city.

Kathryn sighed. "Thank you. For, well, everything. I'm sorry I've been a constant source of trouble for you."

Jenn chuckled. "It's been fun. I'm glad I met you, Kathryn. And I really hope you enjoy the rest of your time in New Orleans. As I said when we first met, there's something for everyone if you just go out and look for it."

Kathryn looked at her, and Jenn momentarily got lost in the soulful brown eyes. She blinked and looked away. She knew down that road led to heartache. She'd had her own fair share of that over the last few years. This was for the best. For everyone.

"Good night, Jenn," Kathryn said, her bright smile not quite meeting her eyes.

34

A TOUCH OF JEALOUSY

"WELL, THAT WAS AN INTERESTING EVENING," Arabella said.

"Unexpected," Rebecca agreed.

They walked hand in hand down the street towards the hotel. Rebecca was enjoying feeling Arabella's soft hand in hers. She wondered if this behaviour would continue when they were back home in London.

Nothing had been mentioned about what they would do when they returned home. Rebecca didn't know if Arabella was ready to start introducing her as more than her just a friend, especially to her father.

While she wanted to know, she also didn't want to rock the boat. She'd take what she could get for now. The going-home situation could be a conversation for another day.

"So, you liked the show?" Rebecca asked, trying to take her mind off their eventual departure.

"I did, very much so."

Rebecca furrowed her brow a little. She'd been convinced that Arabella would like the burlesque show. She knew she appreciated other forms of dance, so it wasn't too big a leap. While some people might attend a burlesque club to see flesh on display, she knew Arabella would understand the complexity of the act and the fitness required.

Although, now she allowed her mind to wander, she did wonder what Arabella thought of Jenn's performance. Did Arabella get turned on by it? She couldn't blame her, Jenn was a very attractive woman. But she was her friend. It would feel weird if Arabella thought of her that way.

"So… you, um, liked the… choreography?" She winced slightly. It sounded ridiculous to her own ears.

"I did. Jenn must have incredible core strength," Arabella said.

Jealously rushed through Rebecca in a way she'd never felt before. Now she wished she'd never gone to Façade. She looked around the bustling street. They'd left soon after the main show had ended, along with many other people from the club.

She suddenly felt extremely possessive of Arabella. They were walking along a street, crammed with women who loved women. Women who would obviously find Arabella attractive. Some who Arabella might also find attractive.

It had never occurred to her before that she might have to compete for Arabella's affections. But it made sense, Arabella was stunningly beautiful. She could easily have her pick of women.

Arabella let go of her hand, and Rebecca looked at her in confusion.

"You were hurting my hand," Arabella explained in reply to her unasked question.

"Oh god, I'm so sorry." She looked at Arabella's hand. It was red from the pressure of her grasp.

"It's okay, you were just holding on a little tight. Are you okay?" Arabella questioned. She placed her hands around Rebecca's upper arm as they continued to walk.

"Do you find other women attractive?" Rebecca blurted out. "I mean, it's fine if you do. I was just wondering."

Arabella laughed that deep throaty laugh of hers. "You ask me that *after* you take me to a lesbian bar?"

"Yeah, I didn't think it through," Rebecca said with a chuckle. "Sorry, you don't have to answer that. It's a silly question."

"Are *you* attracted to other women?" Arabella asked.

Rebecca felt her pulse speed up. She'd really put her foot in it now. She couldn't deny it, she'd dated other women.

"Don't answer that," Arabella replied softly. "I just wanted to make the point. We're both attracted to other women. I may not have dated any, but I can appreciate a good-looking woman when I see one. But, I don't think of it as anything else than that. Appreciation. From afar."

"I'm sorry, I really shouldn't have asked that," Rebecca said. "I just suddenly felt jealous, and I've never felt that way before."

"You've never felt jealous before?" Arabella sounded surprised.

"No. When I've been in relationships, it's always been very secure. We started as friends, became more, and generally lasted a while. I've never been a one-night stand kind of person."

"I see," Arabella said. "Do you think you felt jealous because I'm new to being with a woman?"

Rebecca shrugged. "I don't know. I didn't really get time to think about it like that. The thought was just suddenly there."

Arabella stopped walking. Her grip on Rebecca's arm pulled her to a stop, too. The older woman stood in front of Rebecca.

"I can see another woman and think she is attractive, but I don't want to be in a relationship with her, or kiss her, or sleep with her. I want to be with you. You're like a best friend to me, as well as someone I'm desperately attracted to."

Rebecca's eyes drifted to Arabella's lips. She closed her eyes and shook her head. Now wasn't the time to stare at her beautiful girlfriend's features. Now was the time to talk about something that had been bothering her for a while.

"It's just," Rebecca started. She paused as she tried to think of an appropriate parallel. "You... you wouldn't go into a store and buy the first pair of shoes you tried on."

Arabella's mouth contorted as she tried to smother a grin.

"No," she allowed. "I wouldn't. But, I'm assuming that in this charming analogy, you are comparing yourself to a pair of shoes?"

Rebecca nodded.

"What if I'd passed that shop window every day for

weeks? Looking in the window at those shoes, analysing them, thinking about how they would fit? How they would feel? Balancing if they were the right shoes for me. Before, finally, one day going into the store and trying them on. Would that make sense?"

Rebecca felt a bubble of happiness well up in her chest. That did make sense. She'd been so caught up in being Arabella's first that she hadn't considered that Arabella had spent a lot time thinking about this. She wasn't the kind of person to jump into a new situation without thoroughly examining it first. Arabella had thought about being in a relationship, probably far more than Rebecca had.

It wasn't like her to worry about such things. Or things in general, really. She knew exactly why this whole situation with Arabella bothered her. While Arabella had spent the last few weeks and months figuring out if she wanted to date Rebecca, she'd spent the same amount of time falling in love with Arabella. Not that she'd admit that to Arabella just yet.

"That makes sense," she replied.

"Good. I know I'm new to this, but I assure you that I'm not going to run off with some other woman."

Rebecca took her hand again and continued to walk them towards the hotel.

"The jealous streak is cute, though," Arabella pointed out.

"No, it's not." Rebecca chuckled.

"It is," Arabella argued gently. "It's nice to know you want me."

"You have no idea," Rebecca mumbled.

"Hmm? What was that?"

"I have an idea," Rebecca changed the subject. "Let's head down to the river for an evening stroll."

Arabella regarded her suspiciously for a moment, obviously wondering if that was what Rebecca had said. Thankfully, she didn't push the matter. She simply nodded her head in agreement.

35

GYM BUDDIES

KATHRYN SWIPED her hotel room key card on the door to the gym. The light shone green, and she opened the door. She tossed her towel onto a table by the window and looked at the view for a couple of moments.

Annoyingly, New Orleans was a pretty place first thing in the morning. She really did think that she would hate everything about the Louisiana city, but as time went by she had to admit it had a certain charm.

Unfortunately, she'd learnt that from a person she had deeply hurt. Someone who had asked her to stay away. Kathryn didn't think that she'd ever had someone ask her to avoid them before.

It was a profoundly unsettling feeling.

More so even than her sudden confusion about herself. She kept trying to push down, but it kept bubbling back to the surface. She was pretty sure that alcohol wasn't the reason for her sudden emotional upset, but it was definitely the reason for her headache.

"Never. Drinking. Again." She selected a treadmill with a view of the river in the distance and selected a slow walking speed.

She had no idea if it was the fact she was on vacation, the alcohol, the grief swirling through her mind, or even the heat, but something was taking over her thought processes.

She had never looked at other women in a sexual way, but now she couldn't stop thinking about it. Sleep had evaded her most of the night as she wondered about her reaction to the show, and about her general behaviour since arriving in town.

At first, she had thought that it was the burlesque show itself. The whole art of burlesque was of course tantalising and somehow forbidden, so any reasonable person would find it stimulating.

Shaking her head to remove the thoughts, she cranked up the speed a little on the treadmill.

She closed her eyes and focused on her breathing and her steps. She had to get herself together. She felt like she was spinning out of control. Erica had been right, she needed a vacation. Sadly, the vacation was making her realise just how troubled she was.

The air pressure in the cooled room changed. She opened her eyes to see Arabella coming in. She wore a black tank top and shorts.

"Hi," Kathryn greeted her solemnly.

She couldn't remember too much about the previous evening, but she knew Arabella had been there for her embarrassing display.

"Hi," Arabella said. She placed her water bottle and

key card in the holders of the treadmill beside Kathryn. "Mind if I join you?"

"Feel free," Kathryn said.

Arabella adjusted the settings, and her treadmill whirred into action.

"How are you feeling?" Arabella asked politely.

"Justifiably terrible," Kathryn replied. "I'm so sorry for how I behaved last night."

"No need to apologise," Arabella said.

"You must think I'm some crazy alcoholic, stirring up trouble all over town."

"The thought had crossed my mind," Arabella confessed. "But I'm not here to judge."

"I don't usually drink a lot," Kathryn admitted. "In fact, I hadn't drunk for over three years, aside from the occasional glass of wine at a work function. I've gone a little crazy here, but I'm not touching another drop of alcohol."

"I see," Arabella said.

She thinks I'm an alcoholic, Kathryn realised. *Of course she would, you told her you didn't drink at all for three years. And now you're proclaiming to not touch another drop.*

"It was a personal choice," Kathryn added. "The not drinking."

"You don't have to explain yourself to me," Arabella said.

"I feel like I do."

Arabella sighed, finally turning her head to face Kathryn. "You don't, you really don't. I'm just... puzzled. Rebecca tells me about you and Jenn, and... I don't know your motives."

Kathryn chuckled bitterly. "Neither do I."

"Why were you in a lesbian bar last night?" Arabella asked.

"I didn't know it was a lesbian bar, and I had no idea that Jenn was performing *that* show there. I found out that was where she'd be, and I went to apologise to her. We had a little fight and she neglected to tell me that I was in a lesbian bar, on the night of her burlesque show, and making friends with a known womaniser."

Arabella laughed softly. "Sounds like she got her own back. What were you apologising for?"

"I… kissed her."

Arabella's brow knitted. "I thought *she* kissed *you?*"

"That was the night before," Kathryn explained.

Arabella slapped the stop button on her treadmill and turned to face her again. "So… you kissed her? The night we had dinner together?"

"Yes, it was a mistake. I was d—"

"Drunk," Arabella guessed.

Kathryn pressed the stop button on her own machine. "Yes. I just… I don't know what I'm doing."

"Well, why did you kiss her? I've had too much to drink on the rare occasion, but I don't randomly kiss people," Arabella said. She picked up her water bottle and took a long sip.

"I don't know," Kathryn said. "At the time, I just wanted to. But I've never been interested in women before. I'm straight."

"You don't sound very straight, if you're kissing women. And I saw the way you looked at Jenn during her routine last night." Arabella looked at her pointedly for a few moments.

Kathryn felt a familiar clenching at her chest. Panic.

"Do you like Jenn?" Arabella asked.

"I don't know," she whispered.

"You do," Arabella pressed. "You do, somewhere deep inside. You know."

She did know. Or, at least, she thought she did.

"I don't understand, though." She leaned heavily on the handrail. "I have never, ever been attracted to women. And then I met Jenn. With her ripped shorts and her messy hair. And now I don't know what I'm feeling. Anyway, it doesn't matter. I'm not going to find out, Jenn doesn't want to see me again."

As much as it hurt, she could understand. It wasn't fair to ask Jenn to join her in a journey into the unknown. Especially after Jenn had admitted feelings for her.

"She doesn't want to get hurt," Arabella said. "Something which you seem to be—unwittingly—doing to her. Frequently."

"I know, I know. I feel terrible. I want to apologise to her, and somehow make it up to her. But I tried that, and I made things so much worse."

"What did you say to her?"

Kathryn winced. "I told her I'm confused."

Arabella laughed. "Oh, I bet she loved that."

"She told me she had feelings for me and she didn't want to be my *experimental toy*." Kathryn stepped off the treadmill and over to the water fountain. She plucked a paper cone from the stack and filled it with water.

Arabella regarded her silently for a few moments. She

stepped off her treadmill, walked over to the chairs by the water cooler, and sat down.

"When I met Rebecca, at the end of last year, I thought I was straight. I was engaged to be married—to a man," she explained. "I'd never looked at a woman in any way other than platonically. Ever."

Kathryn downed the water and poured herself another drink.

"Then, we shared a journey home—which we told you about over dinner. We argued, made assumptions about each other… it wasn't exactly love at first sight. It was more frustration at first, second, and third sight."

"Sounds familiar." Kathryn thought back to her first meeting with Jenn at the bar, then the second at the parade.

"But during the journey we talked. Really talked. I got to see another side to Rebecca, not just the person I assumed she was at the start of the trip, but the real Rebecca, or, at least, part of her. And she opened my eyes. She talked about love and relationships in a way that had me thinking she was a naïve child. I thought she lived in some kind of dream world.

"But her words stuck with me. I started to look at my own life, and I realised I wasn't happy. I didn't want to marry Alastair, and I didn't want to do all the things that had been planned for me since I was a child. I wanted to experience things, see sights, meet people who taught me things."

Arabella laughed as she became lost in the memory. She looked up at Kathryn with a sparkle in her eyes.

"Rebecca told me the purpose of life is to grow as a

person." She rolled her eyes. "I thought she was nuts. She said she wanted to be more today than she was yesterday. And it hit me that I hadn't changed for years. And, in fact, what I was was entirely the product of who I *thought* I should be."

Kathryn could recognise that. She herself was the result of stereotypes and family requirements. Only recently had she been forced to take drastic action to keep the status quo. But it wasn't something she was ready to talk about yet. Not with Arabella.

"The last few months have been terrifying," Arabella admitted as she continued. "One moment I felt for sure that I was ready to leap into a new life with Rebecca. The very next I was clinging to my old life as hard as I could. And in between those two extremes, I buried my head in the ground and ignored everything. Hoping that things would somehow resolve themselves."

"What changed?" Despite her bleariness, Kathryn had noticed that Arabella and Rebecca were together at Façade the night before. They'd shared meaningful looks, and, at one point, Arabella had kissed Rebecca. Something had obviously changed since the previous evening. Maybe something had happened when they left early.

"Coming here," Arabella stated, "I made myself stop and think. I couldn't mess Rebecca around anymore. I had to make a decision, even if it wasn't a permanent one. I was stuck in limbo and I didn't want that anymore. I didn't want to do that to Rebecca anymore."

Kathryn smiled. "You two make a great couple. She speaks very highly of you."

Arabella's cheeks reddened. "She's amazing. And I

finally realised that I'm lucky to have her in my life and it was time to tell her how I felt. Or else I'd potentially lose her."

"I wish I could be sure," Kathryn said. "I just… I honestly don't know how I feel. I feel so confused." She raked her hands through her hair. "I know that's not a great answer, but it's an honest one. I find all of this so confusing. And I feel so damn old, like there's a new term to explain someone's sexual preference every week and I have no idea what they mean."

Arabella smiled. "It is hard," she agreed.

"Apparently, Jenn is pansexual. Which I didn't even know existed before this week. I keep telling her I'm straight, but how can I be straight? I can't stop thinking about her, and it kills me to know that I've completely blown it with her."

Kathryn's eyes widened as she realised what she said. She gulped down another cup full of water.

"Sounds to me like you have your answer," Arabella said. "You can't stop thinking about her. Is that usually the case with women you've just met?"

"No."

Arabella looked at her watch. She stood up and walked back over to the treadmill. "Maybe you're meant to be with Jenn, maybe you're not," she said as she pushed some buttons on the panel. "But whatever is going on, you need to figure it out for you. You owe it to yourself to know what it is that you're feeling. You can't live your entire life as a lie. Trust me, it doesn't work. Now, I really need to get on with this workout because my *girlfriend* is waiting for me."

Arabella started to jog as the machine sped up. She turned her attention away from Kathryn and focused on her movements.

She's right, Kathryn thought. *I can't bury my head in the sand about this. I need to figure this out.*

36

SEEING THE SIGHTS

"So, we're on this open-top bus and we're freezing," Jenn explained.

Rebecca laughed as she poured some cola from the bottle into her glass. "It was *so* cold," she reiterated to Arabella. "Like, I've never been so cold in my life."

Arabella put a fond hand on Rebecca's and squeezed. Jenn smiled at the action. It was heartwarming to see the new couple interacting.

Her heart clenched. She missed being in a relationship. There had been some offers, but Jenn was getting fed up with playing the scene. She wanted security, a future. She smiled as she watched Arabella's thumb gently rubbing circles on the back of Rebecca's hand. She wanted what they had.

"December in New York," she said. "And your girl-friend had no idea it would be so cold."

"Hey! I checked the forecast before I travelled, and it didn't seem that cold," Rebecca replied.

"It's a different kind of cold in New York," Arabella said as if it were obvious.

"I know that *now*," Rebecca grumped.

"Anyway, the bus is about twenty minutes out from Midtown—where both our hotels are located—and Rebecca looks at me and dead serious says, 'I don't think I'm gonna make it'," Jenn said. "So, we decide to get off at the next stop and find somewhere to warm up. Because being on that open-top bus with the wind blowing? Not fun. Luckily the next stop was by some stores, so we went into this clothing store and bought jackets that you could go *skiing* in and then we went to a coffee shop to defrost."

"And you've been friends ever since?" Arabella asked in admiration.

"Yep, we toured around New York together after that," Rebecca replied. "Had dinner together a few times, and then stayed in touch."

Arabella sipped her orange juice as her eyes darted between them. Jenn knew what was coming, the question she'd ask if their positions were reversed.

"So... did you two... ever?" Arabella asked.

"No," Jenn and Rebecca replied at the same time.

Jenn laughed. "No, we've never been anything more than good friends. We kept talking about travelling together, but I was busy and then Rebecca's mom got sick."

"And she has a billion jobs," Rebecca said. "Like she would ever be able to coordinate all those jobs to get some time off! Which is why I had to fly out here to this... what did she call it?"

Jenn smirked. "A sordid hellhole."

Rebecca burst out laughing.

Arabella frowned, looking between the two of them in confusion. "Have I missed something?"

"When Kathryn first came to town, she was dropped off by her sister in the middle of Bourbon Street. And she loudly stated that she didn't want to be left in this sordid hellhole," Rebecca explained.

Arabella's eyes widened. "That doesn't seem very wise."

"It wasn't," Jenn agreed. "She's lucky it was early in the morning and no one was around. But, I do have to give her some credit and say that she was in an extremely bad mood at the time. Every time I saw her after that, she was much nicer."

Rebecca played with the label on her cola bottle. "I don't know how you can defend her after what she did."

Jenn shrugged. "I liked her."

You like her, her traitorous brain amended.

"I saw her this morning in the gym," Arabella said softly.

Rebecca looked at her in a way that made Jenn think this was the first she was hearing about the meeting, too.

"How was she?" Jenn asked.

"Embarrassed. Confused." Arabella chuckled. "Hungover."

"I told her to stay away from me," Jenn confessed.

"She mentioned," Arabella said. "I think that's wise, she doesn't seem to know what she wants. I…" Her face contorted as she appeared to try to verbalise her thoughts.

"You?" Jenn asked, eager to know.

"I get the impression that there's something else going

on with her," Arabella said. "I don't know, she seems like she has a lot on her mind."

"No excuse to act the way she has," Rebecca reminded them both.

Jenn knew that Rebecca was just being protective of her, and she appreciated it. But the truth was, Jenn felt regret at telling Kathryn to stay away. Part of her wondered if maybe Kathryn was close to making a breakthrough in her apparent 'confusion'.

It didn't matter now. She'd made her decision and told Kathryn how she felt. Even if she did see Kathryn again during her stay in New Orleans, it would be nothing more than a passing hello. She needed to focus on other things, like ensuring that Rebecca and Arabella had a fantastic time in the city.

Arabella's phone rang, and she rolled her eyes. "Excuse me, I've been expecting this call."

She got up and walked over to an empty part of the coffee shop. Rebecca watched her, concern in her eyes.

"Problem?" Jenn asked.

"Work keep calling her," Rebecca said. "At first it was emails, then last night they called her twice. I know she's the boss, but it's like they can't cope without her. She's on holiday."

"I don't suppose you can tell her not to answer?" Jenn asked.

Rebecca shook her head. "No, her work ethic is off the scale. I would have thrown my phone in the Mississippi by now."

"I don't think she'll get a signal out in the bayou.

Maybe we should suggest heading out there this afternoon, taking a boat trip," Jenn suggested.

Rebecca's eyes shone. "Could we do that?"

"Sure. I know a couple of great companies, as long as you're both okay with gators and snakes?" Jenn had taken a friend from Boston on the tour once, completely forgetting that he was terrified of snakes. He'd screamed so loud she still heard ringing in her left ear, two years later.

"We'll ask her when she gets back," Rebecca said. Her expression became distant, and Jenn knew she was already planning what camera equipment to bring with her to the swamp.

37

GUIDING HAND

A SUGGESTION from the concierge had led Kathryn to a small bistro in Frenchmen Street. The eatery was tiny and only held about a dozen tables. The windows looked out onto the bustling street, the window separating the busy street from the relaxing restaurant.

Just what I needed, she thought. *Some peace and quiet. And good food.*

The waiter approached and handed her a menu.

"Thank you."

She opened the hard-backed menu and looked over what local cuisine they had to offer. She'd only been reading for a few moments when she heard a knocking on the glass window. She lowered her menu and looked up.

Shit.

Echo was smiling at her from outside. She smiled back, hoping it seemed sincere and not terrified. A moment later, Echo entered the restaurant.

Kathryn's heart pounded hard against her rib cage. Echo sat at the table, directly opposite Kathryn.

"I was hoping I'd bump into you again," she said. She looked Kathryn up and down appreciatively.

"Here I am." Kathryn smiled, at a loss for much else to say.

"Are you meeting someone?" Echo asked.

Kathryn knew she couldn't lie. The waiter had already been informed that she was dining alone and had swept away the cutlery and glassware from the other side of the table.

"No, just me," she squeaked.

"Well, I can't have a pretty woman like you eating alone." Echo winked dramatically. She laughed loudly and then waved the waiter over.

Kathryn shifted nervously in her seat. There wasn't much that could be done about the situation, and before long they had both ordered meals and were on some kind of date. Possibly a second date, to Echo's mind.

She'd apologised for getting drunk and vanishing the night before. Echo waved away the concerns as if it were something she was used to. She kept the conversation ticking over, telling Kathryn all about her crazy exploits with various women. She certainly wasn't shy.

But Kathryn felt shy. For the first time in many, many years. She twisted her hands in her lap and wondered if she could escape somehow. She didn't want to be dining with Echo, she didn't want to be dining with *anyone*. She wanted to be left alone to her humiliation. She'd made a mess of the whole trip, and she'd only been there a few days.

She wondered why Erica couldn't have picked a business conference in the Florida Keys to dump her at. At least then she'd have been able to stay out of trouble. Why did it have to be New Orleans? The home of Jenn Cook and of Kathryn's mounting regrets.

It was over the main course that Echo suddenly dropped the bomb on Kathryn.

"So, you're still figuring it all out, aren't ya?"

Kathryn nearly choked on her chicken. She looked up at Echo with confused panic. "Sorry?"

"The gay thing," Echo said. She noisily slurped her beer. "You're not sure, I could see it in your eyes at Façade. You're curious, but you just don't *know* yet."

Kathryn swallowed hard. "Something like that."

Echo nodded knowingly. "You like the dancer, don't ya? Jenn?"

Kathryn could feel the blush rising up her cheeks. She knew lying would be impossible. "I don't know. I think so."

"Ah." Echo chuckled. "You really are having trouble figuring it all out." She interlaced her fingers and rested her chin on them. "So, how far along are we? Any lesbian activity? Touching? Kissing? I mean, I can tell there hasn't been any sex yet."

Kathryn's cheeks felt like they were on fire. She opened and closed her mouth a few times, but nothing came out.

"Oh, wow." Echo smiled sadly and shook her head. "I see, we're in the *very* early stages."

"I'm really not comfortable discussing this," Kathryn tried.

Echo ignored her. "So, let me guess. You're straight,

completely straight, never been with a woman, never even looked at a woman. But now, suddenly—" she placed her open palms on her cheeks and looked shocked, "—you wonder if you like girls. Am I right?"

"N—no," Kathryn stuttered. She lowered her cutlery and took a few gulps of water. She couldn't understand how Echo was so spot on. Was she a walking cliché? Did this happen all the time?

"Come on." Echo drank some more of her beer. "I saw the way you looked at Jenn on that stage. That wasn't just someone appreciating the artistic tones of a good burlesque show. That was someone who wanted more."

Kathryn placed her water glass down on the table. She looked around the bistro to see if anyone was watching them. Luckily, it was a quiet day, and no one seemed interested. She looked back to Echo who was staring at her in wonderment.

"You don't *know*, do you?" Echo asked.

"Know what?" Kathryn questioned. She picked up the wine menu and fanned her face.

"If you're sexually interested in women," Echo answered. "You think you are, but you're not quite sure."

"I—I—" Kathryn stuttered.

Echo turned around to face the waiter and shouted for the bill. She turned back to face Kathryn. Picking up her fork, she reached across the table and stabbed at Kathryn's leftover chicken. "You're not going to eat this, are you?"

It was already removed from her plate before she had a chance to reply.

"Why did you ask for the check?" Kathryn was confused.

"Because you and I are going to hit some of New Orleans finest establishments, and we're going to solve your conundrum for you," Echo explained.

Kathryn had many questions. "Why?" was the only one she managed to verbalise.

Echo shrugged as she threw down some bills on a silver dish that the waiter had laid on the table. "I need a new toaster oven. Come on, let's get out of here."

Kathryn didn't know why she was agreeing to this madness, but she did and soon found herself hurrying after Echo as they walked along Frenchmen Street.

"I don't understand," she said.

"I know." Echo nodded. "That's why we're doing this."

"Doing what?" Kathryn pressed.

Echo turned and looked at her, a wide grin on her face. "Think of it as a scientific experiment. You're not sure if you like women or not. You probably have questions, and the best place to deal with all of this is Heels."

"Heels?" Kathryn looked at Echo with a raised eyebrow.

Echo put her arm around Kathryn's shoulder. "It sounds worse than it is, but you and me are going to work out your sexuality. In order to do that, we need some booze and some dancers. Trust me."

"I'm not drinking anymore," Kathryn protested.

"Fine, then *I* need some booze. Do ya trust me?"

Kathryn didn't know why, but she did trust Echo. There was something about her that Kathryn liked. Probably her no-nonsense attitude. She didn't feel like she needed to pretend with Echo, the woman accepted Kathryn no matter what she said or did.

And the truth was, she needed help and guidance. And if Echo was the only person offering, then she'd accept. She was seeking answers to questions she didn't really understand. Maybe Echo was the answer to finding them.

She gave a vague nod.

Echo turned abruptly and started to enter a seedy-looking club. Kathryn grabbed her hand and pulled her back towards the street.

"Jenn doesn't work here, does she?" Kathryn asked. She tilted her head towards the flashing neon sign.

Echo laughed loudly. "No! Of course not, this is a dive. Your girl is too classy for here."

"She's not *my girl*." Kathryn blushed furiously. She looked around to ensure that no one had overheard Echo's words.

Echo held up her hands. "Okay, okay. Not your girl. Got it."

They entered the club. Kathryn winced at the décor. Echo hadn't been kidding when she said it was a dive. Her eyes scanned the bar.

"There are men in here," she said accusingly.

Echo nodded. "Yes, unfortunately there are. But as a gay woman you have to learn that you are in a minority."

"I told you—"

"Come on." Echo cut her off by dragging her towards a booth in the corner.

Kathryn looked at the leather bench for a couple of seconds. It looked grimy, and the cracked material showed foam that had seen better days. Ordinarily, she'd never sit on a bench like that. But she was already in a dive bar, so she decided to throw caution to the wind and embrace the entire experience. She sat down opposite Echo.

"So, what's the plan?" Kathryn asked. She examined the table, which wasn't as clean as she'd like.

"Drinks," Echo announced. She waved in the direction of a waitress.

Kathryn looked seriously at Echo. "I don't want to get drunk. Seriously."

Echo nodded. "No, you don't want to get drunk. But a little liquid courage to remove that hetero-filter is going to be essential."

It made sense. And something to dull the smell was probably going to be helpful.

A waitress in a tight and skimpy outfit approached the booth. "Hey, y'all," she said. "What can I get ya?"

"Well, hey yourself." Echo smiled, clearly appreciating the bare midriff on display.

"White wine," Kathryn said quickly. The sooner they ordered, the sooner the poor girl could leave and not have to deal with Echo's leering.

Echo ordered a beer. The waitress promised to be right back. As she left, Echo leaned out of the booth and watched her walking away.

Kathryn rolled her eyes. "Is that necessary?"

"What?" Echo shrugged. "I'm not getting any tonight, the least I can do is look."

Kathryn felt relieved that Echo didn't have plans to get her drunk and attempt to seduce her. She knew she'd have to be paralytic with drink before agreeing to anything sexual with Echo. She was nice enough, but she certainly wasn't Kathryn's type.

Kathryn frowned. The thought indicated that she did have a type.

"What's with the frown?" Echo asked.

"Nothing," she quickly covered.

Echo chuckled. "Look, if you want to get anything out of tonight, then you're going to have to start opening up."

Kathryn thought for a moment. It was true. Whatever this bizarre experiment was, it would require opening up. She nodded towards the waitress. "You find her attractive?"

Echo grinned mischievously. "Yeah, but I take it you don't?"

Kathryn shook her head. "She seems like a nice girl, but no, I don't see her... that way. Should I?" She looked over at the waitress and squinted. Was this part of the test? What did a lack of attraction mean?

"Aw, the confused mind of a babydyke springing to life. Look, darling, do you find *all* men attractive?"

Kathryn looked at Echo and shook her head. "Of course not."

"So, if a muscular man was walking down Bourbon showing off everything he had to offer, would you automatically be thinking you'd want you a slice of that?"

Kathryn blushed. "No."

"Exactly." Echo's eyes lit up as the drinks arrived. She thanked the waitress.

After a long slurp of beer, she sighed and rested her hands on the table as if she were a news reader about to deliver an important breaking news alert.

"There is much discussion about lesbian types and categorisations," she began. "Some say there are just five main types of lesbian: butch, lipstick, alpha, athletic, and boy babe."

Kathryn blinked and decided to keep silent on the fact she thought there were only two types.

"But," Echo said with a considered pause, "I don't subscribe to that theory. Yeah, you can find all of those types of lesbian, but I think there are more categories out there. You'll hear terms like dyke, power dyke, diesel dyke, butch, stone butch, gold star, lone star, chapstick, femme, pillow queen, blue jeans, stud, stem, futch, boi. It's endless. Thing is, I personally think that those categorisations are off-putting to newly uncloseted members of our group. They wonder what they are, if they need to get some kind of badge, if they can overlap two. Can they be a power dyke during the week and a pillow queen on the weekend?"

Kathryn took a large swig of her wine. Echo had been right, she would need a drink.

"The straights don't categorise themselves like we do. Even the gays have less terms than us. Personally, I think of sexuality as a scale." Echo drew a line along the table with her finger. "Straight, bi or pan, gay. You can be anywhere along that line. Does that make sense?"

Kathryn looked at the imaginary line and nodded her head a little.

"People are obsessed with labels. I know that we fought for the right to use those labels, but I think it's gone far enough," Echo continued. "We're all individuals. Yeah, we may fit into stereotypical groups. I'd be considered butch, but does that define me? Does that mean I can't enjoy a little lip gloss now and then? No."

Kathryn nodded again.

"So, you need to push all of that to one side. Don't worry too much about what you are, don't spend forever looking for the label that fits the best. Think about you and how you feel. What I'm trying to say is, humans don't fit into neat little boxes and neither should your sexuality. You can slap a name on it later if you really want to, but first you need to figure out what it is for yourself."

Kathryn considered the words. They made sense. She'd spent a lot of times wondering if she was gay or straight. But they were words assigned to people. Did they encapsulate her feelings? Not really.

She sipped some more wine and pulled a face. It tasted like acid. Not surprising. She wasn't at an upmarket wine bar in New York enjoying the latest import from New Zealand.

"So." Echo paused, grinning. Kathryn knew it was going to be a personal question. She took a deep breath and held it in preparation.

"When did you first look at a woman as something other than a potential manicure buddy?" Echo asked.

Kathryn knew she was blushing as she considered the question.

Echo patiently waited for her to reply, drinking her beer.

"When Jenn kissed me," Kathryn admitted quietly.

"Damn, girl." Echo leaned back and placed her arms along the back of the booth seat.

"I pushed her away," Kathryn continued. "I… I had no idea she was gay. Or that she thought I was flirting with her."

Echo's eyebrow raised. "I see. And then?"

Kathryn let out a deep breath. "Then I couldn't stop thinking about it."

Echo remained silent, waiting for her to continue.

"I kissed her," she whispered eventually.

Echo's eyes flew wide open. She stared at Kathryn silently.

"I was drunk," Kathryn explained further.

"Of course you were." Echo laughed. "Because you're straight, right?"

Kathryn sipped some more foul wine.

"Like so many straight women: spaghetti."

"Spaghetti?" Kathryn asked.

"Straight until wet," Echo supplied.

Kathryn wished she hadn't asked. She tried to put the conversation back on course. "She said I was drunk and pushed me away."

"And then?"

"And then I couldn't stop thinking about it. About her."

Echo leaned forward. "Thinking about the kiss or thinking about more than the kiss?"

"More."

"More like kissing and cuddling or more like... more?"

Kathryn wondered if it was possible for her cheeks to melt from her face entirely. "More."

"More like—"

"Do we have to do this?" she interrupted.

"I'm afraid we do," Echo said with a mock serious tone which was belied by the spark of humour in her eyes.

"What I'm trying to find out is, do you want a roll in the hay, or do you want to be baking cookies for your brood of children?"

Kathryn nearly choked on her wine. Echo laughed at her reaction.

She opened her mouth to reply, but Echo held up her hand. She was looking towards the front of the stage where people were moving to seats.

"Hold that thought, the show is about to start."

"What show?" Kathryn questioned.

"Well, it ain't burlesque."

Before Kathryn had a chance to say anything else, music with a forceful bass line started pumping through speakers and bright lights lit up the stage. The stage which Kathryn belatedly noticed was adorned with silver poles.

Her heart sunk as she realised she was in a strip club. She wondered how she managed to get herself into these situations. This kind of thing never happened to her back home in New York.

Young, lithe women appeared onstage in the skimpiest of outfits. Kathryn turned away to examine the sticky cocktail menu on the table. It wasn't right, she couldn't watch.

After a few minutes, Echo tapped her hand. "You like her?"

Kathryn dragged her eyes from the menu. Her cheeks were so hot she wondered if she was creating the red glow of the stage lights.

"Which one?"

"The one in red."

Kathryn shook her head. She looked away from the stage again. "I'm sure she's a nice girl, but—"

"Yeah, yeah." Echo waved her hand. "What about the natural blonde? Are blondes your thing?"

Kathryn sighed and turned back towards the stage. She wondered how long strip shows lasted, how long she would have to endure the torture.

She sought out the blonde. She didn't know what she was looking for, what she was supposed to look *at*. She could appreciate that the woman was toned and exceptionally fit, but nothing else. In the right light, she looked a little like Jenn. But she wasn't Jenn.

She wasn't interested in any of the women. Nor would she ever be. It was a waste of time being there, an uncomfortable waste of time.

"Kathryn? Hello?" Echo tried again.

"I don't think I want to be here anymore," she said simply.

Echo regarded her for a moment and then nodded. "Then let's get out of here."

Kathryn threw down some money on the table. She rolled her eyes when it promptly stuck to the surface.

They quickly exited the club and started to walk along the street to get away from the crowds. Once they were in a slightly quieter area, Echo pulled Kathryn to the side.

"Wanna tell me what revelation you just had?"

"I'm not gay," Kathryn said with certainty. "I was just in a strip club, and I felt nothing. Well, I felt extremely uncomfortable. But I didn't feel anything else."

"Okay," Echo drawled. "Not even for the blonde?"

"Nothing. When I saw her, all I could think was that she's not Jenn."

Echo let out a long laugh.

Kathryn frowned. "What's so funny?"

"You know Jenn is a woman, right?" Echo said. "You know that having strong feelings for one woman rather than all woman can still make you gay, right?"

Kathryn clenched her jaw. "I never said—"

"Look, Kathryn," Echo interrupted. "I meet a lot of baby dykes who come to the city to explore their sexuality. A lot of them choose a type they wanna tap and that's it. They don't care about anything other than getting their kicks. They drink, dance, and screw. Simple as that."

Kathryn looked around the street, hoping no one passing by had heard Echo's crass commentary.

"But you, you're different," she continued. "Which makes me think that Jenn is a lucky girl."

"What do you mean?"

Echo sighed, as if explaining something so obvious was paining her. "You're not in town to scratch an itch, you came to town and you fell in love."

A laugh bubbled up and exploded from Kathryn's lips. "I am *not* in love."

Echo folded her arms and stared at Kathryn. "Really? Do me a favour, okay? Pretend that Jenn is a man. Now, replay all of your interactions with her and your internal monologues and whatever as if she was a man. See if that clears things up for you."

Kathryn rolled her eyes. It was the most ridiculous thing she'd ever heard. She was not in love. She'd felt confused, but she'd gone to a strip club and she'd felt nothing. In fact, she felt dirty and like she wanted to leave as quick as possible.

So, what if Jenn were a man? What difference did that really make?

She swallowed hard.

It made all the difference.

"You're gay," Echo announced. "But you're gay for one woman. It happens. Maybe it's a crush, but you don't seem like the kind of woman who has crushes."

"I—I…" Kathryn stuttered.

The world was spinning. She hated to admit it, but Echo's argument made sense. If Jenn were a man, she wouldn't be so confused about her feelings. The confusion was rooted in the fact that she was debating whether or not she was gay. Wondering if she knew her own mind at all, having never previously felt anything like this for women.

But if she ignored gender, it was very clear that she had strong feelings for Jenn. Very strong feelings. Could they be lo—

"Echo, I hope you're keeping outta trouble?"

They both turned. An older, larger lady was smiling at them. She looked Kathryn up and down. "Well, well, if it isn't Fine Shoes."

"Hey, Miss Mae." Echo smiled. "Just hanging out with my new buddy here."

Kathryn regarded Miss Mae. She seemed familiar. The penny dropped, and she remembered where she had seen her. "You work at the tourist office."

"I surely do," Miss Mae replied. "You didn't like my bus."

"No. I didn't like much that day."

"I thought as much," she said with a knowing smile.

"I'm sorry," Kathryn apologised. She knew she'd been a pain in the ass when she'd first arrived, and she deeply regretted it.

Miss Mae gave Kathryn with a long look. "I'll think about accepting your apology *if* you watch my show tonight."

Kathryn's eyes widened. She wondered what kind of show she was talking about. She'd certainly had her fill of some shows.

"Miss Mae is the best jazz singer in town," Echo explained.

"Oh, well, yes, I guess I could drop by." She was confused as to why she was receiving a personal invitation from the woman.

"Go back to your sinful ladies, Echo," Miss Mae said with soft humour. "I'll look after Miss Fine Shoes here."

Kathryn looked down at her heels and frowned. Her shoes weren't that impressive, but it seemed she'd gotten a reputation and a nickname from them.

Miss Mae took her arm and started to walk down the street with Kathryn in tow. Kathryn turned around and looked over her shoulder. Echo saluted her in farewell.

"Child, you have to be careful who you trust in this city," Miss Mae was saying.

Kathryn noted that the bustling crowds in the street parted for them. Many people greeted her companion as they passed by.

"Can I trust you?" Kathryn said.

"More than you can trust Echo." Miss Mae chuckled. "Girl is trouble. A good heart, but still trouble."

Kathryn wasn't about to argue that fact. She imagined Echo could be a lot of trouble if she put her mind to it.

"Where are we going?" she asked instead.

"The Snug, best jazz venue in town."

"Oh." Kathryn was mesmerised by how friendly people were being to them. It was clear to her that Miss Mae was something of a local celebrity.

"You're going to have a front row seat, I'll see to that," she said.

"Th—thank you." Kathryn couldn't think what she had done to deserve the special treatment she was receiving from the woman.

"I sing for twenty-five minutes, no longer," Miss Mae said. She pulled Kathryn close as though to give her some advice. "Always leave 'em wanting more."

Kathryn chuckled.

"And then you and I are going to talk about my girl, Jenn."

A shiver ran up Kathryn's spine. She felt like a misbehaving schoolgirl who was about to get lectured in the mother of all detentions.

"And don't think about leaving early," Miss Mae said with a shake of her finger. "I know where you staying, Fine Shoes."

Kathryn swallowed and nodded her understanding. She wished, not for the first time that evening, that she had stayed in the hotel.

Miss Mae led her into a small club and guided her to a

seat in the front row. She pointed to her eyes and then to Kathryn. "We'll talk soon," she promised.

Kathryn nodded. Miss Mae walked away, speaking to the bartender before she disappeared behind the scenes.

When will I learn to just stay in the hotel? she chided herself. They have room service. I should just stay there the rest of the trip.

38

EMPLOYMENT

Arabella sat on the sofa and looked around the small apartment. Her professional eye quickly cast over the architectural details of the home, assessing resale potential. Jenn had a good eye for design. The room was sparsely decorated but still homely. She lived on the edge of the French Quarter—convenient for work, Arabella assumed.

Rebecca was in the kitchen with Jenn, helping her make a proper British cup of tea. Rebecca often thought that people needed help in that regard. She'd even taken to watching over Arabella as she made hot drinks, offering nuggets of unwanted advice.

Arabella pulled off her shoes, dropping them beside the sofa. She massaged the heel of one foot. She wasn't used to all the walking they had been doing, but it was worth every second and every potential blister.

New Orleans was beautiful. Vibrant and, at times, chaotic. The thing she enjoyed the most was the constant soundtrack. You never knew when a band would set up in the middle of the road and start playing. And if there was no band, then music was pumped through speakers to keep up the illusion.

She'd added a number of songs to her Spotify list to remind her of the trip when she returned home. Her face fell at that thought. Home. The duration of their stay had seemed perfectly reasonable when they booked flights. Now it seemed painfully short.

How could they possibly see everything, and how would she manage returning to work after realising how much stress it caused her?

Mindlessly, she checked her phone. She'd taken a couple more calls that afternoon, despite being on a boat in a swamp. Three important deals were all tied to each other via a funding scheme, who was refusing to pay out any money until a valuation was complete. Unfortunately, it was hard to value a barren piece of land and a gleam in an architect's eye.

On the smaller end of the scale, two residential sales looked like they were about to fall through. Property deals falling through weren't anything new, they happened all the time in England. But it did mean months of work for nothing and a return to the drawing board, without having been paid.

"I can hear you thinking about work," Rebecca said as she came into the room. She placed a mug of tea on the coffee table in front of her.

"It's hard to turn off," Arabella admitted.

Rebecca looked down at her thoughtfully.

Arabella frowned at the expression. It didn't seem to be a telling-off look. "What?"

Rebecca's shoulders rose slightly. "Nothing, just… doesn't seem like you enjoy your work much sometimes."

Arabella laughed. "Does anyone?"

"I do," Rebecca said.

"I do, too," Jenn said from the kitchen.

"We do." Rebecca offered her a wide smile.

"So I hear."

Rebecca perched on the edge of the table and looked at Arabella seriously. "Do you like your job?"

Arabella sucked in a breath. That was a hard question to answer. Her name was on the incorporation documents. Her family had established the company, and it was a runaway success in its first year. It was now one of the most respected estate agencies in London. She ran a busy office and sat on the board.

It had been her life from the moment she started work. She adored *aspects* of her job, but did she like it as a whole? She didn't know. It was another thing she had never stopped to think about.

The question was ridiculous. As if she would ever walk up to her father and tell him she quit.

She quickly shook her head. "That's not relevant. It's a good, safe job. And my father needs me. I make very good money."

"You're making yourself sick with stress," Rebecca said.

Arabella narrowed her eyes.

Rebecca held up her hands. "Okay, okay, I'll drop it. Just thought I'd mention it."

She returned to the kitchen, presumably to continue helping Jenn. Arabella glanced down at her phone to where she had opened her emails. There were five new messages since the last time she checked, all marked high priority. All about an impending work disaster.

She closed the application and opened her personal email account. As she suspected, no new emails. The last thing she had received was a selfie from Rebecca sent the day before they travelled. Rebecca refused to email Arabella at work, saying she didn't want to rub shoulders with stuffy suit-clad men in Arabella's inbox.

She smiled at the image. Rebecca had angled the phone's camera so her suitcase could be seen on her bed. It was entirely empty except for a bikini. Rebecca issued a thumbs-up and the subject line was 'job done'.

Arabella closed the application down and tossed her phone into her bag.

39

THE SNUG

JAZZ MUSIC PLAYED through The Snug's speakers on a quiet loop. The bartender came over and took Kathryn's drink order. She opted for water and fruit juice in order to remain sober for whatever Miss Mae had to say to her.

In what she was coming to understand was traditional New Orleans style, people started to arrive moments before the show was due to start. They quickly grabbed drinks, and within a few short minutes, the bar was filled to capacity.

Some musicians started to set up on the stage. Kathryn watched with interest how quickly they managed to set up and tune their kit.

A spotlight shone in the middle of the stage, and silence fell over the room. It was the first time in her life that Kathryn had heard a bar completely fall silent. She could hear the ice cubes in her drink chinking together.

A large, worn armchair was brought up onto the stage.

She could feel the anticipation building. The room buzzed with excitement.

Miss Mae stepped onto the stage and the crowd went wild. Kathryn clapped politely, looking around in surprise at the whoops and hollers coming from all around her.

Miss Mae smiled gratefully at the audience. She raised her microphone to her mouth and turned to wink at the musicians. It was an indication for the music to begin, and a moment later Miss Mae started to sing.

Chills ran up Kathryn's arms. She instantly understood the reverence with which people had looked at the older woman on the street. Miss Mae's voice was incredible. She was easily the best singer that Kathryn had ever heard.

The short set flew by. The majority of the audience knew not to applaud in between songs. Those who tried received a quick glare from Miss Mae and were soon silenced.

When the set was over, Miss Mae whispered a soft "thank you" into her microphone and the audience went wild. Kathryn joined then, standing up and clapping loudly. Miss Mae smiled and waved to the audience before walking off stage.

A few moments later, one of the bar staff approached Kathryn and asked her to come backstage.

She nervously entered the small dressing room where Miss Mae sat in an armchair that looked as worn and well-loved as the one on stage. In front of her was a glass of whisky and a glass of water. She gestured for Kathryn to sit on the small sofa beside the dressing table.

Kathryn sat down. "You're extremely talented. You have an amazing voice."

Miss Mae inclined her head. "Thank you, Fine Shoes."

Kathryn glanced down at her heels.

"My Jenn has been moping around," Miss Mae said.

Kathryn looked up but remained silent. She wasn't sure what to say.

"She won't speak to me." The singer shook her head. "She stubborn."

"Yes, she is," Kathryn agreed.

"And she don't want to get her heart all broken up either."

"I… I know."

"So whatcha gonna do about it?"

"Me?"

"You." Miss Mae picked up her whisky and took a small sip.

Kathryn was baffled. She couldn't fathom what Miss Mae wanted from her. Jenn wanted her to stay away, and that was what she intended to do.

"You want some free advice, Fine Shoes?"

Everyone seemed eager to give her advice, but Kathryn nodded.

"You know they call this here fine city the Big Easy, right?"

Kathryn nodded again.

"That was thought up by some fancy marketing types in the sixties. It's supposed to signify our laidback attitude to life. But New Awlins ain't easy, it's anything but easy. Just like the rest of this country, life is hard. We have to deal with unemployment, natural disasters, and tourists."

Kathryn snorted.

"You may laugh, Fine Shoes," Miss Mae took another

sip of her whisky, "but you tourists, man, you cause trouble. Don't get me wrong, we like your money."

Kathryn smiled.

Miss Mae lowered the glass and leaned back in her chair. "You from New York?"

"I am."

"The Big Apple." Miss Mae nodded. "With all your running around, business deals, and coffee to go."

"And our fine shoes." Kathryn indicated her heels.

Miss Mae laughed loudly. "And your fine shoes!" She looked at Kathryn for a few moments. "I can see why Jenn likes you."

Kathryn wondered if Miss Mae wasn't quite up to date on the latest events in her twisting relationship with Jenn.

"We agreed to avoid each other," she explained.

"I gathered. She said you were confused, still figuring things out."

Kathryn broke eye contact. She wasn't comfortable discussing her sexual preference with someone she'd just met.

"Thing is," Miss Mae continued. "Life is short. We may be laidback down here, but we don't go wasting no time. We live our life to the full. We find our happiness wherever we can and we embrace it. Not like you big city folks. Going to doctors every time you have a feeling."

Kathryn chuckled bitterly. She'd practically paid for her therapist's new car following the recent turmoil in her life. She was sure that therapy worked perfectly well for some people, but it didn't for her. Mainly because she purposefully lied to the therapist so he heard what she thought he wanted to hear.

"The way I see it," Miss Mae said, "you got to talk to her. Tell her that you have feelings for her."

"How can you possibly know that I have feelings for her?"

"I saw it in your eyes the first time I mentioned her name." Miss Mae smiled. "If you were here for some pickup then you would have gone with Echo or stayed at that nasty club I saw you come out of earlier. You not like the other girls. You care for her."

"Echo thinks I'm in love," she confessed.

"What do you think?" Miss Mae asked.

"I don't know," Kathryn said. "The whole thing confuses me."

Miss Mae's eyes narrowed. She stared at Kathryn, seemingly taking stock of her.

"How confused can you be?" the woman asked. "You wanna be with Jenn? It's as simple as that."

Kathryn blinked. "Um. Well—"

"No, no. Don't overthink it. Just ask yourself if you wanna be with her. Do you want to talk to her? Walk with her? See sights with her? You getting too caught up on the idea of the future. Live in the now."

Loose fragments of ideas started to fall together in Kathryn's mind. She'd been looking at the bigger picture. Straight or gay. She'd been so bewildered about her sudden lusting for a woman, that she'd forgotten an important piece of the puzzle. It wasn't about whether Jenn was a man or a woman. It wasn't about whether Kathryn was gay or straight or anything in between.

She liked Jenn. She more than liked Jenn. The rest

didn't matter. The idea of hurting Jenn was painful. The idea of not being able to see Jenn was more so.

She couldn't shake the memory of the first kiss from her mind. When she had drunkenly initiated a kiss the second night, it was because she wanted to recreate the feelings again.

It all seemed so obvious.

But she'd ruined everything. She couldn't ask Jenn to give her a chance now. Firstly, she wanted to respect Jenn's request and stay away. Secondly, she couldn't think how she could even begin to convince Jenn of her feelings after all the back and forth that had gone on between them. And, lastly, she couldn't drag Jenn into the mess her life was. How would she ever explain what had happened over the last two years? The decisions she had made?

Addison.

"You overthinking again, Fine Shoes," Miss Mae said. "Love ain't easy. It's one step at a time."

There was that word again.

Love.

"Come to the tourist office tomorrow afternoon," Miss Mae said.

"But I promised—" Kathryn said.

"Jenn doesn't want you to stay away. She wants you to not break her heart. And I don't think you want to break her heart. You may be confused, but I think you're starting to work it out." Miss Mae stood up. "Tomorrow afternoon. Basin Street."

"What time?" Kathryn asked as she stood up.

Miss Mae laughed. "We don't do time around here, Fine Shoes. Afternoon is fine."

40

POSSUM

REBECCA KNOCKED on the interconnecting door. She nervously drummed her fingers on her thigh as she waited for Arabella to open her side.

A few moments passed, she heard soft footsteps, and then the lock being turned. Arabella opened the door and leaned on the frame.

"We literally just said good night. Miss me?"

Rebecca nodded. "Yeah, I did. But I wanted to apologise."

Arabella frowned. "What for?"

"At Jenn's, I asked if you liked your job. I was overstepping." It had played on her mind for the last few hours. Arabella didn't seem concerned about it, but Rebecca wanted to clarify what she had said and why.

Arabella stepped to one side and gestured for her to come in. "Tea?"

"Yes, please." She'd trained Arabella on how to make a

good cup of tea. Why people insisted on putting in the milk last, she'd never know.

She walked into the room and sat on the edge of the bed. It was high, and her feet dangled, which felt appropriate considering her childish behaviour.

"I don't think you overstepped," Arabella said as she set about making two cups of tea.

"I was jealous."

Arabella turned around and frowned. "Oh?"

"You've been taking calls, and I get that you have to. It's your job, and they need you. But I kinda feel like this is my time, and that they are calling and taking you away from me. I asked if you liked your job because I felt jealous that they could so easily take you away, take your attention. But, of course they can, it's your job. And it's not like you have an average job. You co-own the company."

Arabella smiled. "I had no idea you had such a strong streak of jealousy. It even runs to corporations."

Rebecca rolled her eyes and pointedly turned away. She didn't want to be mocked. She was trying to be honest. She'd never really felt jealous before. It was different with Arabella, she kept wondering what would take the impressive woman away from her.

The bed dipped beside her as her girlfriend sat down.

"Sorry, I didn't mean to be flippant," Arabella said softly. "And you don't need to apologise. Asking if I like my job is a reasonable enough question. Arguing with me if I tell you that I do, that would be stepping over the line."

"If?" Rebecca turned to look at her. "*If* you tell me that you like your job?"

Arabella let out a soft sigh. "Yes, if. The truth is; I don't know if I like my job. I love the industry, I find architecture fascinating, as you know. But buying and selling houses, I don't know if that's an interest, never mind a passion."

Rebecca's eyes widened. Arabella didn't like her job. And now Rebecca had opened the floodgates.

"I'm so sorry, I shouldn't have mentioned anything," she said. "I know you've been struggling with change lately… I didn't mean to make things worse."

The kettle finished boiling. Arabella pressed a quick kiss to Rebecca's cheek and stood up. "I know, you didn't."

Rebecca watched her making the tea. She felt terrible. Watching Arabella taking work-related calls on holiday had eaten at her. She hated that Hanley Estates couldn't cope without their boss, but she shouldn't have mentioned anything. It was Arabella's *job*. Her family business. It had to come first.

"I can hear you thinking," Arabella said. She turned around and grinned. "Possum."

"Possum?" Rebecca raised an eyebrow. "Don't they raid trashcans?"

"It's better than Boo-Boo." Arabella turned her attention back to the drinks. "What are you thinking about?"

"Well, now I'm thinking about the fact you just called me Possum."

Arabella chuckled. "Before that."

Rebecca stood up and walked over to her. "I was

thinking that I shouldn't have said anything about your job."

"I thought we'd agreed to speak to each other when things are bothering us? That can't be a one-way street, you know."

"I know." Rebecca peered over Arabella's shoulder and watched the tea being made. *So far, so good.*

"If you don't stop spying on me when I make you a drink, you'll be called worse than Possum," Arabella promised.

"Okay, Boo-Boo." Rebecca turned around. She looked at the bedside table and frowned at the book she saw there. "*Empowering the Unconscious Brain*, huh?"

Arabella was beside her in a second and trying to pull the book out of her hand. Rebecca tightened her grip.

"Give me the book, *Possum*," Arabella ground the name out.

"What are you embarrassed about, Boo-Boo?" Rebecca asked sweetly as she clung to her end of the book.

Arabella let go and Rebecca fell backwards onto the bed.

"I didn't want you to see that book," Arabella admitted. "But you see everything."

Rebecca frowned as she looked at the book, wondering what was so bad about her seeing it.

Arabella noticed her confused expression. "It's a self-help book," she clarified.

"Yeah, I didn't think it was a slice of toast. This is on my to-read list. I'm currently reading one about learning while you sleep, but I'm not sure it will work for me, I toss and turn too much to keep earbuds in at night." Rebecca sat up and placed the book back on the bedside table.

When she looked up, Arabella was looking down at her with something akin to shock.

"What?" Rebecca asked.

"You... read self-help books?"

"Of course I do. You know I love improving myself—wait, are you embarrassed about reading self-help books?"

Arabella's cheeks tinged pink and she turned away. "The tea," she said by way of excuse.

Rebecca watched her retreat. She smiled in wonderment. Arabella really was a complicated, wonderful human being.

"I love self-help books," Rebecca said. "Some aren't that great, but most of them are really useful. They teach you ways to do things, deal with things, understand things. There's no shame in them."

Arabella finished making the drinks and thrust a cup towards Rebecca, keeping her gaze low.

"There's no shame in them," she repeated, refusing to take the tea until Arabella made eye contact with her.

Arabella looked up, her eyes locking with Rebecca's.

Rebecca took the mug.

"My parents would disagree," Arabella said.

"Then you totally need to read *Toxic Parents*," Rebecca told her.

Arabella laughed. "Is that really a book?"

"Yep, the full title is *Toxic Parents: Overcoming Their Hurtful Legacy and Reclaiming Your Life*," Rebecca said.

"I'll put it in my wish list," her girlfriend promised.

Rebecca placed her tea on the bedside table and picked

up the book again. She toed off her shoes and sat up, her back against the headboard. She patted the space next to her.

"Come here, I'll read to you."

Arabella looked at her with uncertainty for a moment. Rebecca could practically see the cogs turning in her mind, wondering if it was a good idea. Questioning if she was going to be mocked.

Rebecca patted the bed again.

Arabella nodded, walking around the bed and grabbing her own mug of tea as she went. She curled up beside Rebecca, wrapping her hands around the tea and resting her head on Rebecca's shoulder.

Rebecca opened to the bookmarked page and started to read.

41

MISUNDERSTANDINGS

KATHRYN DECIDED that three o'clock would constitute 'afternoon'. And so, she walked into the tourist office on Basin Street at precisely that time.

She'd lain awake most of the previous night wondering if coming was a good idea. On the one hand, she wanted to respect Jenn's wishes. On the other, she genuinely worried that Miss Mae would track her down if she didn't do as she commanded.

Kathryn had never been a sentimental person, or someone who became swept away with emotions and feelings. She was practical and pragmatic. Sometimes to a fault.

So, her sudden feelings for Jenn had come as a massive shock to her. Once she had stopped fighting herself and accepted that she felt a great deal of affection for Jenn, the floodgates of her emotions crashed down.

At first, she'd found Jenn fascinating. The long journey on the trams had proved that Kathryn and Jenn could talk about almost nothing for hours and have a great time while doing it.

Then the burlesque show proved that Kathryn had a physical interest. No matter how much she tried to ignore it, she felt sexually attracted to Jenn after that night.

She didn't know if it was love, as Echo had suggested and Miss Mae had implied. She didn't even know if she was capable of love, and she certainly didn't know if Jenn would be able to love her, especially considering her recent history. But that was a bridge she'd cross later, if Jenn would even speak with her.

What Kathryn did know was that she wanted to be honest with Jenn. No matter the outcome.

The outside temperature was becoming more intense, and she was lightly perspiring as she walked into the tourist office. She took a deep breath of cold air.

She knew it wasn't just the weather. It was her growing panic.

"Ah, there you are," Miss Mae called out from behind her desk.

Kathryn looked over to her and nodded nervously. Jenn stood in the large lobby, eyeing her with suspicion.

"So very kind of you," Miss Mae said loudly. She turned to address Jenn, "She giving me a donation for the church."

Kathryn blinked in surprise.

"Hundred dollars, wasn't it?" Miss Mae asked her.

Kathryn narrowed her eyes and approached the desk.

"Excuse me," Jenn said quickly. She walked out of the lobby and into the old station's waiting room.

Kathryn watched Jenn leave. She turned back to look

at Miss Mae, who had her hand held out, palm raised to the sky.

Kathryn rolled her eyes. She got her purse from her handbag and started to count some money into the woman's open hand.

"Why am I giving you one hundred dollars exactly?"

"For my church."

"And when did I agree to that?"

"You didn't." Miss Mae folded the money and placed it in her bra. "But now think how kind and generous you look to Jenn. Ain't no one who don't like a philanthropist."

Kathryn sighed. "What now?"

Miss Mae shrugged. "Don't look at me, Fine Shoes. You did the thinking, you came here. You must have something to say."

Kathryn realised she had just been hustled out of hundred dollars by the wily old woman. She shook her head and muttered under her breath as she walked towards the waiting room.

Air left her lungs as she stepped into the beautifully preserved hall. She knew that the building had been a train station in a past life, and she'd seen signs promising an historical experience in the original Basin Street waiting room. But nothing had prepared her for actually seeing the room for the first time.

For a moment, she forgot why she was even there. She looked around in open-mouthed awe.

Old wooden benches, the high and ornate ceiling, and the display cases made it feel like she had stepped back in time. She approached the first of the display cabinets.

"Impressive, isn't it?"

Jenn stood behind Kathryn, and Kathryn tensed. She held her breath, not wanting to react or say something that might cause Jenn to leave again.

"Very," she admitted. "A wonderful restoration."

Jenn took a tentative step and stood beside her. Her gaze was focused on the contents of the display.

Kathryn continued to peer through the glass. Original tickets, timetables, models of trains, and other historical documents were displayed with information cards.

Kathryn smiled, her sight resting on a shopping list.

"Some things never change," Jenn commented.

Kathryn nodded. "We all still need bread, milk, and sugar."

"I often look at that and wonder whose shopping list it was," Jenn said.

"And did they lose it *before* or *after* they bought the items?" Kathryn supplied.

Jenn chuckled. "Exactly. Did they get to the store and pat their pockets down?"

"And then try to remember what they'd written on the list."

"Then forget the most important item," Jenn added.

"Oh, I hate that," Kathryn confessed. "There's always one thing that you forget, and it's the thing you needed most."

"The thing you originally went out for," Jenn said.

Kathryn smiled. They were communicating, and it felt good. She took a breath and exhaled. It felt good, too. Like a weight had been lifted from her chest.

She gestured to the next cabinet, which housed a conductor's uniform from the turn of the century.

"More formal than your tram outfit," she said.

"Streetcar," Jenn corrected softly.

Kathryn could see her smiling reflection in the glass of the case. "Mmm."

"Why did you come here?" Jenn finally asked.

"To donate to Miss Mae's church."

"She's an atheist."

Kathryn pursed her lips and slowly shook her head. She muttered under her breath.

Jenn laughed. "And with a mouth like that I can't see you as the church-donating type."

"I… I came to see you," Kathryn admitted. She turned around to face Jenn.

Jenn's brow knit in confusion. "Why?" she asked in a whisper.

"I had to see you. I tried to stay away. I really did. I was worried about even bumping into you, and then last night I was in a restaurant and I bumped into Echo." Kathryn looked at her feet, wondering how to explain exactly what had happened the night before.

"Oh?" Jenn's voice was tight.

"She invited herself to dinner with me and we talked. She convinced me to go on to some seedy club—"

"Kathryn," Jenn interrupted.

She paused and looked up. Jenn's face was contorted, she looked pained.

"If this is going to be some story about how Echo helped you with your sexual awakening… I don't… I don't want to hear it. I—I've heard it before."

Kathryn blinked as she processed the words. Then she laughed, so loudly it reverberated in the large space.

"God, no!" she exclaimed. "No, absolutely… just, no. We spoke. Nothing more. In fact, we mainly spoke about you."

Jenn's expression morphed away from hurt and back to perplexed.

"Anyway, we were…" Kathryn let out an embarrassed breath. "At a strip club and I didn't feel comfortable, so I asked if we could leave. Outside, we met Miss Mae and, well, I went to hear her perform and then we spoke."

"Look, Kathryn." Jenn shifted from foot to foot nervously.

Kathryn held up her hand. "No, I need to say this. I still don't have all the answers, I wish I did. Being at that club, it made me realise some things. And speaking with Echo. She explained some things to me. She opened my eyes in many ways. Like I said, I don't have all the answers yet. But I have enough to know that I—"

"Hey, babe."

Kathryn turned to see a tall, slim blonde enter the waiting room, half engaged in something on her phone. She approached Jenn and placed a kiss on her cheek, wrapping her arm around Jenn's shoulder. "Shift over?"

Kathryn stared at Jenn in shock. The blonde interloper continued to look at her phone, unaware of what she had just walked in on.

Jenn licked her lips nervously, still staring at Kathryn. Her hand shook as she lifted her wrist to look at her watch.

"Y—yeah, yeah, sorry. I lost track of time."

Kathryn looked at the two of them.

"Stupid fool," she muttered to herself as she spun

around and ran towards the exit. She couldn't believe she had actually thought that admitting her feelings to Jenn was a good idea. She barely knew her. And now, it seemed as if she wasn't the only one who had fallen for her charms.

She had to get out of there. The embarrassment was too much to take.

She marched across the road, weaving in and out of traffic without any thought for her safety. As long as she was away from Jenn, she would be all right.

She shuddered as she heard Jenn call out her name. There was no way she would stop now. She didn't want to hear explanations or see Jenn's pitying expression.

She'd made it across two lanes, now she had another two to go and she'd be unhindered by any further traffic on her way back to the hotel. She stood on the grassy central reservation and looked up to cross the next road.

Tires screeched. A horn blared. There was an unmistakable thud.

She couldn't move. Ice cold fear ran down her spine. She knew what had happened, without even turning to see. She knew.

All she could do was pray that it wasn't the case.

Her body wouldn't move. As if through sheer willpower alone she could stand still and wait for Jenn to catch up to her. To believe that the thump was anything else.

The longer she stood still, the more she became aware of people pointing, cars coming to a stop, and the sound of someone screaming.

She turned around, breaths coming in large uncontrollable pants. She stepped off the kerb. Jenn was in the road, her back to Kathryn.

She heard the bloodcurdling scream again. The blonde from the waiting room was running towards Jenn.

They reached Jenn's prone body at the same time. Kathryn hesitantly brought her fingers to Jenn's neck, seeking out a pulse.

"Ambulance, I need an ambulance on Basin Street, by the tourist office," the blonde cried into her phone. "It's my cousin, she's been hit by a car. She's... she's not moving."

Kathryn felt a stomach-turning blow at the words.

The blonde was Jenn's cousin. Her *cousin*. The kiss on the cheek was an innocent familial peck. How could she have acted so rashly and run away without being sure?

"Lady?!"

Kathryn realised the blonde, Jenn's cousin, was looking at her with a questioning frown. She got herself together, remembering what she was doing, and focused on her search for a pulse.

Her finger shook. She used her other hand to steady her wrist. She closed her eyes and focused.

She sagged in relief. "There's a pulse. It's weak, but it's there."

Jenn's cousin relayed the information down the phone. Kathryn looked down at Jenn's beautiful face, which was grazed but peaceful. She threaded her fingers through long blonde locks and removed them from her face, tucking them behind her ear.

"What happened?" Jenn's cousin asked as she hung up the call, the ambulance on the way.

Kathryn looked up. She opened her mouth to beg forgiveness, but no words came out.

"Miss Mae called me, and then I saw Jenn running off."

"I—I think she was coming after me," Kathryn said.

"I'm Chloe." She knelt closer to Jenn and picked up a limp hand in her own.

"I'm… just a tourist." Kathryn swallowed. "Kathryn, we… we met a couple of times."

She looked up, wondering where the ambulance was. They were surrounded by onlookers and stopped cars. The driver was getting out of his car and stumbling towards them in shock.

She couldn't believe how surreal it felt. A few moments ago, she was trying to confess her feelings to the woman who now lay unconscious in the middle of the road.

Hot tears streamed down her cheeks.

Where's the damn ambulance?

42

TIME TO LEAVE

ARABELLA STOOD at the hotel reception desk and watched one of the slowest typists ever prepare her final bill.

She could feel herself getting more and more annoyed with each excruciatingly painful keystroke.

Rebecca placed a hand on her forearm. She leaned in and whispered, "If you want to just go, it's fine. I'll deal with your checkout and we can settle up later."

"It's fine," Arabella said. "I have time before the flight. And I don't want to saddle you with the bill."

"It's okay, I know you're good for it," Rebecca replied. She leaned in closer. "I have generous payment plans available."

Arabella felt a shiver run through her. Damn work. Damn the Southbridge account. Damn her office for not being able to deal with things without her constantly holding their hands.

"We can explore that when you get home," she promised.

"Are you sure you don't want me to come as well?" Rebecca asked.

"Absolutely not. You're here to see your friend and explore the area. I won't see your holiday being ruined because my staff are incompetent."

"You're hot when you're all fired up," Rebecca said.

Arabella chuckled. She leant her head on Rebecca's shoulder. "I'll miss you."

"I'll miss you, too," Rebecca promised.

Arabella quickly stood up straight and placed her hand over her pocket. "Damn."

"What's wrong?"

"I think I left my phone in your room. I wanted to fully charge it before the flight, but I left it—"

Rebecca smiled brightly. "I'll go... you carry on..." She gestured towards the slowest checkout in history.

"Thank you. Could you have a quick look in case I left anything else?" Arabella asked. She wondered what had gotten into her, she'd never forgotten her phone before.

"Sure." Rebecca sauntered towards the elevators.

Ah, yes, that's why I forgot, Arabella thought as she watched her girlfriend depart. She turned back towards the desk. "You have two minutes, or I'll assume my room is free. I really don't see what the delay is."

"Sorry, ma'am, it's our computer systems—"

Arabella held up her hand. "Don't talk to me about computer systems."

She could feel the anger coursing through her veins. Her father had called her first thing that morning to give her an update on everything that was falling apart. She'd woken up, fully dressed and snuggled up to Rebecca, to the sound of her mobile vibrating across the bedside table.

At some point the night before, they had fallen asleep while talking. It wasn't something that Arabella had ever done before, and the crick in her neck told her to never do it again. No, the next time she fell asleep on her bed with Rebecca, she'd take the time to actually lay in the bed, holding Rebecca close to her.

Seeing her father's name flash up on her phone had caused her to jump to her feet like a teenager caught in a compromising position. That thought had quickly left her mind once he started to explain disaster after disaster piling up in her office.

There was only one thing for it; she had to go home.

Rebecca had been understanding, had helped her pack and find the first flight home. She'd even offered several times to go back with her. But Arabella felt terrible enough for having to leave, she didn't want to ruin Rebecca's holiday more than she already had. And what would Rebecca do when they got home? Arabella would be busy with work, and Rebecca would be mourning the loss of the end of her holiday, sad to be missing out on spending time with Jenn. No, it was better that Arabella went alone.

But that didn't mean that she wouldn't miss her terribly.

"Miss Foster, I have a message for you," one of the other receptionists called out.

Arabella was pleased to hear that Kathryn was there. It gave her the opportunity to say goodbye in person. She turned around and let out a gasp.

Kathryn's mascara had smeared, her cheeks were red, and she looked like someone who'd just run an impromptu marathon.

"Kathryn?" She stepped towards her, fearing that the woman would collapse if she didn't take her grasping hands.

"They wouldn't let me go with her," she said, her hands taking Arabella's in a death grip.

"Who?"

"Jenn. She was hit by a car."

"Oh my god!" Arabella helped Kathryn into a nearby chair and sat on the arm.

"She had a pulse and then the ambulance came. They wouldn't tell me anything, and they wouldn't let me go with her. I... I don't know what to do."

The receptionist came over with a folded piece of paper. "I'm so sorry to interrupt, Miss Foster, but they said the message was extremely urgent."

Kathryn's shaky hand took the slip of paper. She opened it up.

Call Erica immediately. RE: Addison

Arabella frowned. She didn't know what any of that meant, but she saw all the colour run from Kathryn's face. The woman grabbed her phone and quickly made a call.

"Erica?" she said the moment the call was connected.

Arabella felt like she was intruding, but Kathryn still

held her hand in a vice-like grip so she wasn't going anywhere.

"Michael?" Kathryn asked, her voice tight. "He's… back?"

Arabella looked around, praying for Rebecca's quick return.

"Mother *knows?*" Kathryn cried. "But… you said you wouldn't tell!"

Arabella leaned a little closer. She could hear a woman speaking, presumably Erica, whoever that was.

"Kathryn," the woman was saying, "I didn't tell her anything. Michael came to the office and told her everything he knew. Mother just put the pieces together."

"What is she going to do?" Kathryn asked, her voice barely a breath.

"She's going to Addison. You have to get there first, Kathryn. Before Mother does."

Arabella's head was swimming. *Who's Addison? Or Michael? And what does her mother know?* She could feel Kathryn shivering with fear. She suspected that she was in shock. Whatever was happening couldn't possibly have come at a worse time.

"I… I can't leave, there's been—"

"Kathryn," Erica said sharply. "Mother knows. Do you want Michael to—"

"Of course I don't. You know I don't."

"You have to make a decision, you can't pretend this isn't happening anymore," Erica said.

Kathryn let out a small sob, her hand almost crushing Arabella's.

"I know, I'll leave now. I'll call you when I can."

Kathryn hung up the call. She let go of Arabella's hand and rushed over to the reception desk. She picked up a pen and jotted something on a piece of paper.

"Have my belongings forwarded to this address, I'm checking out now. You have my credit card on file, charge what you have to. I have to go... right now."

The receptionist looked confused but took the slip of paper.

Kathryn spun around, and Arabella took her by the upper arms. "What's happening?" she demanded.

"I... I have to go. I'm sorry. I'm so sorry, I can't stay. Tell Jenn I'm so sorry." Kathryn tore herself away from Arabella's grip. She ran towards the doorman. "I need a taxi, right now."

Arabella stood in shock and watched the woman run off. She had no idea what had just happened, but whatever it was, it was important.

"One phone," Rebecca said as she strolled back into reception.

"Jenn's been in a car accident," Arabella told her. "She's been taken to hospital."

"What?" Rebecca's face paled.

"Kathryn just told me... and then something happened, and she's run off."

"Kathryn ran off?" Rebecca asked, pulling her own mobile from her pocket.

"Yes, she just had a strange phone conversation and then... checked out. But, before that she said that Jenn had been in an accident. She was at the scene, but the ambulance wouldn't let her go with them."

"I'll text her, and her cousin," Rebecca said. "Hopefully someone can tell me what's going on."

Arabella noticed that Rebecca was shaking. She reached out and put her arm around her shoulders. "I should stay."

"No, no, you need to get home. You'll go out of your mind if you don't get back to the office and shake them up soon."

Arabella knew Rebecca was right. She already felt her skin itch at being so far away from work. It was a long way home. It would take many hours of travel and many hours to readjust to the time difference.

But she wanted to stay, to make sure that Jenn was okay and to look after Rebecca. Not that the woman would ever admit that she needed looking after. Rebecca was strong and single-minded.

Rebecca sent a couple of text messages and let out a shaky breath. "There, we'll see what they say."

"Miss Henley?" the receptionist called out. "We have your final bill ready."

Arabella gritted her teeth. She tightened her grip around Rebecca's shoulders. She didn't want to leave, but she knew she had to.

"It's fine," Rebecca reassured. "You have to go. We'll talk or text all the time."

"If you need me to turn around and come back, you call me immediately. You know my flight time, I'll leave it until last second to board."

Rebecca took a small step back and looked her in the eye. "I appreciate that, I really do. But I'll be fine. You need to go and slap some sense into your office. I'll be home before you know it."

43

AWAKE

Jenn opened her eyes and looked around the hospital room. Rebecca was slumped in one of the visiting chairs, asleep. Just as she had been for the last four days. Jenn kept telling her to go back to the hotel where she had a plush bed, but Rebecca remained.

She was a great friend. Of course, other friends had visited in the days since the accident, and Chloe was a semi-permanent feature, but Rebecca hadn't moved. She'd even taken to helping the nurses with Jenn's care. Jenn knew that this was a throwback to when Rebecca had cared for her mum in the hospital back home.

Even though she was surrounded by those who loved her, she was missing one person.

Kathryn.

She couldn't remember much of what happened, but the moment she woke up she'd felt a longing to see her. As if she had been dreaming about her.

Not long after she awoke, disorientated and in pain,

Rebecca had explained the conversation that Arabella had overheard. Kathryn was... gone.

The next day, when Jenn felt a little less like her head was going to explode, she'd asked Rebecca to repeat everything she knew. She tried to piece together the mysterious fragments to figure out what would cause Kathryn to leave like that.

The following day, Arabella called Rebecca. Jenn asked to speak to her, listening to the tale from the source. It hadn't helped. She still didn't understand.

Chloe said that Kathryn had been with her following the accident. And then Arabella explained that she had checked out of her hotel and vanished. Jenn couldn't remember much. The nurse said it was common for people who had been in an accident to forget what had happened just before.

She knew that Kathryn had been at Basin Street. They'd spoken about... something. It was hazy, but she felt like it was important. It felt different from the other conversations they'd shared. Maybe it was wishful thinking. Maybe the bump on the head had warped her perception.

Jenn must have run out into the road, but she couldn't remember doing so. She didn't know what would ever make her do something so foolish.

Her heart was heavy. She was struggling to push thoughts of Kathryn Foster from her mind, but she had to. The truth of the matter was that Kathryn had left. She didn't even know if Jenn was alive or dead.

The door to her room opened. She looked up, eagerly. Despite her determination otherwise, she couldn't help it.

A part of her still expected Kathryn to walk in, apologising for being delayed. She pictured her fussing with blankets and tweaking the air-conditioning unit. Caring for her, like Jenn knew she did.

"Still just me," Chloe said. She walked over and handed Jenn an apple and a bottle of water. "Sorry, she isn't coming back."

"I know," Jenn said. "I wasn't expecting her to."

Chloe gave her a look of disbelief.

Rebecca stirred in her seat. She sat up and started to stretch.

"Sorry we woke you," Chloe said.

"No problem, time to get up anyway," Rebecca said.

"Can you talk some sense into my cousin? She's still looking out for the woman who nearly got her killed."

Jenn rolled her eyes. "She didn't do anything. I walked into traffic, it's my fault."

"And she defends her," Chloe added.

"Technically," Rebecca said, "you don't know what happened, you can't remember."

"Exactly," Chloe said. "Maybe she pushed you."

Jenn ground her teeth. "I doubt it. Especially if she sat with me until the ambulance came, like you said she did."

"If I'd known she was the one who had messed with you and broken your heart, we would have needed a second ambulance," Chloe promised.

"Anyway," Rebecca interrupted before the two cousins got into another debate over Kathryn. "What did the doctor say?"

Chloe turned to face Jenn, trying to cover up her anger with a smile. "He says you can go home today."

Jenn dropped her head to her pillow. "Thank god."

"But you need to take it easy," Chloe said with a serious tone. "Three broken ribs, and you had a concussion. No dancing, no driving, no drinking while on the pain meds."

"I know, I'll take it easy," Jenn promised. She eyed her arm. She hadn't broken it, but the sprain was so bad that it was in a sling.

"I'll come and stay with you," Rebecca said, practically reading her mind.

"I can't ask you to do that," Jenn said.

"I'm offering." Rebecca stood up and tucked her hands into the back pockets of her jeans. "Chloe has to work, and you'll need help at home. I'm here, so I can help. Besides, I've been offered a couple of quick freelancer jobs while I'm here."

"You're dying to get home to Arabella," Jenn pointed out.

Rebecca smiled, but it didn't reach her eyes. "I can stay here a couple more weeks with you. Besides, absence makes the heart grow fonder, right?"

Jenn regarded her for a few moments. She'd love to tell Rebecca to get on the next plane home and be reunited with Arabella, but she knew that she would need help as she recovered. And she was right, Chloe couldn't take any more time off work. She doubted she could convince Rebecca to leave anyway. She'd been stuck to Jenn like glue since she'd woken up.

"If you're absolutely sure?" she asked.

Rebecca nodded. "I am."

"Great," Chloe said. "Then it's all settled. Maybe you can talk some sense into her about this Kathryn woman."

"I don't need anyone talking sense into me. It's not like I'm ever going to see her again, she left," Jenn said.

"Then why do you keep looking anxiously at the door?" Chloe asked. "You're expecting her to walk in. And, judging by the look on your face, you'd forgive her if she did. Despite the fact that she clearly doesn't care about you. Who leaves town after something like this happens? No one, that's who. No one."

Jenn swallowed. Chloe was right. She couldn't think of one good reason for Kathryn to vanish like she had. And she hadn't attempted to call to see how Jenn was.

Kathryn really couldn't have known if she was dead or alive.

Obviously, she didn't care either way.

Two Weeks Later

44

LONDON CALLING

ARABELLA HUNG up a call and let out a frustrated groan. She lowered her head to her desk, slowly thudding her forehead against the cool wood.

Her assistant, Helen, entered the office and placed a pre-packaged sandwich and a bottle of orange juice in front of her.

"Lunch," she announced.

Arabella looked at the unappealing sandwich and let out a sigh. She sat up straight and stretched out her back. She missed Dhia. The spa technician in New Orleans had been nothing short of a genius. She'd quickly found and eradicated each of Arabella's knots, knots that were so common she had taken to naming them.

"Your father called again. He said he'll be back from Portugal a day later than he originally thought," Helen said. "Something about another meeting."

Arabella rolled her eyes. She doubted it was another meeting at all, more like a round of golf. Not that she could begrudge her father having a holiday. He was in his seventies and deserved a break from work. It was just mildly frustrating that he had refused to postpone his holiday at the same moment she had felt forced to return from her own.

"You have fifteen minutes before Lannaker and Hardcastle get here for their meeting," Helen continued. "We're printing out the amended contracts, and we're trying to get the last of the survey results from the solicitors. Can I get you anything else?"

Arabella half-heartedly reached for the sandwich. *At least it's brown bread*, she noted. She shook her head and started to pull at the packaging.

"It's one-thirty," Helen said.

Arabella looked at the clock on the wall. A smile graced her face before she could cover it. It was finally a reasonable time to be able to call Rebecca. She'd probably wake her, but it would be an *acceptable* time.

Helen returned her smile. "I'll hold your calls and give you some privacy."

She left, closing the door to Arabella's office behind her before she could say anything else. Arabella didn't know how much Helen knew, she didn't exactly spill her heart and soul to her personal assistant, but it was clear that Helen knew enough.

She knew that Arabella's afternoons were infinitely better than her mornings. She knew that Arabella frequently made overseas calls around lunch time. Afternoons meant she could contact Rebecca. She could finally speak to her again and engage in text conversations throughout the rest of the workday.

She pushed her sandwich to one side and picked up her phone. She called Rebecca, waiting for the international dial tone to sound. It was a sound she loved and hated in equal measure. She loved it because the technology allowed her to stay in touch with Rebecca. She hated it because it reminded her that she was thousands of miles away.

"Afternoon," a throaty voice answered.

"Good morning," Arabella said softly, as if she were personally there to witness Rebecca waking up.

"I miss you," Rebecca said. She said it every time they spoke.

"I miss you, too. Very much," Arabella admitted. "How are you? And Jenn?"

"I'm good. Jenn is going back to work today, just a couple of hours in the morning, easing herself back into it."

Arabella's heart soared. Of course, she was happy that Jenn was feeling better and finally able to get back to work. But a part of that happiness was rooted in the knowledge that it meant that Rebecca would be able to return home shortly.

"But one of my freelance jobs I committed to has pushed back the date of the shoot…" Rebecca trailed off.

"But you had a contract in place," Arabella stated firmly. She paused. It wasn't Rebecca's fault, and she could tell from her tone that she felt bad about the delay. "How much have they pushed back?"

"Three weeks."

Arabella took a calming breath. It was the last thing she wanted to hear. She understood Rebecca's taking freelancer roles while she was in town. It was a great opportunity to diversify her portfolio, make some extra money, and keep busy doing something she loved. But she'd been looking forward to when Jenn could get by without Rebecca's help, so Rebecca could come home.

Now that was looking even further away.

"Are you angry?" Rebecca asked quietly.

"No. No, just disappointed. I miss you," Arabella reassured. "But I understand. There's nothing you can do."

"I took another couple of roles. If I'm going to be here, I might as well make the most of it," Rebecca said. "I'm doing some work for the tourism office. I think Jenn convinced her manager to take me on as a way of thanking me for helping her out."

"Sounds nice," Arabella said, trying to insert some enthusiasm into her tone. "It's a wonderful building, and the waiting room is amazing."

"Yeah, I'm looking forward to it. Well, I'm… I'm missing you, and I'm missing home. But I'm keeping busy, you know?"

"I know. I understand." Arabella pushed her sandwich into her desk drawer for later, she'd lost her appetite.

"When's your dad back from sunning himself in Portugal?" Rebecca asked.

"Oh, he's staying another day," Arabella said. "Apparently, he has a meeting."

Rebecca laughed. "Oh, in the golf club restaurant or on the green?"

Arabella chuckled. "It's cheeky, isn't it?"

"Yep," Rebecca said. "He's taking advantage of your good nature."

Arabella leaned back in her chair. Her eyes wandered to the giant prints that adorned her office walls, a gift from Rebecca following their drive home. She'd had many a positive comment about them from clients.

"How come when you help Jenn, you're being a good friend, and yet when I help my father, he's taking advantage of me?" Arabella asked with a wide smile.

"Because Jenn doesn't *expect* me to help her, and she's eternally grateful. And I know she'd do the same for me in a second. Your dad went on holiday not long after you had to cancel yours. And he dumped you with a load of his work. And he isn't grateful, he expects it from you."

Arabella stilled. Her hand reached for her necklace, and she ran the charm along the chain, deep in thought.

"Shit, sorry," Rebecca mumbled. "It's early, I just spoke without thinking."

"No, you're right. He does expect it, he does take advantage," Arabella admitted. "I'd just not thought of it in such black-and-white terms."

There was a knock on the door. Helen poked her head around the corner, an apologetic look on her face. "They're early."

Arabella rolled her eyes and nodded her head. Helen closed the door again.

"My meeting has turned up early, I need to go."

"I had a dream about you last night," Rebecca said. "It was a bit like when we were at the water aerobics, except it was just you and I in the pool. And I think your bathing suit—"

"Rebecca," she growled in warning. She didn't need to

sit through a business meeting with *those* thoughts in her mind.

Rebecca chuckled. "I'll tell you another time."

"You better. I'll text you later," Arabella promised.

"Later," Rebecca said.

She hung up the call and tossed the phone onto her desk. It was 4,624 miles from London to New Orleans. She'd checked. Lately, she was feeling every single one of them.

She stood up and brushed down her skirt, checking her appearance in a mirror by the door.

"Back to work," she murmured.

45

ADDISON AND LUKE

JENN SAT on the rickety stool behind the bar at CeeCee's. It was almost three weeks since her crash, and two since she'd gotten out of the hospital. It felt good to be back at work and getting her life back to normal. Even if she could only work at some of her jobs at the moment. She certainly wasn't performing at Façade yet.

She sucked in a deep breath, relishing the fresh air even if it was hot as hell outside.

It was great to be out of the house. Rebecca had been a godsend. Without her care and attention, Jenn wouldn't have been back at work so soon. But Jenn wasn't used to doing nothing. She was used to being busy, running all over the city, and meeting hundreds of people every day.

She'd started morning shifts at CeeCee's a few days earlier. It was nice and casual. Not too many customers, no heavy lifting. She turned her head to face the anti-quated fan, trying to enjoy the pathetic breeze from it.

An elderly man entered the bar. Jenn lowered herself gently from the stool.

"Morning, sir," she said with a warm smile. "What can I get you?"

"Just a bottle of water." He looked at the handwritten sign on the bar and put his hand in his pocket to scoop out the correct amount.

Jenn picked up a bottle of water that was floating in the bucket of half-melted ice and placed it on the bar. She picked up the bills as he slowly slid them towards her, one at a time.

"Where is Basin Street Station?" he asked.

"You need to head down Bourbon," Jenn said as she stood on the bottom rung of her stool and leaned over the high bar to gesture the direction. "About another five-minute walk, you'll come to a café with an outside seating area, take the next left. Keep going and you'll see it right in front of you."

"Wonderful." He picked up the water bottle. "And that's where the tourist office is?"

"It is, I highly recommend the open-top bus," a familiar voice sounded from the doorway.

Jenn looked up in shock.

The elderly man turned and regarded Kathryn. "That sounds great, thank you."

"No problem, enjoy your stay in town," she said as he passed by her on his way out.

Jenn continued to stare at Kathryn, belatedly realising that something about her seemed off. Her eyes widened as she realised what it was. She stared at what Kathryn was holding in her arms.

A child.

A boy, she thought. Asleep in Kathryn's arms, balanced on her hip, legs dangling on either side.

"Hello, Jenn," Kathryn said in a whisper.

"You have a son," Jenn said, incredulously.

"Yes." Kathryn nodded. "His name is Luke."

"Luke," Jenn said softly. She continued to stare at the slumbering brown-haired boy.

Kathryn sat at one of the barstools. When Luke started to stir she adjusted her grip on him so they would both be more comfortable. Jenn looked at his soft features and messy hair, stuck to his forehead with perspiration. She swallowed hard at the adorable sight.

"I'm sorry I left without seeing you," Kathryn said.

"You could have called me," Jenn pointed out bitterly.

"I didn't know what to say," she confessed. "I wanted to come and see you, to explain everything... face to face."

Jenn tore her eyes from Luke. She took a protective step back; the bar didn't seem like enough of a barrier between them. She folded her arms.

"Are you married?"

"No," Kathryn said simply.

"Engaged? Boyfriend?"

"No, and no. I'm single."

Jenn frowned, looking at Luke. She wasn't one to judge, but babies came from somewhere.

"I had an affair... with a married man," Kathryn admitted. "It was stupid, and I deeply regret what I did. He convinced me that he would leave his wife, but he never had any intention of that. I thought he loved me.

We only slept together twice before I came to my senses, but by then I was pregnant."

Jenn felt her eyebrows raise at Kathryn's bad luck. And poor judgement of character.

"I told him. He'd always told me that he didn't love his wife. I thought the pregnancy would finally make him break the relationship and be with me. But that didn't happen. Instead, he and his wife moved to Europe."

Jenn sat on her stool again. She wanted to be angry, but she found it impossible. Kathryn was back, and she was pouring her heart out.

"My mother couldn't have stood the scandal of my being pregnant out of wedlock. She's very traditional, and Erica was always the wild child, I was the golden girl. I didn't know what to do, so one day I confided in my father. He was recovering from a minor heart attack. He'd had one years before, so we all thought it was nothing serious."

Kathryn coughed slightly, seemingly trying to keep the tears at bay and remain calm while Luke slept in her arms.

"He came up with a plan. We'd both travel to see my Uncle Addison in Brazil. My father to convalesce and me to join him, to keep him company. Supposedly."

Addison, Jenn thought. She remembered the exchange she'd heard between Kathryn and her sister, Erica. *Tell Mother about Addison.* And then Arabella's retelling of what she had overhead in the hotel lobby.

Luke started to fidget in Kathryn's arms. She adjusted her grip and whispered some soothing words into his ear until he calmed down again.

"I... didn't want to keep him." Kathryn's cheeks

burned with embarrassment. "My father convinced me otherwise. He promised me that he would make everything okay. He told me to leave Luke with Uncle Addison for a while, until he had the chance to speak with my mother."

"Is your mother that bad?" Jenn asked. She couldn't imagine a mother who wouldn't be thrilled with a grandson, regardless of the state of the relationship between the parents.

Kathryn looked at her with a smile. "Worse. She would disown me, cut me out of the family business. Freeze my assets. Religion is critical to her. She's not exactly... maternal."

Kathryn wiped her lightly perspiring brow with the back of her hand. Jenn fished a bottle of water from the icy bucket. She unscrewed the cap and placed both on the bar in front of Kathryn.

"Thank you." Kathryn took a sip. "Uncle Addison has been a foster father in Brazil for many years. He adores children. I have fond memories of visiting him when I was growing up. I knew it would be a good life for Luke. And my father seemed convinced that he would be able to tell my mother without her imploding. So, I agreed to his crazy plan. I had the baby and we stayed for a couple of months, then my father and I went home."

Darkness crossed her expression. "A few months later, my father and I were arguing one evening. He wanted to tell my mother, he wanted to bring Luke home, to have a grandson. I was terrified. I felt for sure that he'd have a better life with Addison. Especially if my mother would disown me and leave me penniless. Not that the money made any difference to me personally, but for Luke's sake. I wouldn't be able to provide for him. And I didn't think I could be the mother he deserved anyway. We fought and… my father had a heart attack that evening and died."

Jenn had known that Kathryn's father had passed away, but that didn't prevent the shock she felt at hearing how and when he had died.

"I'm so sorry," she breathed.

"I felt like it was my fault. I guess it *was* my fault," Kathryn continued. "I forced a sick, old man to keep my secret. I fought with him endlessly. It was too much for him."

"You can't blame yourself," Jenn said.

"I did… I do. I couldn't stop thinking that maybe it wouldn't have happened if I'd made different choices. But I messed up my life, and then I ruined Luke's and my father's. My sister suspected that something had happened. Eventually I confided in her because I was losing my mind. She spent the last six months watching me go off the rails, throw myself into work and into an emotionless pit. Which is why she dumped me here. To give me the time she knew I needed to process everything."

"So, you changed your mind and went to get Luke?" Jenn asked.

"No. Well, not exactly," Kathryn admitted. "After your accident, I got a call from my sister. My secret was out in the open. I found out that Michael had told his wife everything. Including that I had been expecting his child. They'd never been able to have children and Michael's wife wanted the baby. They returned to New York to speak to me, but I was here. They spoke to my mother. She put two and two together and realised that I hadn't simply visited Brazil with my father."

Kathryn took another drink of water. Jenn noticed her hand was shaking.

"They were on their way to Brazil to try to take Luke. I realised I couldn't let that happen. Not just because I didn't want *them* to have him, but because he was mine. I did a lot of soul-searching when I was in New Orleans. I realised that I'd spent my whole life doing what other people wanted me to do. Michael wanted a warm body when his wife was out of town. My mother wanted me to be the perfect daughter. My sister wanted me to take the reins of the business, so she could party. And everything I did, every decision I made, was to fit into these roles they had assigned to me.

"I was terrified of losing those roles, as if I would cease to exist without them. I didn't know who I was. If my mother disowned me, who would I be? I didn't know. But the moment I heard that Michael was headed towards Brazil, I knew. I'd be a mother. A single, unemployed mother. And that didn't matter, because it was what I wanted."

Jenn smiled. Kathryn was speaking with such passion, such warmth and love. Something had changed in the last few weeks. It was like the woman was alive again. Jenn had seen hints of it, but this was as if Kathryn was now in full bloom.

"The second I laid my eyes on Luke again, I fell in love with him. I knew I could never let him go," she said.

"He's adorable," Jenn agreed.

"He is." Kathryn looked down at the child wrapped around her. "Addison had shown him photographs and videos of me, so he knew who I was when I got there. I cried for half an hour straight."

"How old is he?"

"Thirteen months," Kathryn replied. "I had him five months into our year in Brazil. For the next few months I… I was in a bad place. I didn't connect with him very well. I didn't want to connect with him because I didn't think I'd see him again."

"And what about Michael and his wife now?" Jenn asked. Her eyes scanned the outside of the bar, fearful that some terrible child snatchers might be lurking there.

"My father was a lawyer," Kathryn explained. "He'd registered Luke's birth in New York, citing me as the sole parent. Michael believed that Addison was fostering Luke, in which case Michael could have had grounds for a custody battle. Of course, it helped that a lot of my communication with Michael took place over email. I had a paper trail proving that he'd abandoned me the moment he heard about the pregnancy." She kissed her son's cheek. "He's mine, and mine alone."

"Motherhood suits you," Jenn said.

Kathryn looked at her over the top of Luke's head. "Not quite the words my mother used."

Jenn winced. "What happened?"

"Well…" Kathryn sighed. "Suffice to say I was right. I got disowned and fired immediately."

"She fired her own daughter?" Jenn asked incredulously. "One who has a baby?"

"Of course." Kathryn chuckled. "My mother is, well,

she's a real piece of work. She was appalled to find out that her daughter was an unmarried mother with gay tendencies."

Jenn blinked in surprise. "G—gay tendencies?"

"Yes." Kathryn looked steadily at her. "I told my mother about this amazing woman I met while I was in New Orleans. She was extraordinary, a free spirit with a real zest for life. I explained that she taught me I didn't have to follow some conventional pattern to fit in with the world around me. I should be able to do what I wanted to do, whatever made me happy. I told my mother that the woman had brought me back to life."

"Me?" Jenn breathed.

"You." Kathryn confirmed with a wide grin.

"W—why are you here?"

"I wanted to see you. I know I have been a thorn in your side, but I've had time to reflect on a lot of things and I want to get to know you. Properly. If you would like that?" Kathryn gestured to Luke. "I understand if not, I'm not exactly—"

"I'd love to get to know you. Both of you," Jenn admitted.

46

NEED SOMEONE ELSE TO BITCH ABOUT

REBECCA ADJUSTED the settings on her camera and lined up for another shot.

"What you up to, shutterbug?" Miss Mae asked.

"Getting some new shots for your website," Rebecca replied.

"Does anyone go on our website?"

"No idea," Rebecca replied. "But your boss wanted some new pictures for it, and for your leaflets, too."

Miss Mae looked around the tourist office lobby. "Ain't much to photograph."

"True," Rebecca agreed. So far, she'd been taking pictures of the signs more than the actual space. The desks were old and beaten up, and the chairs were worse.

"If you need a little glamour then you know where I am," Miss Mae said. She plonked herself down in a chair and grinned at Rebecca.

Rebecca took a couple snaps of her. "I'll get these over to *Vanity Fair* post haste."

Miss Mae chuckled. "I'll take my usual fee."

Rebecca looked down at her camera and started to adjust the settings again. Her mind kept wandering, back to London to be exact. Jenn was well enough for her to head home once she finished up her contracts in a couple of weeks. But Jenn was still moping about in a depressive funk because of the Kathryn situation. She didn't want to leave her until she thought she was doing better.

But she missed Arabella so much. The video calls, voice calls, and text messages just weren't enough. She wanted to touch her, kiss her, hold her in her arms. She'd never missed anyone so much in her life.

"Good afternoon!"

Rebecca looked up to see Jenn step into the building with a spring in her step and a wide smile on her face. Rebecca frowned. It was the happiest she'd seen Jenn for weeks. She shared a confused look with Miss Mae.

"How is everyone today?" Jenn asked as she unstrapped her backpack and placed it behind the desk.

Miss Mae's eyes narrowed as she looked Jenn up and down. "What up with you, dove?"

Jenn looked at Miss Mae, biting her lip as if debating whether or not to share her news.

"Kathryn's back."

Miss Mae sighed and turned in her swivel chair. She picked up a crossword puzzle and focused on it, so Jenn turned to face Rebecca instead.

Rebecca just looked at her in surprise. She didn't know how she felt about that news. Kathryn had messed Jenn around and ultimately broken her heart. She had probably played a small part in Jenn's accident, even if it was primarily caused by Jenn ignoring basic road safety. But Jenn was obviously deeply smitten with Kathryn... and now she was back.

"She explained everything," Jenn was saying. "She had family stuff happening, she had to drop everything and go and deal with some things."

"She didn't know if you were alive or dead," Miss Mae mumbled, not fully focused on the crossword after all.

"She... has a son," Jenn said carefully.

"A son?" Rebecca's eyebrows rose. She looked over to Miss Mae who hadn't reacted to the news. The older woman counted the boxes in her puzzle with the tip of her pen.

"It's a complicated story," Jenn said. "She had to give him up, but now she's back with him again. His name is Luke, and he is so cute."

"How old is the boy?" Miss Mae asked.

"Thirteen months," Jenn replied.

Miss Mae shook her head ruefully. "She got you wrapped around her little finger. Or if she didn't before, she will now. You love a toddler."

Rebecca nodded her agreement. It was common knowledge that Jenn was obsessed with toddlers. Babies she could take or leave, children she didn't mind, but the certain qualities of a toddler left her weak at the knees.

"Fine Shoes waltzes back like nothing happened and you forgive her?" Miss Mae looked up. "Dove, you nearly died."

Jenn chewed her lip as she looked from Miss Mae to Rebecca. "She had to go, there's this guy, Michael—"

Miss Mae waved her pen in the air to silence Jenn. She

turned back to her crossword. "I'm sure she had reasons," she said. "And whatever those reasons were, you have already forgiven her."

Jenn looked at Rebecca hopefully.

Rebecca let out a sigh and shrugged her shoulders. "I want you to be happy, Jenn. If Kathryn does that for you, then great. But don't forget what happened. We don't want to see you hurt again."

Jenn pulled her friend into a hug. "I'll be careful, I promise."

Rebecca chuckled. "You better."

Jenn rushed around to Miss Mae and hugged her, too. Miss Mae didn't move. Instead, she ignored the woman wrapped around her and tried to continue with her crossword. Jenn bent down to look her in the face, grinning at her co-worker's pout.

"Oh, come on, be happy for me. Please?" Jenn smiled.

Miss Mae looked up at her. She let out a sigh and then shook her head as she slammed her pen down on the crossword puzzle.

"Okay, but we need to find someone else to bitch about," she said.

47

YOU DIDN'T CALL

LATER THAT EVENING, Jenn was walking down towards the river to meet Kathryn and Luke for an early dinner. When she woke up that morning, she never thought that this would be the day that Kathryn would walk back into her life. Certainly never with Luke.

She'd not had a chance to properly meet Luke that morning. Kathryn had been eager to get them checked into a hotel, and Luke slept through their entire conversation at CeeCee's.

Dinner would be her first real meeting with him. She hoped her natural ability with children would work on this particular child.

She was still struggling to process everything that happened. Over the hours, her relief at Kathryn's return as well as her understanding of the circumstances had given way a little to anger. Kathryn had never contacted her to find out if she was okay. She had simply vanished, and then turned up again when it suited her. With a child, an explanation, and… what? An assumption that Jenn would accept it?

Jenn took a deep breath and pushed that thought to one side. She'd deal with it in due course. For now, she wanted to enjoy Kathryn's company before deciding what to do next.

She walked along the boardwalk, spotting Kathryn and Luke at a table covered by a large parasol. Kathryn was speaking animatedly to Luke and laughing happily. Jenn smiled.

She's beautiful.

Miss Mae had lectured Jenn before she left the tourist office that afternoon. She'd spoken about Kathryn's erratic behaviour and asked again how the woman could leave without knowing what had happened to Jenn after the accident. And, most importantly, how she could go from not wanting Luke to suddenly wanting him in her life again.

Jenn could feel her forehead furrow. They were all good points. Points she needed to clarify with Kathryn. As elated as she was to see her again, she needed to ensure that Kathryn wouldn't vanish again.

She couldn't take it if she did.

She approached the table and stood by Luke's high-chair. The attached food tray was filled with colourful stacking cups that he was playing with.

"Luke," Kathryn said softly to get his attention.

Luke looked at his mother and noticed that she was looking beside him. He turned and looked up at Jenn.

"Jee-en!" he exclaimed excitedly.

Jenn's heart clenched at the adorable boy mispronouncing her name. And the fact that Kathryn had clearly taught him her name.

"Hey, Luke." She took a seat beside Kathryn, opposite Luke.

"Jee-en," he repeated. He looked at Kathryn as if to assure himself that his mother had seen their guest.

"Yes, Jenn," Kathryn said softly, attempting to correct the boy. "Jenn's having dinner with us."

A waiter approached the table. He handed each of the women a menu and placed a drawing sheet and some crayons beside Kathryn in case she wanted Luke to have them.

"I'm glad you could come," Kathryn started. She cleared the stacking cups and replaced them with the paper and the crayons.

"Me, too," Jenn admitted. She watched Luke pick up a blue crayon and excitedly run it over the paper. "You're good with him."

"Thank you." Kathryn smiled.

"It's quite a change," Jenn said carefully as she flipped through her menu.

"What do you mean?" Kathryn asked as she fondly watched Luke.

"Well, going from not wanting to be a p-a-r-e-n-t to this."

Kathryn's face crumpled. She looked destroyed for a moment before she sat up and picked up her menu. She focused on the page, but Jenn knew she wasn't really reading it.

She felt terrible, wishing she had taken a little more time to think about what she wanted to say. "I'm sorry, that was tactless, I didn't mean it like that." She lowered her menu and regarded Kathryn.

"Yes, you did," Kathryn replied with a small nod of her head. "I understand, I… I sound impulsive and unreliable. You're wondering if I'm suited to this—"

"No! No, not at all," Jenn exclaimed. She reached her hand across the table to take Kathryn's. "I'm sorry, that really came out wrong. I shouldn't have said anything."

"You're right, though. It is a big turnaround. I didn't want to… be a mother. But I think it was more concern about not being a good enough one. Worry that when my mother cut me off, because I knew she would, that I would be alone and wouldn't be able to offer Luke the best. It was fear."

Jenn understood that. It must have been a shock for Kathryn to discover that she was pregnant, especially with a mother who would react so badly to a grandchild out of wedlock.

"But now that I've done it, I wouldn't change it for the world," Kathryn continued. "We'll be a family, no matter what."

"I'm really glad to hear that. I'm sorry about what I implied, though. That was rude."

Kathryn opened her mouth to answer. She looked at Jenn for a moment and then frowned as if realising something. She closed her mouth and turned to see Luke staring at them with a wide grin.

"Nosey!" she said in a playful tone. She removed her hand from Jenn's and gently tweaked Luke's nose. "Nosey Luke Foster, that is your new name."

"Ugg," Luke stumbled over the letters.

"Luke," Kathryn said, exaggerating the first letter.

"Ugg," Luke repeated with a nod of the head. He looked away and continued to massacre his piece of paper with random colours.

"Clearly, I didn't predict this when I named him," Kathryn said as she turned back to Jenn. "But I also didn't predict I'd see him ever again. I was a different person last year. Hell, I was a different person five weeks ago."

"What changed in five weeks?" Jenn asked.

"Honestly?" Kathryn asked before letting out a disbelieving chuckle. "You."

"Me?" Jenn frowned in confusion.

"Yes, you," Kathryn repeated. "You with your own way of tackling this thing called *life*. You with your nonconformity and happiness. You with your twenty-seven jobs—"

"Nine, actually."

"Saving lives, pouring drinks, driving trams—"

"Streetcars."

"You're full of life, Jenn," Kathryn said pointedly. "You are living your life, you're doing the things you want to do, and you're not following the conventional rules. And it's working for you. I didn't know that it could be like that."

"What did you think it had to be like?" Jenn asked with interest.

"Work commitments, family commitments. Find a man, get a house, get married, have children. Work up the corporate ladder."

"Sounds boring."

Kathryn laughed. She caught a crayon that rolled off Luke's food tray and handed it back to him. "It *is* boring, I just never really considered that there were alternatives. You opened my eyes to that, and you made me analyse what I had done, what I was doing, and where I wanted to be. I can never thank you enough for that gift."

Jenn blushed. She didn't think for one second that she had done anything special, certainly not anything life-changing, but Kathryn seemed to think so.

The waiter returned, so they ordered food and non-alcoholic drinks, both wanting to be clear-headed for whatever lay before them. Kathryn ordered a children's meal for Luke, asking about the vegetable options. When the waiter listed the vegetables, Luke looked up and happily started shouting for peas. Peas were ordered.

The waiter left, and as Jenn opened her mouth to speak, Luke sent a piece of paper flying in her direction.

"Jee-en."

Jenn picked up the colourful swirling mess and smiled. "Wow, Luke, this is very good!"

Luke beamed with pride. He held out his hand in a grabbing motion, and Jenn handed him the drawing back. He turned the paper over and started colouring the back of the sheet.

She looked at Kathryn. "The New Orleans creativity vibe has gotten into him already."

Kathryn smiled lovingly at her son. "Yes, obviously I didn't have anything for him when I went to Brazil, so I picked him up some crayons and a blank notebook for the flight to New York. He has been drawing ever since."

Luke quickly ran out of space on the back of his sheet. He turned it over and over again as if expecting a new blank sheet to appear. Kathryn reached into a baby bag—

until now tucked under her seat—produced a blank sheet of paper and placed it in front of him.

Jenn watched the interaction and smiled. Her mind was turning with different questions, but the biggest one that kept presenting itself was the next to fall from her lips.

"Why did you come back?"

"To see you."

Jenn swallowed at the serious look in Kathryn's eyes.

"You left, after… after my accident. You left."

Anger flashed in Kathryn's eyes. "You know why I had to leave—"

"But you didn't know if I was dead or alive. You didn't even call!"

"I called every day," Kathryn breathed.

Jenn blinked. "What?"

"I—I called every day. I spoke to the same nurse. I told her I was your aunt from out of town, and she kept me advised of your progress. She told me she shouldn't be telling me anything, but I think she could hear the panic in my voice. She told me when you woke up at six in the evening the day after your accident. She told me about the three broken ribs, numbers 5, 6, and 7. The concussion, and the relief when there was no internal bleeding."

Jenn swallowed and stared at Kathryn in surprise.

"I'm sorry, I know it was a breach of your privacy. But I was too frightened to call you."

Jenn knew she should be angry at her personal medical details being so readily handed out, but she was too overcome with joy. Kathryn had called *every* day. She even remembered details that Jenn herself had forgotten.

"Are you angry?" Kathryn asked, obviously concerned by her continued silence.

It was enough to break Jenn out of her daze. "No, no, sorry I... I thought you..."

"You thought I didn't care."

Jenn winced and slowly nodded.

"Well, I can't be surprised that you would feel that way." Kathryn sighed. "After I left, I thought I should have said something else to Arabella, get her to pass a message on to you. But I didn't know what to say. And, at the time, I was in a state of shock."

Jenn understood. She didn't think she'd be able to, but she did. She often thought of Kathryn coming back, what reasons she might give for her disappearance, but she never really accepted them. Now, sitting beside her and listening to the words, seeing the expression on her face—it made it real.

They both turned to regard Luke and his colouring for a moment.

"I cared... I mean, I care about you. Very much," Kathryn said. For a moment, Jenn thought she meant Luke. She had spoken so softly and was still facing him. "I know that seems ridiculous. We hardly know each other."

"Not at all." Jenn sucked in a quick breath. "I... feel the same."

She cares about me. And she came back, she thought. *But what does that mean?*

It seemed too soon to bombard Kathryn with questions about what would happen next. For now, she was happy to just enjoy her company.

Soon their meals came. Jenn noticed that Kathryn's

food was getting cold while she tended to Luke and his meal. She silently stood up and took the seat beside the boy. She took the cutlery out of Kathryn's hands and started to cut Luke's food and feed him herself. They took turns eating their own meals while the other fed Luke before switching again.

The women kept to lighter topics, mainly Luke and Kathryn getting to know each other. Jenn spoke of her recent return to work. It was casual, light, and airy, but there was an undercurrent of all the things left unsaid.

When the meal was finished Kathryn insisted on paying despite Jenn's protests. They stood, and Jenn helped to put Luke into his stroller. It hurt her ribs, but she already knew she'd carry him for miles if it would make him or Kathryn happy.

"Sorry," Kathryn apologised. "Dinner with a child isn't exactly a long affair, and I need to get him ready for bed."

"It's okay, I understand," Jenn replied. She remained crouched in front of Luke and gently tickled his stomach.

"Maybe we could see each other again soon?" Kathryn asked hopefully.

"Sure, I'd really like that," Jenn said. "Maybe you and Luke would like a trip on the steamboat tomorrow? I'm working, but I can spare some time for my favourite visitors."

They began to walk along the boardwalk.

"That sounds wonderful, as long as you're not going to throw yourself in the Mississippi after some worthless drunk again," Kathryn said.

"I can't make any promises," Jenn joked.

They walked silently. A question that Jenn was dying

to ask kept tossing over and over in her brain. She eyed the calm waters of the Mississippi, so she didn't meet Kathryn's gaze.

"So…"

"So?" Kathryn questioned.

"Was there… anything else I opened your eyes to? You mentioned something about gay tendencies?"

Kathryn chuckled softly. "I think you know."

"I'd like to hear it."

Kathryn paused. She pointed Luke's stroller towards the railings, so the boy could see the ships passing. She turned to face Jenn. "I like you. A lot."

"Is that what you meant by gay tendencies?" Jenn asked.

"Yes," she admitted. "I'm still struggling with the labels."

Jenn felt herself deflate. Was she still just going to be an experiment? "I see, so… you're still confused?"

"Well, I don't know if I'm straight, bi, pan, gay… but I do know one thing with absolute certainty."

Jenn frowned. "What's that?"

"I'm Jenn-sexual," Kathryn replied with a flirtatious grin.

"J—Jenn-sexual?" she stammered.

"Yes," Kathryn replied mock-seriously. "I realised I was getting too caught up in the more conventional questions again. Things like, am I interested in men or am I interested in women? But the answer was staring me in the face all along. I'm interested in the person who caused me to initially question myself. So, I decided. I'm Jenn-sexual."

Jenn felt her mouth turn dry. She stared longingly at

Kathryn's lips as her brain attempted to catch up with events and process data. The last kiss she had initiated was devastating in its aftermath, and the last thing she wanted to do was make another error.

"Car!" Luke cried as he pointed at a large cargo ship.

Both women looked at him and chuckled.

"Your kid's broken," Jenn joked.

Kathryn slapped her arm playfully. She knelt beside his stroller and pointed at the ship.

"That's not a car, Luke, that's a ship. Can you say 'ship'?"

Luke stared at it for a long while. Kathryn tried again, and eventually, Luke mumbled something that could have been anything at all. The boy let out a long yawn and looked expectantly at Kathryn in an attempt to convey his boredom.

"We should go," Kathryn said sadly as she stood up. "He's had a lot of travel and excitement, and I want to get him into a normal routine as quickly as possible."

"I understand." Jenn nodded as she looked down at the adorable boy who was staring up at her.

Kathryn stepped closer and placed a light and yet lingering kiss on her cheek. She handed Jenn a business card. "Here's my new number, let me know when and where to meet you tomorrow."

Jenn nodded. Kathryn turned Luke's stroller and continued along the boardwalk. Luke leaned out of the stroller and waved goodbye to her.

She waved back.

48

CERTAINTY

REBECCA WAITED for Jenn to get home. The moment she'd left the tourist office, she'd called Arabella and told her all about Kathryn's return and the appearance of a child. Arabella had known there'd been something going on with Kathryn, she'd called it quite early on.

Rebecca had caught her up on all the gossip she had, which wasn't enough for Arabella's liking. She promised that she'd find out everything and would report back as soon as she could. Now she was waiting for Jenn to return from dinner with Kathryn, hoping that her friend wouldn't be dismayed again by something Kathryn had said or done.

She mindlessly flipped through television channels while plucking kernels of popcorn out of a bowl. She heard a key in the door and turned the television off. She turned expectantly in her seat, watching as Jenn entered the apartment.

"Hey." Jenn put her keys on the hook by the door.

"Hey, how did it go?" Rebecca asked.

Jenn regarded her suspiciously. "You really want to know? Or are you about to try to convince me to stay away from her?"

Rebecca shrugged. "I've not decided yet. Depends on what you tell me. But I do really want to know how it went."

Jenn pointed to the kitchen. "Want a drink?"

Rebecca pointed to her bottle of cola on the coffee table. "I'm good, thanks."

Jenn vanished for a few minutes, probably longer than she needed.

She's stalling, Rebecca thought. *She thinks I'm against this.*

She couldn't blame Jenn for thinking that. She'd not exactly been complimentary about Kathryn since she'd left. But then, she did think that Kathryn left her friend for dead in the street. That was not a great quality in a person.

When Jenn did finally return she sat in the armchair and opened her bottle of water. She took a few long sips.

"She's interested in me. She apologised for her behaviour. She called a nurse every day to check on me in the hospital. She wishes she didn't have to leave, but she had to go and get her kid. She loves that kid with all her heart, I can see it in her eyes. She kissed me, on the cheek. She says she's Jenn-sexual," Jenn listed.

Rebecca stared at her. "Wow... right, I need a recap on some of that."

Jenn started to laugh. "Bex, it was great. She... she likes me... like, really likes me. We're seeing each other again tomorrow. I don't have all the answers yet, but I really think this is going to work out."

"What is Jenn-sexual?" Rebecca asked, latching on to the point that had stuck in her mind.

"She said she'd been hung up on figuring out labels. Wondering if she's straight, bi, et cetera. But she's decided she's Jenn-sexual. She has feelings for me. She even told her uptight, religious, bitch of a mother that she had 'gay tendencies.' She then proceeded to fire her and disown her."

"For being gay?"

"That and having a child out of wedlock."

Rebecca couldn't fathom it. "What kind of mother doesn't want a relationship with her daughter and grandson?"

"One who is making a big mistake. Kathryn said she wants nothing more to do with her. She's fully focused on her and Luke now. He calls himself Ugg. It's so damn cute, Bex."

"Ugg?" Rebecca laughed.

"Yeah, can't pronounce L's or K's yet. Ugg."

Rebecca smiled. "I'll have to meet this kid."

Jenn nodded quickly. "You should, he's adorable. And… I think this is serious. I mean, she came all this way to talk to me. We didn't discuss the future yet, it's been a full-on day. But I think that's where it's heading."

"Are you ready for that?" Rebecca asked. "Remember how badly she hurt you."

"I do." Jenn took another sip of water. "But she hurt me because I really liked her, and I was sure she liked me despite her protests. And now, I know she likes me, and she's ready to admit it."

"She has just appeared in town again, suddenly assured of her sexual preference, with a child and no job," Rebecca pointed out.

Jenn nodded. She pointed around the small apartment. "If she was looking for a sugar momma to take her and Luke in, do you really think she would seek me out? I'm hardly a target for that kind of thing. Some young nothing from NOLA with a load of part-time jobs and no savings."

"You're not a nothing," Rebecca argued.

"You know what I mean. No one is going to use me for the money I don't have."

It was true. Jenn lived a comfortable life, but she didn't have much money. She worked low-paid part-time jobs because she enjoyed them, but they didn't leave much for a nest egg.

"Okay…" Rebecca ran her hand through her hair. "But, do you really know her? You've hardly spent any time with her."

"We have talked *so* much in that time," Jenn said. "When she was here before, and today. I feel like I know her inside out. She was born in Brazil, though she's never been able to get used to the heat of the country because she left when she was a small child. She idolised her father. Her mother is a hard-ass, but she feels duty bound to appease her."

Jenn took another sip of water, smiling as she remembered the details of past conversations.

"She works with her mother and sister at a PR

company in New York. She doesn't like it much, but she's good at it, so she stuck with it, mainly for her mom. She's travelled to a lot of places in Europe. She takes a lot of photographs, but she never has time to look at them, so she reckons she has over ten thousand pictures to organize someday. She loves animals and donates her time to an animal sanctuary in Jersey every other weekend."

Rebecca held up her hand. "Okay, I get it…"

"She's hot-headed and quick to judge, but when she gives something a chance she's fair. She's very honest—in a refreshing way. She'll tell you if she doesn't like something and she'll explain why. She likes to read biographies because she thinks it's interesting to understand why people make the choices they do."

"Jenn," Rebecca said.

"She has a lot of money, but she doesn't treat herself much. She's too practical for that. She buys nice clothes because she needs them for work. When she travels to Europe, she always ties it in with seeing a client. She never thought she'd be any good at being a parent, and, although she looks like the best mother in the world, I know that she's analysing every single decision she makes one hundred times over."

She stopped and looked up at Rebecca. "I know everyone thinks that this was just some vacation fling. I know people think that she's hot and I lusted over her and that was it. But you know what? I'm a big girl. I'm an adult and I spoke to her, I got to know her, and I fell in love with her. I hated her when I first saw her, it wasn't love at first sight. I got to *know* her."

"It's not you I'm worried about," Rebecca said quietly.

"I know," Jenn said. "But… I have a good feeling about this. Really. She's the one for me. I'm so happy right now. So incredibly happy."

Rebecca let out a sigh and reluctantly smiled. There would be no stopping Jenn now. She was completely enamoured with Kathryn. Rebecca just hoped that Kathryn felt the same way. It wasn't her place to tell her friend what to do. She needed to be the best friend she could be and support her either way.

"So… Luke's adorable, right?" she asked.

Jenn grinned widely and nodded her head. "Oh, man, he's amazing. So fucking cute."

Rebecca laughed. "Better stop swearing if you're gonna be a mommy."

The grin vanished from Jenn's face. "Mommy?"

Rebecca stared at Jenn. "Has it escaped your notice that your new girlfriend has a kid?"

Jenn blinked a couple of times. Rebecca could tell that Jenn hadn't had time to put two and two together yet. It was only now falling into place that she was potentially about to enter into a relationship with someone who had a child. Which meant she'd have a child, too.

"If things work out," Rebecca said, "you'll be Mommy Two. Maybe even Mama."

"Mama," Jenn whispered as her eyes glazed over.

Rebecca grinned. "You have been saying that you were looking for something serious."

"Yes," Jenn whispered in agreement.

"When is she going back to New York?" Rebecca asked.

Jenn's eyes snapped up to meet hers. "I— I don't know. She didn't say anything."

Rebecca felt terrible for bringing it up. It was obvious that Jenn was only just catching up to the fact that Kathryn was in town. She hadn't properly considered the point that she'd presumably soon be leaving again.

"Long-distance relationships aren't that hard," Rebecca said. "With Skype and stuff. Or maybe you could move to New York?"

"I doubt there are many open positions for streetcar drivers or steamboat hosts in New York," Jenn said with a sigh.

"You need to talk to her," Rebecca said. "Before you get in too deep."

"I know, I know." Jenn flopped back into the sofa. She winced.

"Mind your ribs," Rebecca said.

"Screw my ribs," Jenn mumbled.

"Hey." Rebecca came to sit on the arm of the sofa. She wrapped her in a one-armed hug. "You'll work things out, I know you will."

49

BACK ON BOARD

As she had so many times before, Jenn entertained the passengers waiting on the dockside with jokes and stories, but her heart wasn't really in it. Not because of the pain in her ribs, nor the lack of sleep she'd had the night before. It was because of the heavy black cloud that she felt hanging over her.

Rebecca had been right, of course. Kathryn would have to go home at some point, and Jenn couldn't live in New York, even if she wanted to. She loved New Orleans too much, and she'd never be able to find employment in New York, nor the funds to rent an apartment.

That was if Kathryn would even want her there. The possibility that this was a fling, an experiment, weighed heavily on her mind.

Out of the corner of her eye she saw Kathryn arrive with an excited Luke bouncing in his stroller. "Excuse me a moment," she said to the couple she'd been talking to.

She weaved her way through the rope maze that

contained the queue. She approached the little party and smiled as warmly as she could. It was a tough sell considering she had been up all night with Rebecca drinking and agonising over what to do.

Jenn was sure that there was something important between her and Kathryn, something that deserved to be explored. But she was also adamant that she didn't want her heart crushed when Kathryn finished her vacation and went home.

"Jee-en!" Luke said excitedly.

"Hey, little man," Jenn said as she smiled down at the cute boy.

"Are you okay?" Kathryn asked. She frowned slightly as she looked at Jenn. Clearly her concerns were written all over her face.

"Yeah," Jenn said, quickly brushing off the concern. "Just tired. Didn't get much sleep last night."

"Ah." Kathryn nodded. "That makes three of us."

"Oh?" Jenn looked at Luke to see if something was obviously wrong that would have prevented him from sleeping.

"I think it was the room," Kathryn explained quietly. "He's not used to there being any noise at all when he sleeps. We're close to Bourbon Street, and when all that died down even the hum of the minibar kept him awake."

Jenn smiled in understanding. "I'm the same. There's no electronics in my bedroom. I hate the noise they make."

"Maybe we'll have to stay at your place," Kathryn said. She blushed as she looked up at Jenn. "Oh! I didn't mean…"

Jenn laughed and waved off the rest of Kathryn's apology. "It's fine, I know what you mean."

A crackling from the walkie-talkie caught her attention. She turned to face the boat and nodded her head at the captain on the deck. "We're ready to start boarding," she said. "Ready, Luke?"

Kathryn looked at the crowd of people by the dock. "Shouldn't you let them on first?"

"Lady," Jenn said with a serious tone, "I'm in charge of boarding the ship. Brunettes with cute kids are first. Sorry but it's a safety thing."

Kathryn bit her lip and grinned. "Sorry, I don't understand these things. Lead the way."

Jenn unhooked a rope and gestured for Kathryn to follow her up the ramp and onto the steamboat.

Kathryn held onto Luke's hand as they walked around the ship for a second lap. On their way, they had made a number of friends as Luke stopped and waved to everyone they passed. Kathryn would usually have hated the attention but seeing how enamoured everyone was with her son was heartening.

As they circled the ship, Kathryn watched Jenn interacting with the other passengers. She frowned, noticing Jenn's eyes glaze over a little with sadness whenever she spotted them.

Kathryn knew something was up. Jenn's whole demeanour had changed from the previous night. It was clear they needed to have a conversation sooner rather than later.

"Luke, let's go in here," she suggested when she saw Jenn in the dining area where the jazz band was playing.

Luke happily turned. A passenger held the heavy door open for them as they entered. Kathryn thanked him, but the man was too busy smiling from ear to ear at Luke to notice.

Her son's eyes lit up at the first strains of the jazz band. He stopped in the middle of the room and began to stomp his little feet in an attempt to dance along to the tune.

A few passengers noticed, and their interest got Jenn's attention. She walked over to them at the same moment that Luke pulled his hand away from Kathryn's and walked towards the band. He stood right in front of the drummer, staring up at the man in awe. His chubby legs thudded up and down in time with the beat.

"A career in dancing?" Jenn asked with a smile as she stood beside Kathryn.

"Doubtful." Kathryn grimaced at the terrible, wobbling thrusts Luke was attempting. She turned to Jenn. "May I ask what's wrong?"

"Nothing," Jenn said unconvincingly.

"Oh, please, you look at me and Luke like you might cry," Kathryn said softly. "What is it?"

Jenn swallowed and looked around the room. When she seemed satisfied that everyone was focused on the band, or on Luke, she spoke again. "I... I guess it occurred to me yesterday that I'll miss you."

"Miss us?" Kathryn frowned.

"Yeah, when you go back to New York," Jenn explained.

"Oh." Kathryn nodded. Her eyes drifted to Luke. "What if I didn't go back to New York?"

Jenn's jaw dropped. "What?"

"There's nothing for me there. I... I hadn't intended to go back."

Jenn continued to stare at Kathryn open-mouthed.

"This is why I didn't say anything last night," she acknowledged. "I know it looks odd, suddenly uprooting my life and moving to a city I hardly know. I hadn't made any firm plans. My father's inheritance money means I'm able to take some time off of work and spend it bonding with Luke. I figured it doesn't matter where that happens, and New Orleans is as good as place as any."

"You're... staying?" Jenn confirmed.

"I'd like to, if that's okay with you," Kathryn continued. "Besides, Luke's taken to jazz. I can't tear him away from his passion."

Jenn turned to a colleague. "Watch that kid as if your life depends on it," she instructed.

She grabbed Kathryn's hand and pulled her towards a staff door. Kathryn allowed herself to be dragged along, watching as Jenn's colleague approached Luke and started to dance along with him.

Once they were alone, in a dimly lit corridor, Jenn let go of her hand and turned to face her. "I need to know, for sure," Jenn said breathlessly. "Because I'm ready for this. I need to know if you are. If I've misread this, tell me now."

"I'm trying to give you space and time to be sure of things," Kathryn said. "I don't want to bombard you with this, me being here, *Luke* being here. I don't want you to feel pushed into anything."

"Are you staying?" Jenn asked, a forceful undertone to her voice.

"Yes."

"You and Luke, staying in New Orleans... for, like, more than a week."

"We'll be here for no less than six months. Hopefully more, if you'll have us."

Jenn's eyes sparkled. "And... you... want to be together?"

"I want to take you out, on a real date. Where we will kiss, and no one will claim it was a mistake," Kathryn confessed. "If you can find a babysitter, that is."

Jenn lunged forward, lips connecting with hers. Kathryn threw her arms around Jenn's shoulders, careful to avoid pressing against her ribs. She returned the kiss with everything she had, wanting to express her true feelings as best she could through the act.

She pulled back. "If I upset you again, I'll leave," she promised. "This is your city. If you don't want to see me again, just tell me."

Jenn cupped her face, her expression dark and serious. "Never. Leave. Again."

"I won't. Fate keeps bringing me to you, and who am I to argue with fate?" Kathryn whispered.

"You don't believe in fate, or true love," Jenn reminded her.

"Things change," Kathryn said.

She threaded her hand through Jenn's locks and pulled her in for another kiss.

50

SURPRISE

Rebecca lowered her camera. She walked over to the curtains of the luxury hotel suite and adjusted them slightly. She returned to her spot in front of the open door and brought her camera back to her face.

Much better, she thought. It was the little details that made the difference between a good shot and a great shot. Picking up on all the small things that combined to make an image. Especially places that were supposed to denote luxury such as the five-star hotel she was currently free-lancing for.

Rebecca took a couple of pictures of the new layout. She stepped further into the room and tried for a different angle. She placed her camera down on the desk and walked over to the bed. She fluffed the pillows up a little and ran her hand over the sheet to iron out the few tiny creases.

"How the mighty have fallen."

She spun around.

Arabella stood in the doorway, watching her with a smirk. "A professional photographer, now a hotel maid," she continued.

Rebecca looked around in shock. "What—what are you doing here?"

"Seeing you."

"You're supposed to be in London!" Rebecca rushed across the room and pulled Arabella into a hug.

"I missed you," Arabella whispered in her ear.

"You couldn't tell me that you were coming?" Rebecca asked. She stepped back and looked Arabella up and down. She took another step back and folded her arms, trying to look disagreeable. "I can't believe you didn't say anything."

"Surprise?" Arabella was grinning from ear to ear.

"No, you don't get away with it that easy," Rebecca said. "I'm very annoyed with you."

"Oh? Then why are you smiling so much?" Arabella asked.

Rebecca narrowed her eyes. "I've been missing you so much. How long have you been planning this? I could have been happily *expecting* your arrival, not miserably *missing* you. I could have... have picked you up from the airport!"

"They have taxis," Arabella told her. "And I honestly thought you'd enjoy the surprise. That, and I only made the decision last night. Which meant I had to fly to New York yesterday and get a connecting flight today."

Rebecca shook her head. "Wait, what? You only decided last night? What about work?"

"This isn't the greeting I expected at all," Arabella said,

but she was still smiling. Presumably she was happy that she had Rebecca so off kilter. It was so like her to enjoy something like that.

Rebecca smiled. "You're unbelievable, you know that?"

Arabella stepped forward, raising her arms. "Does this mean you forgive me?"

Rebecca nodded and stepped into the hug. She squeezed her momentarily before kissing her, cupping Arabella's face in both hands and showing her just how much she'd missed her. She pulled away only when she'd used up all the air in her lungs.

"How long are you here for?"

"As long as you need," Arabella said.

Rebecca's brow furrowed. "I don't understand."

The last time they spoke, Arabella was just as busy with work as she'd always been. Deals were failing all around her, her father was useless, a key member of staff had left, and they still couldn't find a receptionist who didn't cut off calls when transferring them.

"I hired a very expensive expert," Arabella explained. "I poached him from a rival company in an act of brilliant corporate sabotage. I told my father that I was taking a sabbatical, and that my replacement is called Kevin. And then I told Kevin that I'd be in New Orleans if he needed me, and if he needed me there would be a high likelihood that he'd be fired for not being the expert he claimed to be."

"You got a Kevin," Rebecca said happily.

"I got a Kevin," Arabella confirmed. "They're marvellous, I highly recommend them. Running costs are high, but that can't be avoided." Her tone turned serious. "I needed to see you."

"I'm so glad you're here. Sorry I reacted like that… I've just been missing you so much that I've been feeling depressed lately."

"Noted. In the future, I'll give you some notice. This just seemed romantic, somehow."

"Romantic?" Rebecca bit her lip. It wasn't like Arabella to try to be romantic, but this was a side to her that Rebecca looked forward to exploring.

"Silly, I know." Arabella flushed.

"Not silly." Rebecca kissed her again. More chastely this time, now that she remembered the door to the corridor was still open. "I am so glad you're here. Where are you staying?"

"Here."

"Here, here?" Rebecca asked.

"Yes. I told the manager I needed a room immediately after seeing some fabulous photographs on Instagram from a top London photographer I follow. He seemed very pleased."

Rebecca chuckled. "You don't have an Instagram account."

"No, but you told me you uploaded some snaps to Instagram the other day before you started your project here… I listen." Arabella smothered a yawn behind her hand. "Sorry, I'm still not a very good traveller. I'm told I get grumpy when I travel."

Rebecca noted the dullness in her eyes and the blush on her cheeks and neck. Now she was looking, she realised that Arabella looked exhausted. Then she heard Arabella's stomach rumble lightly.

"Go and get some rest, I can catch up with you later," Rebecca instructed.

"I'm not going to argue. There's a protein bar in my bag with my name on it," Arabella said. "I'm in room 521. Come and see me when you're done."

"Sure you don't want to sleep?" Rebecca asked. She didn't want to interrupt her.

"I'd rather see you," Arabella said. She looked around the room. "There's a cobweb in that corner."

Rebecca turned around and followed Arabella's pointing finger. Sure enough, there was a cobweb in the corner of the room. Trust Arabella's eye for detail to pick up on it.

"Damn," she said, wondering how she hadn't noticed it herself.

"If you want to photograph my room…" Arabella winked.

"I'll take you up on that later," Rebecca promised.

Arabella let out a tired yawn. "Right, I'm going. Room 521."

"Room 521," Rebecca confirmed. "Thank you for coming, I can't tell you what it means to me."

"You can tell me over dinner, I have expensive tastes," Arabella told her. She gave her a peck on the cheek and turned and left the room.

Rebecca smiled so hard her cheeks started to ache. She couldn't believe that Arabella had chosen her over work. And surprised her with the romantic gesture of just showing up like that.

She reached for the phone and called down to the hotel reception.

"Hi, it's the photographer. I'm in room 802 and there's a cobweb in here, and the bedding needs sorting out. Can you ask someone from housekeeping to come up? That's great. Oh, and is the kitchen still open? Brilliant. There's a really important property developer from London staying in the hotel. And I know she loves an egg white omelette with spinach. One word from her would put this place on the map! Fantastic, I'll come down and get the omelette and deliver it to her myself. Also, I'm going to order some flowers to be delivered to the front desk... can you let me know when they arrive?"

When she was finished, she lowered the phone.

If she wants romance, I'll show her romance, she thought.

51

BLUBBERBYES

Arabella let out a breath and looked up at the blue sky. It was another beautiful New Orleans day. She'd not heard a word from work, only a quick email from Helen informing her that Kevin was coping wonderfully and reminding her to have a lovely holiday.

She'd taken the advice to heart, spending the next few days bolted to Rebecca's side and spending every waking moment with her. Some days they saw sights, some days she accompanied Rebecca on her freelancing jobs, some days they sat outside coffee shops and read books in companionable silence.

"Bella. Play."

She tilted her head to regard Luke who was staring at her, a grubby tennis ball in his hand. She lifted herself from the picnic blanket, placing her drink away from him.

"Play? I don't know how to play," she joked.

He giggled. "You do."

She turned around and looked at Rebecca. "This

young man wants me to play, I must now leave you," she said formally.

"Farewell," Rebecca replied in between mouthfuls of a portion of beignets she was sharing with Jenn.

Kathryn gestured for Luke to come closer to her. She pulled a wet wipe out of her baby bag and gave his mouth a clean. "Mucky," she teased him. "How did you get to be so mucky?"

Luke shrugged. He strained to turn around to check Arabella was still there and still intending to play with him. She gave him a smile, reassuring him that she wasn't going anywhere.

She looked around the park while she waited. It was a quiet weekday. There were a few other picnic blankets around, and some children playing in the distance. It was sheer bliss.

"Before you go," Kathryn said to Arabella, "help me figure out the ninth job."

Arabella laughed. She looked at Jenn with a curious expression. "I don't know what it could be, I think we've guessed just about everything there is."

Rebecca snorted a laugh. "I don't think astronaut, belly dancer, and oil tycoon could really count as reasonable guesses."

Kathryn looked at Luke. "Luke, ask Jenn what her ninth job is. She can't deny you anything."

Luke frowned. He turned to Jenn and opened his mouth. His eyes dropped to the beignets between Rebecca and Jenn. Jenn tore off a piece of a beignet and handed it to him. He put the sweet treat in his mouth and sat down in front of her.

"Traitor," Kathryn whispered.

"Remember, you only have one guess per day," Jenn reminded her.

Arabella laughed as Kathryn rolled her eyes. She'd been limited to one guess per day after endless guesses threatened to derail a cinema trip a couple of days before. Arabella had loved watching Luke that night, as well as cuddling up on the sofa with Rebecca while they waited for Jenn and Kathryn to return home from their date.

"And remember she told you that it's not anything like any of her other jobs," Arabella added.

"True." Kathryn nodded. She held up her hand and listed the jobs she knew. "So, we know you are a steamboat host, bartender, tram driver—"

"Streetcar," Jenn and Rebecca corrected.

Kathryn smirked and then continued. "Voodoo museum attendant, casino worker, burlesque dancer, water aerobics instructor, and a tour guide. So… it's not like any of those."

"Right." Jenn dipped her finger in powdered sugar and then put her finger on the end of Luke's nose. He giggled and brushed it away with his hands.

Arabella smiled. Jenn was so good with him, and Luke adored her. Rebecca had told her that Jenn was planning to cut back on some jobs in order to spend more time watching Luke while Kathryn set up her new PR company in the city.

"Oh, I don't know." Kathryn threw her hands in the air. "Zoo keeper."

"Nope! You're close, though." Jenn darted a hand

towards Luke's tummy and tickled him. He fell to the ground and giggled.

"Stop, stop!" he cried through laughs.

Arabella swept in and picked him up. "I'll save you from that evil tickle monster," she told him. He put his chubby arms around her neck and smiled down at Jenn.

Arabella noticed Rebecca watching her wistfully. She knew that look. It was the 'you'd make a great mother' look. She'd seen Rebecca use it a few times recently. Not that she minded. She felt the same way when she saw Rebecca playing with Luke.

"Close?" Kathryn asked. She scooted closer to Jenn. "How about another clue?" She fluttered her eyelashes.

Jenn melted.

Arabella rolled her eyes. "You're not actually going to fall for that are you, Jenn?"

"She is," Rebecca said.

"Bella. Play," Luke reminded her.

Arabella looked at the adorable boy in her arms. "Of course. What would you like to play?"

"Blubberbyes."

Arabella blinked. "I'm sorry, sweetie. What was that?"

Jenn was on her feet and taking Luke from Arabella's arms. "No, no, that's our secret, remember?" she told him as she stepped away from the picnic blanket. Her cheeks were red.

Arabella and Kathryn shared a look.

"Luke, honey," Kathryn asked. "What did you say? Blubberbyes?"

"Yes, like Jenn!"

Jenn shushed him and took a few steps away. Rebecca was howling with laughter at the whole display.

Arabella's eyes widened. "This is something to do with the ninth job," she realised.

Kathryn got to her feet. "Blubberbyes... what could he mean?"

Arabella shook her head. "I don't know, but she's stolen your son." She watched as Jenn playfully ran away with the boy in her arms. She turned to Kathryn. "What letters does he struggle with most?"

Kathryn chuckled. "Most of them. There's a speech therapist in his future. But L's, T's, G's, F's."

A grin crossed Arabella's face. She walked over to where Rebecca lay giggling on the blanket. She bent down and pushed Rebecca onto her back, straddling her stomach.

"Tell me what you know, Edwards," she demanded. "What is Blubberbyes?"

Rebecca looked up at her. "I'll never tell."

Arabella raised an eyebrow. She picked up the last beignet on the plate.

"Fine, eat it," Rebecca said. "It would be an honour to see you eat sugar."

"Oh, I'm not going to eat it." She picked up a half-drunk takeaway coffee mug. "Tell me, or this beignet... the last of the beignets... goes for a swim."

Rebecca looked at her in horror. "You can't do that! It's the last beignet. You know I save the best beignet to the end."

"It's not my fault you're a slave to tradition," Arabella told her.

"Butterflies!" Rebecca cried. "Blubberbyes are butterflies."

Arabella looked at Kathryn in confusion.

"She's... a butterfly?" Kathryn asked.

"You clearly don't think I'm serious," Arabella said. "Say au revoir to Monsieur Beignet." She dangled the pastry over the cup.

"No, wait! She *is* a butterfly. She dresses up as a butterfly at the Audubon Butterfly Garden. You know, for kids' parties and stuff. She wears a leotard and some big papier-mâché wings and paints her face."

Kathryn laughed loudly. "That is priceless, no wonder she didn't want to tell me." She looked up to where Jenn was hiding behind a tree. "I'm coming to mock you!" she shouted before running towards her.

Arabella lowered the beignet and the coffee cup.

Rebecca looked up at her, a sparkle in her eye. "I won't lie, this is kinda hot," she admitted.

Arabella reached down and picked up the beignet, taking a big bite of it. She moaned as the sugar and doughnut mixed on her tongue. She chewed slowly and then swallowed. It was pure heaven.

She put the rest of the beignet down on the plate. "You're right, they are good."

Rebecca reached up for her arms and pulled her down into a kiss. After a moment, Rebecca pulled back, held Arabella's face still, and, painfully slowly, traced her tongue around Arabella's lips.

"Sugar," she explained when she was done.

"I'm hungry," Arabella whispered.

Rebecca's eyes widened.

"You told me to tell you in the future when I was hungry," Arabella reminded her. "Rebecca, I'm hungry." She stared at the woman beneath her, impressing upon her that she didn't mean food.

"Let's go back to your hotel," Rebecca suggested.

"Excellent suggestion," Arabella agreed.

PATREON

I ADORE PUBLISHING. There's a wonderful thrill that comes from crafting something and then releasing it to the world and hoping that others enjoy and appreciate it.

In my short writing career, I've published a number of books and I intend to write many, many more. However, writing, editing, and marketing books take up a lot of time… and writing full time is a treadmill-like existence.

Don't get me wrong. I feel very grateful and lucky to be able to live the life I do. But being a full time author means there are other things I simply do not have time for. Teaching others and developing my career being two of the most important ones to me.

This is why I had set up a Patreon account. With Patreon, you can donate a small amount each month to enable me to hop off of my treadmill for a while in order to reach my goals.

At the time of writing this, I'm currently writing my tenth novel in around the two and a half years since I started my publishing journey. In that time, I've won a Lambda award and been lucky enough to have multiple best-selling novels in the Amazon charts.

Now, I want to help others to achieve their own writing goals by sharing the knowledge I have. Freeing up some of my time enables me to reach out and help aspiring and established authors alike.

In return for any kind donations you are willing to give are a series of benefits including exclusive first looks at new works, insight into upcoming projects, monthly Q&A sessions, all the way up to special gifts and dedications. There is a tier to suit any budget.

https://www.patreon.com/aeradley

JOIN THE FUN!

I LOVE CONNECTING with my readers and one of the best ways to do this is via my Facebook Group.

I post frequent content, including sneak peaks of what I am working on, competitions for free books, and exclusive easter eggs about my work.

I'd love to see you there, so if you have a Facebook account please join us.

https://www.facebook.com/groups/aeradley

I sincerely hope you enjoyed reading The Big Uneasy.

If you did, I would greatly appreciate a short review on your favourite book website.

Reviews are crucial for any author, and even just a line or two can make a huge difference.

ABOUT THE AUTHOR

A.E. Radley is an entrepreneur and best-selling author living and working in England.

She describes herself as a Wife. Traveller. Tea Drinker. Biscuit Eater. Animal Lover. Master Pragmatist. Annoying Procrastinator. Theme Park Fan. Movie Buff.

When not writing or working, Radley indulges in her third passion of buying unnecessary cat accessories on a popular online store for her two ungrateful strays whom she has threatened to return for the last seven years.

Connect with A.E. Radley
www.aeradley.com

BRING HOLLY HOME

She's lost everything. Can one woman bring her home?

Leading fashion magazine editor Victoria Hastings always thought that her trusted assistant quit her job and abandoned her in Paris.

A year later, she discovers that Holly Carter was injured in an accident. Brain trauma led to amnesia and Holly cannot remember anything about her life.

Guilt causes Victoria to bring Holly home and into her life to aid her in recovery. But when guilt turns into something else, what will she do?

BRING HOLLY HOME | PREVIEW

BY A.E. RADLEY

Louise took a deep breath and quickly started to recite the schedule to her boss.

"So, as you know, the gala is tonight. The table plan is in your room for final approval as you requested. Your car arrives tomorrow at ten o'clock to take you to Charles de Gaulle. I'll be checking out of the hotel earlier to get the Guerlain samples that you requested for your sister, so I'll meet you at the airport at quarter to eleven."

Louise knew this was an exercise in futility. Her boss knew the schedule back to front, and yet she felt the urgent need to fill the awkward silence that permeated the back of the limousine. She subtly turned her wrist in her lap to look at her watch.

"Hm," Victoria murmured.

Louise looked up to see if her boss would say anything else.

Victoria continued to look over the top of her glasses at the passing Parisian scenery.

Louise debated if she should say something else. Maybe give another rundown on the first-class menu on offer on-board the flight from Paris to New York. Maybe attempt to get a tiny amount of kudos for having changed the red meat option from lamb for the entire cabin, simply because Victoria couldn't abide the smell of lamb.

Not that Victoria would ever acknowledge any of the backbreaking, soul-destroying work that Louise did on a daily basis for the impossible-to-please woman. But she lived in hope that a nugget of gratitude would work its way into Victoria's conscience.

Maybe enough to promote her from her role of assistant. Being an assistant to Victoria Hastings was certainly prestigious. Sadly, it didn't pay the therapy bills that Louise would need if she managed to survive the role.

Louise's mobile phone rang, and she answered immediately. "Yes?"

It was that awful French man from the gazette again. Blathering on about something or other and making little sense.

"Look, I've told you before, Victoria will not be doing any interviews. If you wanted to speak to her then you should have called *before* she arrived in Paris for Fashion Week. Do you have any idea how busy she is? Of course you don't."

The man continued talking hurriedly. Louise just shook her head, not even bothering to listen to what he was saying. She couldn't believe the audacity of the man. Thinking that Victoria Hastings of all people would be able to drop everything and speak to some nobody. Did he have any idea who she was?

"Absolutely not, and don't call this number again!"

Louise huffed, hung up the phone, and tossed it into her bag.

"Damn French," she mumbled under her breath.

"Problem?"

Louise looked up and realised that Victoria had turned to glance at her. Louise took pride in her appearance, checking her reflection at least every twenty minutes to ensure she was looking her best. But the second Victoria looked at her, she felt certain that she must appear a wreck.

Victoria was the kind of woman who always looked perfect. She must have had a long conversation with Mother Nature in which she put her foot down and insisted she wasn't going to age another minute. And so, forty-seven-year-old Victoria Hastings looked like a perfectly turned-out woman in her mid-thirties. Not a hair was out of place in her fashionable blonde bob. Her makeup was light but always on point, just enough to rouge her cheeks, plump her lips, and accentuate her steely green eyes. Nothing less could be expected of the editor of one of the world's leading fashion magazines.

Louise realised that she had been silent for too long. Her panic at potentially not looking her best under Victoria's frosty glare had thrown her.

"Um. No, no problem, Victoria. Just a journalist, some awful little French man. You know what journalists are like. I don't even know why I bother sending out press guidelines. He has been calling me here and Claudia back in New York every single day... I... He..." Louise swallowed nervously.

She'd said too much, she'd bothered Victoria with details that were of no interest to her.

Victoria simply stared at her in silence. Slowly, she rolled her eyes. Louise was sure that Victoria was internally questioning the incompetence she was surrounded by. She usually did. Now it was just a matter of whether Victoria would deliver a softly spoken, but scathing, remark, or if she would ignore her. Louise held her breath while she waited for judgement to be passed.

After a few more frosty seconds, Victoria turned and looked out of the car window again. The conversation was over.

Louise released the breath she had been holding. Silently.

Paris Fashion Week was everything she'd hoped it would be. The shows, the designers, the clothes, the city. But now it was drawing to a close. Three months of doing nothing but planning Victoria's schedule had paid off. It had been a success. Not that anyone would know it from Victoria's expression.

From the moment they had landed in Paris, her boss has been quiet and detached. More so than usual. At the best of times, no one would ever accuse Victoria of being friendly or talkative. In fact, Victoria was famously known for destroying careers with a simple look.

But the last few days had been worse than usual.

Louise reminded herself that there was just one more night between her and her comfy bed back home in New York. And the next morning she would be getting to the airport bright and early and thankfully not travelling with Victoria.

The elevator doors slid open, and Victoria put on her over-sized Gucci sunglasses. She walked through the lobby of the Shangri-La Hotel, her heels tapping loudly on the marble flooring.

She could sense the receptionists discreetly looking at her as she walked past them. She imagined that they were breathing a sigh of relief at her departure.

The doorman, dressed in a top hat and a knee-length, forest green overcoat, opened the door as she approached. She breezed through and down the steps.

She let out an audible sigh at the fact that her limousine wasn't in place. She looked up with annoyance to see that the vehicle was on its way down the hotel's driveway, just passing through the wrought iron gates.

"Apologies, Ms Hastings."

She turned to see the manager of the hotel rushing down the steps. He waved his arms frantically to hurry the black limousine up. The moment it came to a stop in front of the steps, he opened the back door and gestured into the car.

"Thank you for your stay. I do hope you found everything to your liking?"

Victoria hummed half-heartedly. While the Shangri-La was slightly above average in some respects, there had been some issues. For starters, the intolerable noise of the fan in her room and the maintenance imbecile who said he couldn't even hear the noise when she had been positively deafened by it.

She passed the grovelling man and got in the back of the limo.

"We do hope to see you again next year," the man continued, holding the door open and looking at her with a pleading expression.

Victoria felt that it was very unlikely that she'd ever come back should he continue to delay her. She wanted to get to the airport and take a few private moments to call her children to see how they were doing. She travelled a lot, but she never stopped missing them.

She was about to instruct the driver to go, regardless of the position of the passenger door, when she noticed the manager looking up the driveway with a frown. She could hear some kind of commotion from behind the car.

"*Excusez-moi,* Madame Hastings!"

She glanced out of the back window. A scruffy-looking man was running towards the car. It looked like he had run through the gates as they were being closed. He held up a piece of paper and was running determinedly towards her. Two doormen and a security guard were chasing after him.

She turned around and called out to the driver in a bored tone, "Go."

The hotel manager closed the passenger door and the car slowly started to edge forward, the sharp turn of the driveway making a quicker departure impossible.

She heard shouts behind the car and rolled her eyes. It seemed nothing was going to go right during this trip.

There was a thump on the window. The scruffy man stood beside the car, holding up a Polaroid photograph. Victoria felt her mouth fall open in shock at the image.

It was Holly Carter. Her former assistant. The one who had abandoned her without a word exactly one year ago. However, there were vast differences between the Holly she had known and the woman in the photograph.

In contrast to Holly's long locks, the photograph showed a woman with short hair. Victoria's artistic sensibilities balked at the change. Long hair was finally back in fashion and the girl had chopped all of hers off. Not that Holly was ever one to toe the line when it came to fashion trends.

But the real shock was the unresponsiveness in her eyes. They no longer sparkled, there was a dullness to them that Victoria had never seen before. And Holly's already pale skin seemed paler, almost sickly in appearance. The forced smile failed to distract from the fact that she looked quite frightened.

As quickly as the photograph had been slapped onto the glass, it was pulled away. Each doorman grabbed one of the scruffy man's arms and dragged him away from the car.

"Wait," she instructed the driver.

Victoria felt the brakes being applied, and the car came to a jolting stop. She opened the door and stepped out of the car.

The man was now on the tarmac, the two burly doormen on top of him, trying to hold him down. He looked up at her.

"You know her?" he asked, his voice thick with a French accent.

"Let him go," she commanded in a soft tone.

The doormen looked in confusion at the manager who

was standing helplessly by. He quickly waved his hands up to indicate that they should let him go.

Slowly, the man climbed to his feet. He clutched the photo in his hand and looked at Victoria expectantly.

She looked him up and down. She had no idea who he was or what he wanted, but he seemed to know Holly. And that was enough to grant him a few moments of her time. Even if she was running late.

She pointed to the car.

"Get in," she instructed.

CLIMBING THE LADDER

Getting the job of your dreams is fantastic, until you bring the company to its knees in your first week.

Chloe Dixon just got her life back on track following an emotional break up. When she trusts the wrong person, she finds herself in the middle of a PR storm. She needs to fix her mistake if she is to keep her long-coveted job and save one of the most influential magazines in the country.

If you like laugh-out-loud romantic comedies, witty dialogue, and characters you'll fall in love with, then you'll love Climbing the Ladder.

CLIMBING THE LADDER | PREVIEW

BY A.E. RADLEY

CHLOE DIXON HELD onto the handrail above her head. She looked out of the train window at the dark tunnels of the London Underground. A book hung loosely from her free hand. It hadn't managed to hold her interest, or stop her from fretting about her new job, as she had hoped.

She turned away from the window and surveyed her fellow commuters. It had been a while since she'd commuted into Central London for work. She felt as if she had rejoined an exclusive club. A club where getting up hideously early, paying an arm and a leg to travel under the city streets, and wearing uncomfortable work outfits was the price of membership.

Despite the shocking cost of a monthly travel card, she was ecstatic to be back in London. Or, in the rat race, as her dad had called it. As per usual, it had taken her parents around fifteen seconds to turn good news into bad.

Her celebration over getting a new job, working for a company she had dreamed of, was soon extinguished under their barrage of questions. What time would she have to get up for work? How much was the cost of travel? How many extra hours would she be away from home due to commuting?

Chloe shook her head to dispel her parents' negativity. They were good people, just overly practical. She loved them both fiercely, but she was also aware of their pessimistic attitudes. She, on the other hand, tried hard to find the silver lining and keep cheerful. She had a lot to be cheerful about.

She didn't know if it was a result of her getting older, or if the world had turned into a more negative place in recent years. She wondered if curmudgeonly old people had always been grouchy or if it was something that happened to many people as they aged.

Whatever the case, Chloe had decided years ago that she would maintain a positive attitude. No matter what life threw at her, she would smile through it.

The commuter train rattled into a station. The platform was packed with commuters desperate to get on the already-bursting-at-the-steams train. Chloe squeezed herself into a corner as people pushed into the carriage.

Five million souls used the London Underground every day. Or so her dad had told her.

It was getting ridiculously hot and crowded. More people pushed their way on board. A signal beeped, indicating that the doors would soon attempt to close. Everyone took a simultaneous deep breath, as if attempting to squeeze into a pair of jeans from the previous summer. The doors started to close, hitting a tall, bald man on the head. He didn't care, as if this were a daily occurrence and being smashed in the side of the head by an automated door was the price one paid for using public transport.

People leaned over her to grab at handrails, leaving Chloe to stare at a stranger's armpit. The train started to move, causing everyone to lean into the gravitational forces.

Her enthusiasm for joining the morning commuters was already starting to fade. She brought up a mental image of the Tube map. She was close enough to the office to be able to walk if she got off at the next stop. If she could get off at the next stop.

She shuddered at the memory of the poor woman who had tried to get off at Green Park. She'd been so engrossed in her newspaper that she hadn't realised it was her stop until the train doors had opened. She'd tried to fight against the tide of people trying to board the train. It wasn't pretty.

Trying to squeeze her way off of the train and then walking at ground level was definitely preferable to being crushed into the wall of the carriage. Next to a man with an unhealthy-sounding cough. And a woman who had forgotten to shower that morning.

Chloe angled her face away from one armpit and found another straight away.

Definitely getting off at the next stop, she told herself.

On her way through Soho, Chloe opened the door to the

newsagent. Before she had a chance to enter the shop, a man walked in front of her.

"You're welcome," she mumbled under her breath.

Hot Monday mornings in London were rapidly losing their charm. Everyone was overheated and miserable to be going back to work after a weekend in the sun. But Chloe was doing her best to stay cheerful. Today was going to be a great day, she could feel it.

She entered the cramped shop and started to look at the magazine rack. Despite the store being so small, the selection was extensive. Fishing, photography, crafts, pets, and the oddly titled 'women's interests.' Women mainly appeared to be interested in knitting and getting rid of cellulite.

She couldn't find what she was looking for, and so she started to look behind some of the magazines. She stood on her tiptoes and looked at the top shelf. Her eyebrow rose, and she quickly lowered her gaze again. While most of the covers were now obscured, she still got an eyeful of some of the more moderate covers that were allowed to be on display. She swallowed and pushed down the desire to flip through the article about losing cellulite.

She crouched down and started to look at the back of the bottom shelf.

The man who had barged past her to get into the shop physically stepped over her to get out again. He sighed in annoyance that Chloe seemed to continually be in his way. She shook her head at his behaviour and wondered what super important job he must have to act like that.

She returned to looking at the magazines on the

bottom shelf, moving some out of the way to see what lurked behind.

Nothing.

She stood and grabbed a bottle of orange juice from the fridge. She approached the counter and put the drink down.

"Excuse me," she said, trying to get the attention of the bored man operating the till.

He glanced up at her. An eyebrow rose, but nothing else was forthcoming.

"Do you have any copies of *Honey Magazine*?"

"*Honey*? Have you checked in cooking? Or women's interests?" He scanned the orange juice. "Three pounds."

"It's not a cooking magazine. It's a lesbian magazine." Chloe handed him a five-pound note.

"Oh, right." He seemed unfazed. He put the note in the till and handed her back the change. "Not heard of it. I can order it in for you, if you want?"

"No, I want a copy now. I work there. Well, I'm starting work there today. I've not read this month's issue because it came out on Friday and I was away this weekend…" She stopped as she realised he wasn't interested in her life history. "You really don't stock it? It's, like, the biggest lesbian magazine in the UK. And Europe."

"Never heard of it," he said. "No one has ever asked for it."

Chloe's heart sank. She was in a busy newsagent in Soho and no one had ever asked for a copy of *Honey* Magazine?

"Try the internet? Or get one from work?" he suggested.

"I don't want to look like I haven't read it," she said.

"Well, you haven't."

"I know that, I don't want them to know that. Are you sure you don't have it?"

"I'm sure, I order all the magazines in myself. We don't have it. As I say, I can order it for you?"

A cough behind her indicated that she was in the way. It was a busy Monday morning and people were in a rush to get to work. Most eager to get into air conditioning and out of the blazing early morning sun. She was surprised someone hadn't climbed over her to be served yet.

She grabbed her orange juice and left the shop. She wandered along the street deep in thought. She didn't expect *Honey* to be one of the shop's best-sellers. But she didn't expect it to be missing in action either.

She'd read *Honey* religiously since she was a teenager. She'd never been in a shop and bought a copy, preferring to have it delivered instead. But her subscription was still being delivered to her parents' house and she'd moved out three months before.

Being at her parents' house for six months while she got back on her feet had been demeaning and exhausting. She thought the break-up had been bad, but the aftermath had been worse. She'd temped and worked all the hours she could during those six months. Partly to make as much money as possible to scrape together a deposit for her own place, and partly to only be at home when it was time to sleep.

Today was the day her life started to get back on track. She was in her own room in a house share in south London, she was starting a well-paid job in digital for a company she had adored for the last fifteen years. No more temporary positions, no more working all the hours she could. It had taken nearly a year, but she felt like she was in a good place again.

She smothered a yawn. Last night had been a sleepless one. She'd tossed and turned for hours as she worried about her first day. Especially meeting all of her new work colleagues. She desperately hoped that she would fit in and maybe even make friends.

The day hadn't been off to the best start. She was sleep-deprived and felt like she could still smell the sweaty odour of the Tube ride. The various armpits she'd stared into would no doubt haunt her dreams that evening.

Not being able to get her hands on the latest copy of *Honey* before work was another blow.

She stopped dead in the middle of the street. She stared down at the orange juice in her hand.

"THREE POUNDS? What a rip-off!"

Published by Heartsome Publishing
Staffordshire
United Kingdom
www.heartsomebooks.com

Also available in paperback.
ISBN: 9781912684137

First Heartsome edition: October 2018

41453496R00231

Made in the USA
Lexington, KY
07 June 2019